MAGGIE CHRISTENSEN

Coming Home to Bellbird Bay

Cover and interior design: J D Smith Design
Editing: John Hudspith Editing Services

Dedication

To my own soulmate who I met later in life

Also by Maggie Christensen

Oregon Coast Series
The Sand Dollar
The Dreamcatcher
Madeline House

Sunshine Coast books
A Brahminy Sunrise
Champagne for Breakfast

Sydney Collection
Band of Gold
Broken Threads
Isobel's Promise
A Model Wife

Scottish Collection
The Good Sister
Isobel's Promise
A Single Woman

Granite Springs
The Life She Deserves
The Life She Chooses
The Life She Wants
The Life She Finds
The Life She Imagines
A Granite Springs Christmas
The Life She Creates
The Life She Regrets
The Life She Dreams

Mother's Story

Bellbird Bay
Summer in Bellbird Bay

One

On the morning of the Christmas Day Grace Winter knew would be the last she'd spend in Granite Springs, she waited till everyone was gathered on the veranda with the traditional glasses of champagne and orange and slices of succulent mango, before speaking.

'I wanted to tell you. I've made a decision. I've put the property up for sale. I'm moving to Bellbird Bay to be closer to your Aunt Dorothy and Uncle Kevin.'

There was a stunned silence, broken only by the distant clamour of a flock of cockatoos and the rustling of animals in the neighbouring paddock. Then all three of her children began to talk at once.

Grace put up her hand. 'Steady on, one at a time. I can't hear what you're saying.' Her stomach clenched. She'd been afraid of their reaction.

'Mum, you're not serious. You can't do this.' Lou looked at Grace in amazement. Being the eldest, the others always deferred to her in times of stress. 'It's our home.' Her outburst reminded Grace of all the times when Lou was a child, when she'd been told something she didn't want to hear.

The others nodded, only Lou's husband, Greg, appearing unconcerned.

'Where will we go when… when…' Mel wailed, gazing around as if the house was suddenly going to disappear. 'What would Dad say?'

Grace's middle child, Mel, had been her father's favourite. She'd always floated through life expecting everything would work in her favour. And, so far, it had. After leaving school, she'd found a position in the office of a friend's father, content to stay there as a glorified personal assistant in a bustling advertising agency with no desire to move on or into a more senior position. She was the one Grace had been most worried about. When the city got too much for her, Mel would arrive on Grace's doorstep seeking what she called R and R and spend a few days soaking up the ambiance of her childhood home before returning to her life in the city.

Trust Mel to bring her father into this. Grace opened her mouth to reply, but before she could say anything, Ben spoke.

'I think Mum's right. This place must take a lot of work, and none of us has time to help out. But are you sure about moving so far away, Mum? Why not a little place in town?'

Grace smiled at the words of her youngest child. She knew parents shouldn't have favourites, but Ben, born when she and Russ had given up hope of having another child, of having the son they'd always wanted, would always hold a special place in her heart. Always a rolling stone, he'd spent the past few years somewhere in Europe investigating a pile of ancient ruins, part of an archaeological dig organised by a UK university with which he was loosely associated. But he emailed and texted regularly, assuring Grace he was thinking of her. And he always made it home for Christmas.

Lou snorted. 'What difference would that make? How could you bear to leave here?' She swept her arm around to encompass the twenty acres of the property Grace and Russ bought when they arrived in Granite Springs all those years ago.

Meeting at university in Sydney, she and Russ had moved to the country when he was offered a position at William Farrer University.

Grace remembered the day like it was yesterday. Russ had picked her up and twirled her around in the tiny kitchen in their one-bedroom apartment. 'Can you believe it, Gracie?' he'd asked. 'Me, a university lecturer!' Then he'd put her down gently and gazed into her eyes. 'You're happy for me, aren't you? You'll be able to get a teaching job there, and we can start a family.'

They'd spent the rest of the day checking out on the map exactly where Granite Springs was located. It was a new university, and Russ had been interviewed by phone. Neither of them had travelled to that part of New South Wales before, but were pleased it seemed to be a flourishing town and was within driving distance of Canberra. It would be a good place to put down roots.

And that's exactly what they'd done. Russ and Grace had bought this small acreage, one of many such soldier settlements on the outskirts of town, land made available to returning soldiers after the Great War. They'd lived here ever since, brought up their children, and dabbled in various types of animals over the years, finally settling on a few sheep and goats, just enough to keep the grass down.

'It's time, sweetheart.' Grace looked at her three children, aware she was trembling, and wondering for the hundredth time if she was doing the right thing. Then she remembered how she'd felt when she wakened only a week earlier.

It had been as if a weight had been lifted from her shoulders. Her eyes still closed, she could feel the sunlight warming them as it poured in through the window beside her bed. The kookaburras were screeching their morning greeting from the top of the fence around the house, and the scent of the tall lemon gum filtered in through the open window.

As her eyes slowly opened and became accustomed to the light, she remembered her decision. The night before, after much soul searching, she'd made up her mind. It was a relief after the weeks of worrying. The meeting with Gordon Slater had clinched it. He was a good solicitor and had been a good friend to Russ over the years.

'You've made a wise decision, Grace,' he'd said. 'It can't have been easy. Not with Russ in recent times. Maybe you can find something smaller in town.'

But she wouldn't be doing that. She was going to make a complete change. A call to her sister, Dorothy, had been the catalyst.

'Why don't you move up here? You can stay with us while you look around. It would be wonderful to have you close by. What you need is a fresh start.'

While Grace resented being told what she needed as if she had no mind of her own, Dot was right.

She'd enjoyed her life in Granite Springs. But now Russ was gone, the children moved away with lives of their own, there was nothing left for her here.

Grace had always enjoyed visiting her sister and brother-in-law in their coastal retreat. Now it would become her home, too. She'd move forward to a new life. A smaller house. A yard she could enjoy without animals to care for. She'd been lonely since Russ was diagnosed with dementia. It was a slow-moving disease that gradually ate away at the man she'd known and loved.

These past few years had been difficult, trying to cope with everything on her own as Russ had disappeared more and more into his own little world. It had used up all her energy. The children were good, but they had their own lives to lead and had seldom been able to make time to travel to visit their aging parents.

Maybe she could even find something with a view of the ocean, certainly close to the beach. It would be different. For a time, she'd hesitated about leaving the family property with all of its memories. But last week she'd realised the memories would go with her. She could almost hear Russ's voice talking to her as he'd done when he was alive and healthy.

'Gracie, girl, don't saddle yourself with this old place for ever. We'd have moved on anyway. It was getting too much for me. And don't let our kids stand in your way. It's your decision, not theirs.'

'Your dad would agree with me,' she said. 'The property was getting too much for us even before he became ill, and since…' She pushed a hand through her short hair, the dark waves now silver with age.

Since Russ's death, the three of them had been overly solicitous, wanting to know she was all right, offering suggestions as to how she should spend her time. As if she suddenly had nothing to do. Caring for the acreage took all the hours in the day. It was too much for her to cope with without Russ to do the heavy work.

When Russ died, Lou had been especially concerned, even suggesting Grace spend a few weeks with her and Greg to 'get over things'. As if a week spent in their inner-city apartment would help assuage the grief Grace harboured at the loss of her soulmate – though it was as if she'd lost the man she loved some time earlier when he stopped recognising her and often ranted and railed like a man deranged. But she never stopped loving him.

Lou and Greg were both busy in their respective careers, Lou as a senior public servant and Greg in an IT position Grace had never been able to understand. What would she do all day when they were at work and she was stuck in their tiny box in the centre of the city?

No, if she was going to leave her familiar surroundings, she'd prefer it to be for somewhere she'd chosen herself, and the peaceful ambiance she'd experienced on her last visit to her sister in Bellbird Bay was exactly what she needed.

Two

Grace's phone rang as she sat sipping her morning cup of fennel and cardamon tea and gazing out at the ocean in Bellbird Bay, the view she never tired of. At her feet, lying in a pool of sunlight, was Tiger, the tortoiseshell cat who'd adopted her when she moved into the small cottage in Bellbird Bay a few months earlier.

At this time in the morning the beach was almost deserted, apart from a group of early morning surfers determined to make the most of the waves before starting their working day. Later, she knew, the surf lifesavers would appear to position the red and yellow flags, then groups of walkers and swimmers would populate the now empty stretch of sand, and the busy day would begin. But now, it was as if it all belonged to her and her alone.

Grace had been lucky. When she arrived in Bellbird Bay in late January, having found a buyer for her twenty acres in Granite Springs – a young family eager to escape the city and try country living had bought at first sight – her sister, Dot, and husband, Kev, had welcomed her with open arms. But, despite their warm hospitality, Grace had known it would soon stifle her. Finding this cottage, one of a string of former beach shacks with only a narrow walkway separating it from the beach, was a miracle. She'd moved in as soon as she could and loved her new home.

The only fly in the ointment was the ongoing disapproval of her two daughters, neither of whom had shown any interest in her new life, or desire to visit. It seemed they hadn't recovered from the shock of her announcement on Christmas Day.

Now, although speaking to them on a weekly basis and sharing her newfound joy in her life here, the calls tended to be one-sided, their contributions limited to stilted accounts of their life.

Ben was different from the two girls. Although his work meant he'd been unable to visit, he was always interested to hear of Grace's experiences and eager to share aspects of his own life with her. Without his weekly communication, Grace would have felt bereft. As she said to Dot, 'It's as if the girls have shut me out of their lives. They're not interested in anything I do here. I don't know how to get through to them.'

Only last night, she'd sent all three of the children an email reminding them it would soon be Easter and she'd love to see them. Given their usual indifference, she hadn't expected to hear so soon. Now, recognising Lou's number on the screen, Grace picked up the phone.

'Hello, darling,' she said.

'Mum. Easter.' Lou didn't beat around the bush.

'Yes, dear.' Grace's heart began to beat madly. If Lou and Greg agreed to visit, maybe Mel would, too. It would mean so much to her to see them here, to have them accept her new life. She had no worries about Ben. She knew he was planning to come, telling her he couldn't wait to see her new home.

'I'm not sure of our plans.'

'Oh!' Grace's heart plummeted.

'We were thinking of going somewhere exotic, perhaps Bali.'

'Bali?' Grace knew she sounded like an imbecile repeating Lou like this, but she couldn't stem her surprise. 'But we always spend Easter together.'

'Yes, well…' Lou blustered. 'Greg…' She stopped, perhaps aware her mother would smell a rat. Lou was the decision-maker in that family. It wouldn't be Greg who wanted to fly away for the holiday weekend.

Grace swallowed, trying to remain calm and wishing Russ was still alive. He'd always been able to handle their elder daughter. But if he was, they wouldn't be having this conversation. 'It would mean a lot to me, sweetheart. It's the first Easter since…' Her voice faded.

'I know, Mum. But it'll all be different this year – without Dad, without Brigadoon. That's why…' There was a pause during which Grace wanted to imagine Lou fighting back tears. But her daughter's voice was as self-contained as ever when she continued, 'Look Mum, I have to go now. Talk later.'

Grace looked at her phone as if she could will it back to life. Why had Lou even bothered to call? But there was no way of figuring out her daughter's actions. It had been the same when she was a child. Lou had always been the one to come up with the most far-fetched explanations for her behaviour and misdemeanours, whereas both Mel and Ben had been more straightforward.

She sighed and rose to take her now empty cup into the kitchen, dislodging Tiger from his spot as she went, leading him to emit a loud meow of annoyance. He padded behind her into the kitchen to stand expectantly over his bowl.

'Greedy puss,' Grace said. 'I already fed you.' But she poured a little cat food into his bowl. Tiger had been a scrawny kitten when he arrived shivering at Grace's back door one stormy night, and the cat still craved both food and affection. Grace gave him both, to the surprise of her sister who claimed to be allergic to cats.

'I don't know why you bother with that creature,' Dot said, when Grace chose to give the stray cat a home. 'He'll turn out to be more trouble than he's worth. Mark my words.'

Grace ignored her sister's advice and was glad she had. Tiger had proved to be good company, her best friend and the one who would always listen to her complaints without protest.

Thinking of Dot reminded Grace she'd promised to meet her sister for coffee. Life here in Bellbird Bay hadn't proved to be as quiet as Grace anticipated. Only a few weeks after her arrival, she'd found herself talked into a casual position in the local library which had soon morphed into her becoming the part-time children's librarian. Then there was the book club Dot had persuaded her to join. She'd had every intention of volunteering with the local meals-on-wheels group but hadn't got around to it yet. But her activities kept her busy and helped her forget her disappointment with her two daughters. She wanted to show her children her new home, to persuade them to agree she'd made the right decision, the right decision for her, if not for them.

Grace remembered her first few weeks in Bellbird Bay, weeks when she wondered if she *had* made the right decision. Dot had insisted she stay with her and Kev until she found a place of her own, perhaps in the same over 50's village they called home. But as soon as Grace drove through the gates proclaiming it to be *Bay Village Lifestyle Resort*, she knew it wasn't for her. It was a very peaceful community, the residents were friendly, but Grace found it too organised. It was a relief when, on one of her early morning beach walks, she discovered the For Sale sign on the cottage she now called home.

*

'Hi, Dot. Glorious morning.'

'Morning, Grace. How are you? You're looking a bit peaky.' Dot hugged Grace and gave her a peck on the cheek

Grace returned the embrace and slid into the seat opposite her sister in *The Bay Café*. This café in a shopping precinct on the esplanade with a view of the ocean was one of their favourite meeting spots. Coming here always reminded Grace of the wisdom of her decision to move to Bellbird Bay.

'I'm fine,' she said in response to her sister, wondering if she should have added more rouge this morning, if her disappointment in Lou's call showed on her face. 'Just wishing Lou could see my point of view. Sometimes I think you and Kev are lucky you never had children.'

'You don't mean that.'

'No, sorry.' Grace knew it was a longstanding regret to her sister that she'd been unable to have children, and wanted to bite her tongue. She loved all three of her children dearly, even if she often wanted to shake them. 'But sometimes, I think they cause more pain than I need in my life.'

'Lou?' Dot guessed.

Grace nodded. 'Skinny cap, please,' she said to the waitress who appeared at their table. She needed the buzz of caffeine to help her get over Lou's call.

'I'll have a pot of English Breakfast tea,' Dot said. As soon as the waitress disappeared, she turned back to Grace. 'What's my niece done now?'

'She and Greg are planning to go to Bali for Easter.'

'Oh!'

'I wouldn't mind so much, but…' Grace took off the hat she wore to protect her from the sun and carefully placed it on the chair next to her, '…I know she's doing it out of spite.'

'Surely not?' Dot had always been quick to defend Lou, Grace remembered, even when she was a child, when she and Russ brought the three children here for holidays. 'She couldn't be so vindictive. Is Easter so important to you?'

'It was always a special time for the family, both Easter and Christmas. When Russ was alive, before he got sick, even in the early stages of his dementia, they were happy times. When the children were little, we used to hide Easter eggs in the paddock and the three of them would compete to see who could gather the most on Easter Monday.' She smiled at the memory. 'We'd planned to do the same when the grandkids arrived, but…' She spread her hands.

'Last Christmas was different, sad, but until I broke the news I was selling up, we were all trying to make the best of it, to keep up the traditions Russ and I established. I was hoping…' Grace's eyes misted over, '…we could make some new ones here in Bellbird Bay.'

'And Mel and Ben?'

'Oh, Ben will be here. He never lets me down. I don't know about Mel. She's likely to follow whatever Lou suggests. I haven't heard from her.'

'She's still in the same job?'

'Mmm. I wish she'd find something else, something more suited to her. She's a bright girl and is wasted in such a menial position. Mel's always underestimated herself. I used to wonder if she felt overshadowed by Lou's confidence, but…' She shook her head. 'Russ said she'd find herself eventually. I hope he was right. She took his death harder than the others – and the loss of Brigadoon.'

'Mmm. You must have been sad to lose it, too.'

'Yes, but I couldn't keep it up. Russ and I talked about it before he got sick, and we always planned to sell at some stage. But it didn't make it any easier. So many memories.' Grace closed her eyes for a moment, remembering when she and Russ had found the block of land for sale when they were out driving one Sunday afternoon. It was soon after they arrived in Granite Springs and were debating whether to buy an old Queenslander in town or move into a new development. As soon as they laid eyes on the twenty-acre block, looking so peaceful with the stand of trees and the ruins of an old dwelling surrounded by bushes, their decision was made. It was as if for this place, time had stood still. Russ immediately christened it Brigadoon after the mythical Scottish Highland village in the old movie they both loved.

'But you don't regret the move?'

'Absolutely not. Russ will always be with me, wherever I am. I just wish the girls would come round to my way of thinking.'

Three

Ted Crawford checked the weather on the Bureau of Meteorology website, pleased to see a fine week was forecast. It was turtle hatching season and he and the others in the band of volunteers were scheduled to meet on the beach below the headland to ensure the baby turtles made it safely into the ocean. Once there, they were on their own, and it was anyone's guess how many would survive.

In all the years he took part in surfing competitions up and down the coast, he'd never thought he'd be spending much of his retirement taking care of these little creatures. But it was strangely rewarding. Over the past few months, Ted, along with other members of the local community, had been rostered to assist with monitoring the nesting conditions and populations, the emergence of the hatchlings, and in attempting to minimise the presence of foxes which preyed on them.

Now it was almost over for another year. He'd be sorry, would miss his early morning forays to the beach. But it would mean he could get back to surfing. There was nothing quite like the thrill of catching a wave as the sun was peeking over the horizon, and the surf around Bellbird Bay was some of the best on the coast.

Ted grimaced at his image in the mirror, the white hair and lined face looking back at him bore no resemblance to the way he felt inside. The years might have worn his body much as the ocean wore away the rocks, but at heart he was still the eighteen-year-old who had taken first prize in the Bay Surfing Championships three years running. But that was before university and a career in the law had put paid to his days on the water.

Now he was back home, and living the life he'd always dreamt of, even though these days he was a tad slower, his eyes needed the assistance of glasses for reading, and it took him longer to climb up from the beach.

He glanced at his phone before locking up, seeing a message from his son. He frowned, wondering what Aaron wanted. Since he and Tanya divorced, Aaron seemed to have lost direction. He continued in his role as project manager for an engineering firm in the city, but Ted felt his heart wasn't in it. The boy – hardly a boy at almost forty, but he always would be to his father – had sounded like a lost soul when they spoke the previous weekend. It had taken all Ted's powers of persuasion to get him to agree to come to stay over the Easter break.

See you late next Thurs. May stay beyond the weekend. Need to talk. A

Ted sighed at the sign he'd come to recognise. He knew without Aaron's confirmation his son was in trouble again. He'd either left his job or found himself in some other pickle and wanted Ted to help him out of it. Sometimes, Ted despaired his son would ever grow up and learn to stand on his own two feet. He'd had great hopes of him when he and Tanya married. But it was soon clear who wore the trousers in their relationship, and it was no surprise when the marriage didn't survive.

Once at the beach, Ted had no time to worry about his son. He was kept busy ensuring the surviving young turtles made their way to the ocean. He always experienced a thrill of delight at the sight of the small creatures flapping their way across the sand to finally reach the sea and disappear in the waves. It was a miracle how so many of them survived to find their way back here to their nesting placc to lay their eggs year after year.

'That's it for another year,' one of the other volunteers said, as he and Ted made their way back up from the beach. Kev Butler and he had been school friends. They'd lost touch for years while both pursued their careers and had been delighted to be reunited when Ted returned to Bellbird Bay in his retirement. Kev had never left, having married a city girl he'd met when she was here on holiday. Now he and Dot lived in *Bay Village*, and he was never tired of expounding the virtues of retirement community living to his old friend.

But Ted preferred the privacy of the old fisherman's shack he'd renovated, and which looked out onto the Pacific Ocean. It was where he intended to end his days.

'Fancy a beer?' Kev asked, as they approached the entrance to the surf club. 'Dot's meeting her sister for coffee this morning, and if I know her, she'll be tied up for hours.' He chuckled.

Ted checked his watch. 'A bit early for a beer for me, but coffee sounds good.' He grinned at his friend's comment. It was a long time since he'd had to consider the comings and goings of a wife. He'd lost Alison to a drunk driver when Aaron was only in primary school and, if he hadn't exactly avoided women ever since, he had managed to keep away from any scent of involvement.

'It's great that you're still surfing.' Kev nodded to the larger-than-life image of Ted along with several others of his era painted on the wall on the way up the stairs in the club. His name was also etched on the board at the top of the stairs, one of the club's champions.

Ted flinched as he always did at this permanent reminder of his glory days. He was happy to leave the competition to the younger guys these days, had been for years, and had never enjoyed being deemed a local hero. He'd hoped when the club was renovated several years earlier, the outdated mural would have been one of the things to go, but it was still there for all to see and admire.

'I go out when I can. Not so agile these days. The old body's not what it was.' But Ted knew he was downplaying his level of fitness. He'd be out in the surf again early next morning, able to match many of the younger surfers if not outdo them.

The two men placed their coffee orders and went out to the deck. There, they had a good view of the beach where a group of young recruits were learning the skill in the surf school which was located close by. Will Rankin was one of the younger guys who'd taken over Ted's crown, but even he had now given way to another generation of surfers, while he made a living from teaching others and hiring out surf boards. Ted had heard Will's son was now emulating his old man.

'This is the life,' Kev said, leaning back in his chair and picking up the small complimentary biscuit served with each coffee. 'Glad you came back?'

'Sure am. I never intended to stay away for ever. But life has a habit of getting in the way. It was more profitable to practice law in Brisbane and when Alison died, with Aaron in school there… It would have been too much of a disruption to pull him out. Then…' he sighed, '…I guess I got caught up in the hype of city living. It took the advent of retirement to force me to make what was a wise move.'

'That reminds me.' Kev carefully placed his cup on the table as if aware what he had to say wouldn't be welcome. 'Dot wants me to invite you to dinner.'

Ted raised one eyebrow. This was a first, though not altogether a surprise. Given the demographic in Bellbird Bay, women outnumbered men, especially in his age cohort. It was a well-known fact the fairer sex lived longer than their male counterparts and since moving back, Ted had found himself prey to the machinations of more than one designing woman. 'Oh?'

'It's none of my doing,' Kev stammered. 'Dot's sister moved up from the country a couple of months ago. She doesn't know many people in Bellbird Bay as yet, and Dot is having a few people over to meet her. You'll come, won't you?'

Ted almost laughed at Kev's doleful expression. It was clear he was under his wife's thumb. A bit like Aaron's marriage, he thought. Keen to put his old friend's mind at rest he said, 'I suppose I could manage it, but I'm not in the market for another wife.'

'Oh, no, nothing like that,' Kev said with a sigh of relief. 'It's the wife's way of introducing Grace around. I don't think…'

Maybe he didn't, but Ted knew those women. They were never content to see a man on his own without trying to match him up with one of their cronies. He'd been there so often and managed to escape the trap each time.

He wondered what this one would be like.

Four

'There's someone I'd like you to meet.' Dot had been chatting on for some time about the joys of community life in *Bay Village* and the various activities she and Kev were engaged in. Grace had stopped listening, preferring to gaze around at the occupants of the surrounding tables, trying to identify those who lived here and those who were tourists. She had almost made up her mind the group of lively women at the corner table were locals while the quiet couple who appeared to have little to say to each other were here on holiday, when she realised Dot was waiting for her to say something.

'Sorry, I'm afraid my mind was wandering.' Grace was embarrassed at being caught out. Was the fact she couldn't always concentrate on what was being said to her a sign of old age, or was it only that her sister sometimes bored her? She was only sixty-one after all. That wasn't considered old these days. She didn't feel old, only sometimes when she forgot why she'd gone into a room or couldn't remember a name, but that was normal, wasn't it? 'What did you say, Dot?'

'I was saying I'm having a small dinner party on Saturday and there's someone I want you to meet.'

'Oh!' Grace knew exactly what her sister had in mind. Dot had always been a bit of a matchmaker and the someone was no doubt a man who Dot had decided was perfect for her younger sister. 'I don't think…'

'You've been here for a few months now and, as far as I can see, have made no effort to make friends. Apart from the book club, I don't know what you do with yourself.'

'I do have my work in the library.'

'Pooh. That doesn't count.' Dot dismissed what Grace considered to be a valuable contribution to the community with a wave of her hand. 'You need to make friends, become part of the community. After living in Granite Springs, I'm sure you know how important that is. So, Saturday?'

Grace knew what she was talking about. But, having been a stalwart member of the community in a small town for years, it was a relief to lead a more insular existence. And there was her writing. It was her secret, one she wasn't prepared to share with anyone, especially not her sister who could never keep things to herself.

In her role as children's librarian, albeit part-time, Grace had rekindled her love of small children and had been inspired to put pen to paper and begin writing the children's book she'd dreamed of for years. It was still in its early stages and not something she wanted to talk about, but it consumed her evenings when others might watch television or participate in one of the many social groups which proliferated among women of her vintage.

Dot was waiting for an answer, and Grace knew her sister wasn't going to accept any excuse she might come up with. It would be easier to agree, be polite to whoever Dot had invited and leave as soon as she could. Her sister meant well and couldn't imagine Grace might be content with the solitary existence she'd chosen. 'I'll be there.'

'Good.' Satisfied she'd succeeded in her quest, Dot gathered up her belongings. 'My treat,' she said as they rose to leave. 'See you on Saturday at seven. No need to bring anything.'

The pair hugged again before going their separate ways.

Alone, Grace wandered around the plaza, peering into shop windows, stopping in front of one which caught her eye. The window of *Birds of a Feather* was filled with a variety of garments in bright colours and the name of the shop appealed to Grace. It reminded her of a television programme of the same name she'd watched years earlier, though she couldn't remember what it had been about. A new outfit was just what she needed to cheer her up. Grace pushed open the heavy glass door.

Inside, she was confronted by racks of beach clothes for all shapes and sizes in every colour under the sun.

'Can I help you?' A smart woman wearing one of the creations Grace had seen displayed in the window appeared as if from nowhere. 'I'm Greta. We haven't met, but I know who you are. You're Dot Butler's sister.'

Surprised, for a moment Grace was lost for words. How could she have forgotten the way news got around in small towns? Bellbird Bay was like Granite Springs in that regard. 'Grace,' she said, taking the other woman's outstretched hand. 'I just wanted to have a look around.'

'Fine. Let me know if I can help with anything.' Greta moved back to the counter where she had been pricing new stock.

Grace wandered around the shop, checking out several garments, unsure if she really wanted to make a purchase. She had plenty of clothes and certainly wasn't in need of another outfit. But, eyeing the dresses, pants and tops on display, the clothes which had satisfied her in Granite Springs now seemed dull and old-fashioned, and she felt the urge to restock her wardrobe.

As if reading her mind and, just as she was fingering a wildly patterned blue dress with wide straps and a v-neckline, Greta appeared at her side.

'You'd look great in that. Would you like to try it?'

Tempted, Grace nodded and was soon standing in the small fitting room at the back of the shop admiring herself in the mirror. The dress was very different from the self-coloured linen garments which graced her wardrobe at home, and which had been her mainstay for years, but there was something about it that called out to her. Deciding to take it, the curtain which protected her privacy opened, and Greta appeared with a handful of other garments, all equally colourful.

'I thought you might like to try these while you're here,' she said, eyeing the beige capri pants and white linen blouse Grace had been wearing and which were now lying on a chair.

In for a penny, in for a pound. Grace's mother's old saying rang in her ears as she allowed Greta to hang up the dresses, pants and blouses – all patterned in vibrant colours – before disappearing again.

Half an hour later, Grace emerged from the shop carrying several bags, her bank card severely depleted, but with a smile on her face. Just wait till the children saw her in her new outfits. Wouldn't they be surprised? Then she remembered. Ben might be the only one to see her new image. Well, at least he'd appreciate it, she consoled herself. And there was this dinner party of Dot's to get through first. Maybe she'd use the occasion to christen one of her new dresses.

*

By the time Saturday arrived, Grace was regretting having agreed to Dot's invitation. She viewed herself in the full-length mirror in her bedroom, wondering if the bright fuchsia pink dress emblazoned with images of peacocks made her look like mutton dressed as lamb, before finally deciding she didn't care. The dress, so different from what she usually wore, gave her the confidence she needed to face whatever and whoever Dot had in store. She checked her makeup, gave her hair a last pat and was ready to go.

'Be good, Tige,' she said to her cat who, having already been fed, was curled up on the sofa and sending baleful looks in Grace's direction. It wasn't often she went out at night. In fact, apart from the book club, this would only be the second time since she moved here. The last time had been to Dot and Kev's, too, but then there hadn't been any other guests. 'I won't be late,' she assured the cat, wishing she could curl up beside him with a good book or her laptop.

Grace had a knot in her stomach as she drove into the gated community after entering her sister's gate code into the keypad. She supposed there was some benefit to be gained from this degree of security, and Dot insisted it gave her peace of mind, but Grace felt safe enough in her little house. She parked in the visitor parking, took a deep breath, walked across to her sister's house and knocked on the door.

Even before it opened, she could hear voices and music coming from inside. How many had Dot invited to this *small dinner party* of hers?

'Here you are!' Dot greeted Grace with a hug and a kiss, before holding her at arm's length. 'New dress? I heard you made it into *Birds of a Feather*. Not my cup of tea, but it looks good on you. Come in and meet everyone.'

Grace allowed herself to be led into a living room which seemed crammed with people whose names Dot quickly reeled off and which Grace knew she'd never remember. But by the time she was seated at the dinner table with a glass of wine, she could see there were only two couples besides Dot and Kev, and a man with tanned skin and thick white hair who looked as uncomfortable as she felt. It appeared from the conversation that the other two couples were neighbours of Dot and Kev in *Bay Village*. It wasn't clear about the man whose name was Ted and who didn't have much to say. *Did the poor fellow know he'd been invited solely to meet her, part of Dot's plan for Grace to move on with her life?*

Her sister might not have put it in as many words, couching it as *making more friends and becoming part of the community*, but Grace knew what Dot intended. She thought it was time Grace stopped grieving for Russ and looked to the future. What Dot didn't realise was that Grace was quite happy on her own and had no intention of replacing Russ in her life – as if anyone ever could.

Somehow, she made it through the evening, helped by several more glasses of wine than was wise. The group had made attempts to include Grace in their conversation with Dot trying to talk Grace up to Ted who mostly responded by grunting. Grace wished she could have done the same, but made an effort to be polite while saying very little about herself. She hoped the two cups of black coffee she drank before leaving would ensure she could safely drive the short distance home. Once there, she gave a sigh of relief, slipped off her shoes and joined Tiger who was lying on the sofa where she'd left him, only lifting his head slightly in recognition of her return, before closing his eyes again and purring softly.

Whether from the effects of the wine or going to bed later than usual, Grace slept soundly, only wakening next morning when Tiger leapt onto her bed to remind her it was time for him to be fed. As she did every morning on waking, Grace checked her phone for messages. She smiled at the one from Ben with an emoji of a chicken popping out of an egg, a message saying how much he was looking forward to Easter, and a photo of his latest find which she had trouble identifying. But there was no message from Lou and still nothing from Mel.

Shrugging on her robe and making her way through to the kitchen, Grace replenished Tiger's food and water bowls before making herself a cup of fennel and cardamon tea and heating a croissant she'd bought yesterday at the local patisserie. Then she took her breakfast out to the deck. It was a glorious March morning, the sun rising over the water turning the sky to pink, the white crest of the waves breaking on the beach below.

She was looking forward to sharing it with Ben, to enjoying Easter next weekend, even if it was to be only the two of them. But she couldn't help worrying about Mel. At thirty-one, she should have some direction in her life. When Grace was her age, she was married with three children. What did the future hold for her younger daughter?

Her thoughts turned to the previous evening. It hadn't been as bad as she expected. The two couples were amiable people, happy to chat about local events and the possibility of the town hosting another food and wine festival. The man, who no doubt Dot had earmarked for Grace, was a different matter. Grace suspected he was another neighbour, one who had been recently widowed and was as disgruntled as she was at being roped into the fiasco. For a brief moment, she'd wondered about him. Why was he here? Had he always lived in Bellbird Bay? But now she'd done her duty to Dot, she need never see him again, and hopefully her sister would give up and let her be. Bellbird Bay was a bit like a coastal version of Granite Springs. There couldn't be many single men of her age around, and those who were would quickly be snapped up. She almost felt sorry for the poor man.

Five

Rising before the sun was up, Ted made his way across the boardwalk and down the steps to the beach. It was a glorious morning, the waves perfect for surfing, an ideal way to put the embarrassment of the previous evening behind him.

What had possessed him to agree to being bait for Kev's wife's machinations? It had been so obvious – Kev and his wife, two other couples and the single woman. She appeared to find the situation as distasteful as he did and didn't contribute much to the conversation which centred around local matters, but he caught her sending curious glances in his direction on several occasions. Of course, it meant he'd been looking at her, too. Her gaudy dress stood out beside the conventional garb of the other three women and proclaimed she was of an independent mind. She was pretty, too, unusual, her silver hair falling in waves around her face and those bright blue eyes and clear complexion. Hell, he'd noticed more than he thought.

By this time, Ted had reached the water's edge. He put all thoughts of the woman and the previous evening behind him and waded into the water carrying his board.

*

'You're still a match for those youngsters, Ted.'

Walking out of the surf, his board under one arm, Ted shook the water from his hair and looked around to see who was speaking.

Will Rankin was standing there, hands on his hips.

'Will. G'day, mate. Not out today, yourself?'

'Not today. Need to get back to the van. Owen is looking after it for me while I check out his competition for the Bay Surf Carnival next weekend. I have a couple of kids coming for lessons at…' he checked his watch. 'I'd better run. Good to see you. Hope we'll see you next Saturday.' He hurried off without waiting for Ted's response.

Of course. How could Ted have forgotten? The Surf Carnival held every Easter weekend was one of the highlights of the Bellbird Bay events calendar, it and the Bay Triathlon which took place later in the year. There were some who would disagree, of course, who'd list the flower show and the food and wine festival which had been one of the topics of conversation last night. But for the surfing community, there was nothing to beat those sporting events.

It was a long time since Ted had been a contestant, but in his day, he'd taken awards in both the Carnival and the Triathlon. It might appeal to Aaron to come down to see the surfers next Saturday, see what his old man used to get up to. It should be a good day out, and they could have lunch at the club afterwards.

Ted hadn't heard from his son since the brief text, confirming he'd be here for Easter. He hoped whatever was bothering Aaron wasn't something needing his intervention. With a brief hiatus when he was married to Tanya, Ted seemed to have been pulling his son out of scrapes since he was five years old.

What saddened him most about the break-up of Aaron's marriage was the loss of contact with his grandson. Zack would be twelve now, have started high school, and Ted couldn't remember when he'd last seen him. If it hadn't been for the odd post on Tanya's Facebook page, he wouldn't even know what his grandson looked like these days. Aaron's divorce had been messy, his ex moving in with her new man and taking Zack with her. Aaron hadn't pushed for custody, unwilling to make Zack the centre of a legal dispute.

He'd ask Aaron for news of Zack next weekend. The agreement had been for the father to see his son for part of each school holiday, but according to Aaron, Tanya blocked him at every turn, finding excuses to deny access.

*

Ted unpacked the last bag of groceries and finished loading the fridge with meat, vegetables and enough beer to keep both him and Aaron happy all weekend. The boy should be arriving soon if he'd managed to leave the city early, and they could maybe have a swim before lunch, then a chat. The sooner Aaron could unburden himself the better, then they could enjoy the weekend together.

While he was waiting, Ted checked Facebook on his phone. As he expected, Tanya had uploaded another batch of photos. She and her new husband, along with Zack, appeared to be lazing on a beach somewhere. The boy looked withdrawn, not how Ted would expect a twelve-year-old to look on holiday in some exotic location. He frowned as his phone pinged with a text.

Got away later than expected. On my way now. ETA midday for lunch. My shout. A.

It was closer to one o'clock when Aaron's BMW finally drew up outside Ted's house.

'Sorry, Dad. I didn't allow for the traffic. Every man and his dog are heading up the coast for the weekend. I thought by leaving on Thursday I'd miss the worst of it, but seems everyone had the same idea.'

'No worries, son.' Ted pulled Aaron into a hug, clapping him on the shoulder as they parted. 'You mentioned lunch. Hungry?'

'I could eat a horse. Where do you recommend?'

'Why don't we head to the surf club? We can walk from here, and you'd probably like to stretch your legs after sitting in the car for so long.'

'Good idea.'

'Want to freshen up first?'

'Thanks.' Aaron headed to the bathroom while Ted slid his feet into his Birkenstocks and picked up his wallet.

'Ready, Dad?' Aaron appeared, having combed his wild, dark blond hair into some semblance of order. He looked just like Ted had at his age but there the resemblance ended. Aaron had never been as goal-driven as his father, had tended to look for the easy option and was easily led.

'Let's go.'

Exiting onto the deck, the two stood admiring the view before moving off.

'You have a great spot here, Dad. I wish…'

Ted gave Aaron a curious glance, but his son didn't expand on what he started to say. Maybe he'd open up over lunch.

'You haven't brought me here before,' Aaron said, as they signed in at the desk where the staff member welcomed Ted like an old friend.

'No?' Ted couldn't remember what they'd done on Aaron's last visit, and he'd gone down to stay with Aaron in Brisbane for Christmas, stayed for the New Year celebrations and the fireworks. He'd been glad to leave the city again and return to the relative peace of Bellbird Bay. Despite the influx of tourists, it was still a lot quieter than Brisbane. To think he'd spent all those years there when he could have been enjoying life here.

'Wow! Is that you?'

They'd started to climb the stairs, and Aaron stopped to gawk at the mural.

'It was a long time ago.'

'I know you said you were a surfing champion, but I never thought… Hell, Dad. You're a local hero. You still surfing?'

'When I can. I try to get out most mornings. Speaking of which, there's a surf carnival this weekend, I thought you might enjoy it.'

'Hmm. Maybe we could give it a whirl.'

Give it a whirl? What sort of talk was that? 'Let's order then go out to the deck.' Ted steered Aaron in the direction of the bar. He ordered two schooners of light and two servings of burgers and chips, and they took their beers out to the deck which was beginning to empty of the lunch crowd.

'Now, what's up?' Ted asked, when they'd downed their beers and made inroads on their meals.

'This is good. You should have let me pay, Dad.'

'Nonsense. The day I can't treat my son to a meal, I'll give up.'

'Thanks.' Aaron ran a finger around the rim of his glass. 'I'm in trouble.'

This was what Ted had been afraid of. 'Work?'

Aaron nodded. 'It's not my fault, but…'

Ted's heart sank. In Aaron's opinion, it was never his fault, but somehow he managed to find himself embroiled in a mess, and expect Ted to help him out. 'What is it this time?'

Aaron launched into a complicated description of a project he'd been working on, something to do with a mine in the north of the state where a crucial piece of equipment had failed. 'I did the design,' he said at last, 'but I used the specs I was given. It wasn't up to me to query them, was it?' he asked piteously. He pushed away his plate

'Now let me see. What you're saying is you were responsible for designing a piece of equipment which failed, which could have caused the deaths of miners, but it wasn't your fault?'

'That's right. You see that, don't you?'

While Ted wanted to reassure his son, he needed to know more about the circumstances. Engineering and mining weren't things he was familiar with. His law practice had been involved in civil and criminal cases. He'd never had to investigate or defend anyone for negligence, which is what Aaron appeared to be referring to.

'While I hear you don't accept culpability, I'm not familiar enough with the case to advise you, Aaron. Can you provide me with more information?'

'I knew you'd wrap it all up in that legal jargon of yours. I'm innocent, I tell you.' Aaron's voice rose, causing the only other diners on the deck to look round.

'Keep it down, son. You don't need the whole club to know.'

Aaron looked around, then said in a low voice. 'What am I going to do, Dad? They've asked me to take leave till it's all sorted.'

'Ah!' So, this was why Aaron had mentioned staying a few more days. No wonder he wanted to get away from the city for a time. 'If you can put it all down in writing for me – who was responsible for what and the implications of the inaccurate design, I'll talk to a few people I know and…'

'You'll be able to prove it wasn't my fault, that I acted in good faith.'

'Leave it with me.' Ted thought for a few moments. 'It didn't occur to you something might be amiss when you were drawing up the plans?'

Aaron looked uncomfortable. 'Well, it wasn't up to me,' he blustered. 'So, I can stay with you till it's resolved?'

'Of course, you can,' Ted said, seeing his beloved peaceful existence disappearing.

Six

Grace was checking everything was ready for Ben's arrival when she heard a car stop outside. She'd offered to pick him up at the airport but independent as ever, he said he'd hire a car. This must be him. She rushed to the front door, Tiger weaving around her ankles in his eagerness to be part of the welcome committee.

The brightness of the sun made her blink as not one, but two figures emerged from the little Kia.

'Look who I found at the airport,' Ben called, just as Grace recognised the second figure.

'Mel!'

A warm glow suffused her. Mel hadn't replied to her email, hadn't answered her phone, but she was here. 'I'm so glad to see you, sweetheart.' She pulled her daughter into a warm hug. 'You, too, Ben.' She hugged her son, too, and the three walked back into the house arm-in-arm.

'So, this is the place I've been hearing so much about?' Ben said, as soon as he walked inside. He made straight for the kitchen and out to the deck. 'Wow, Mum, what a view. No wonder you love it here. A big change from paddocks of sheep and goats.'

'Don't you miss Brigadoon?' Mel asked, following them out and throwing herself down into one of the cane chairs without even glancing at the view.

'Of course, I do… sometimes. But I love it here, darling. You'll come to love it, too.'

'Don't be such a pain, Mel. Have we time for a swim before lunch, Mum? I feel as if I've been sitting on a plane for days, and the ocean looks so inviting.'

'Sure. It's a cold lunch. We can have it any time. I might join you on the beach though I won't have a swim. I already had one earlier.'

'Mel?' Ben asked.

'Not me. I don't have any swimmers.'

'But you'll join us on the beach?' It was just like Mel to come to a beach town without any swimwear. 'We can get you sorted later. There's a great beach and swimwear shop. *Sassy's.* It's where I bought mine.'

Mel pouted. Not a good look. It hadn't been when she was four and was even less so now. 'I guess.'

While Ben changed, Grace fetched towels, sunscreen and hats while Mel continued to sit and stare into space, only rousing herself when Ben reappeared.

'I'm glad you decided to come after all,' Grace said to her daughter, when Ben had launched himself into the sea and was swimming strongly towards the headland. 'How are things?'

'Okay. There was nothing happening in Sydney over Easter, and Lou and Greg are off to Bali.'

'Yes.' Grace's lips tightened. She hadn't forgiven her older daughter for going off overseas instead of coming here. Though Lou had said something about visiting later.

Mel didn't say anything else, and Grace decided not to question her any further. Not now. She tried to make out her daughter's expression but the large sunglasses she was wearing, combined with the brim of her baseball cap, hid her eyes completely. There was something bothering Mel, and Grace was determined to discover what it was. She had the whole weekend to find out.

'It was amazing. You should have come in,' Ben said, grabbing a towel and dripping water all over his mother and sister.

'Oh, get off!' Mel yelled, moving out of his reach.

'That's enough, Ben. Leave your sister be.' Grace wiped the drops of water from her face with a laugh. When would she be able to stop mediating between the two of them? Ben had always been able to get a rise out of his sister and it seemed he still did. Grace sighed. Perhaps this weekend wasn't going to be as happy as she anticipated.

After a lunch of cold meats and salad, Ben opted to rest, claiming jetlag had caught up with him. Grace suggested to Mel that she show her the town and to her surprise Mel agreed. 'I'd like to drop into the garden centre,' Grace said. 'I want to buy an azalea to replace one which has died and get some potting mix. Okay with you?'

Mel nodded, disappeared into her room and reappeared having changed from the jeans and tee-shirt she'd arrived in into a pretty dress.

'You look nice in that, darling. It suits you,' Grace said.

'It's warmer here than I expected,' was Mel's only reply.

Grace sighed inwardly. This was going to be hard going but she was determined by the end of the weekend, she'd have found out what was wrong, why Mel was behaving even more awkwardly than usual. It was out of character for her to be so tight-lipped, when she normally found no difficulty in stating her views to all and sundry, whether they wanted to hear or not.

Before driving to the garden centre, Grace parked the car on the esplanade so they could wander past the shops there.

'Is this the place you were talking about?' Mel asked, when they passed the sign which said *Sassy's*, the window filled with a variety of swimsuits, bikinis, shorts and sarongs.

'Mmm. Want to go in?' Grace held her breath.

'I suppose… if I'm going to be here and want to swim.'

Mel pushed open the door and they walked into the airconditioned shop.

Grace took a seat while Mel flicked through rails of swimsuits of all shapes and sizes, finally choosing several to try.

'Your daughter?' asked the assistant, when Mel was ensconced in the fitting room. 'You look alike.'

We do? No one had ever commented on this before. But in Granite Springs, there was no need. Everyone there had known both Grace and Mel since Mel was born. Grace supposed they shared the same bone structure – high cheek bones and a pointed chin – and they both had blue eyes. But her hair was now silver while Mel's was a darker brown than Grace's had ever been, and the younger woman wore hers long and tied back instead of waving around her face.

'I'll take this one.' Mel emerged from the fitting room to hand a black and white garment to the assistant while Grace tried to see the resemblance the assistant had remarked on. She shook her head. She must have been imagining it. Mel lacked the determination of which Grace had always been proud, and which Russ told her shone through everything she said and did.

'Happy now?' Mel asked when they left the shop.

'You didn't need to buy a swimsuit to please me.' Grace's heart plummeted again. Could she do nothing right for Mel?

'No?' Mel swung the bag in one hand. 'Garden centre, you said.'

'Yes.'

At the garden centre, Mel seemed content to wander while Grace made her purchases, loading them into a shopping trolley before going to find her daughter.

'Is that a café through there?' Mel asked, pointing to a gap in a carefully trimmed plumbago hedge. A sign indicated it was the entrance to *The Pandanus Café*.

'It is. Feel like a coffee?'

For the first time since she arrived, Mel appeared to take the initiative. 'Yes, please.' She led the way through the deep blue blossoms to where small tables had been artistically placed among a series of low bushes and towering palm trees. In its centre was a large pandanus tree, and in the far corner the kitchen was neatly hidden from view by a screen of grevillea.

'I often stop here when I come to the garden centre,' Grace said, choosing a table and parking the shopping trolley by her side.

'It's nice.'

Grace sighed with relief. Mel had found something she liked here in Bellbird Bay. Maybe the weekend wouldn't be such a disaster after all.

They sat in silence while waiting for their order – lemon and ginger tea for Grace and a macchiato for Mel. Grace was trying to work out what to say to encourage Mel to open up to her.

It wasn't till they'd been served that Mel finally met her mother's eyes. 'Was Dad disappointed in me?' she asked.

Surprised, Grace put down the cup she'd been raising to her lips. 'Disappointed? No. You know we both loved you. We only wanted you to be happy. But…' she bit her lip, '…you don't seem happy, Mel.

What's the matter? Is it work or…' Grace knew nothing about Mel's private life. Her daughter kept it just that – private. Whereas both Lou and Ben had been accustomed to sharing the ups and downs of their lives, her younger daughter had always preferred to keep things to herself. Even as a child, Mel had been reluctant to talk about her friends despite being free with her opinions.

Mel didn't answer immediately. She took a drink of coffee and shifted in her seat. Then she said, 'I don't know what to do, Mum. Graham's told me I need to smarten up if I want to keep my job, but…' she raised her eyes to meet Grace's, '…what else can I do? I'm not like Lou or Ben. I didn't go on to university after school. Selma's dad offered me this job and I took it. I thought… I don't know what I thought. But it seemed a good idea at the time.'

'But maybe not any longer?' Grace asked gently.

'I'm turning thirty-two this year. All my friends are married and have good jobs and I'm still flailing around trying to find myself. What's wrong with me?'

'Nothing's wrong with you, sweetheart. It just takes some people longer than others to work out what they want. What would you like to do?'

'That's what everyone asks me. I don't know!'

'Everyone?'

'Well, Lou. We had dinner together before she and Greg jetted off to Bali and she tore into me, told me it was time I grew up, that the world didn't owe me a living, that I was a disappointment to Dad. I wasn't, was I?' her eyes filled with tears.

So that's where it came from. Lou had chosen to tell her sister a few home truths. Though what she said about Russ wasn't true. 'Dad didn't feel that way. He loved you exactly as you are.'

'He did? I miss him so much. I want him to be proud of me. If only he was here, I could…'

'Oh, my darling. He *was* proud, we both were. And wherever he is now, I'm sure…' Grace's eyes misted over. She wished Russ was here, too. Luckily the café was almost deserted. There was no one to see the pair of them sitting there in tears. 'I'm here. Will I do?' She handed Mel a tissue.

Mel wiped her eyes. 'Maybe, but… if I leave the agency, what can I do? I've no qualifications and I'm not trained to do anything.'

'It's never too late, and you don't have to decide anything today. I'm glad you chose to share with me, darling. Maybe together we can come up with something. Is everything else in your life okay?' This was the closest Grace was willing to go in asking about Mel's love life.

But Mel shook her head. There were clearly some things she wasn't ready to share.

Seven

Easter Saturday promised to be another glorious day. Friday being a public holiday, they'd spent it lazing around the house, Ted with his nose in a book and Aaron on his iPad. This morning, Ted rose early and, leaving Aaron asleep, headed out to have a surf before the carnival began and the beach became crowded. Once there, he discovered he wasn't the only one with that idea. The parking lot was filled with the rusting vans loved by young surfers, and out in the ocean he could see dark heads bobbing in the waves which were at least two metres high – perfect for the day ahead.

It was a good time to be there, but as soon as the lifeguards arrived to start setting up for the day, he knew it was time to leave.

Back home, he roused a sleepy Aaron and started breakfast, deciding a fry up of bacon, eggs, tomatoes and mushrooms would set them up for the day. He chose to leave any discussion of Aaron's problem till later. There was nothing to be done over the weekend anyway, and hopefully he could manage to take his son's mind off his difficulty by keeping him busy.

'Something smells good.' Aaron appeared in the kitchen wearing a pair of old shorts and a ratty tee-shirt with an AC/DC logo, running his fingers through his sleep-tousled hair. 'Is there any coffee?'

'Making it now.' Ted turned on the coffee maker and the kitchen was soon filled with the aroma of coffee beans.

'Thanks, Dad. I needed that.' Aaron gulped down the contents of his cup and held it out for a refill, before slouching into a chair. 'You still want to go to the carnival thing? You look as if you've been up for ages.'

'Went for a surf as the sun was coming up. There's nothing like it. You should try it.'

'Ugh.' Aaron took another gulp of coffee.

'And about the carnival, yes. I think you might enjoy it.'

'Hmm.' Aaron turned his attention to the plate of food Ted placed in front of him. 'If you say so.'

'How's Zack?'

'What?' Aaron looked up from his breakfast in surprise. 'What prompted you to ask about Zack?'

'Zack's my grandson, the grandson I haven't seen for some time. It's a normal question to ask. I see from Tanya's Facebook page that they're off somewhere for Easter.'

'Yeah.' Aaron grimaced. 'I'm sure she arranges these trips so I can't see him in the school holidays. But Zack's good, though I'm not sure how keen he is on the private school she and Mark have put him into. My half of the fees makes a hole in the bank account, but… if I want to see him… She's got me between a rock and a hard place, Dad.'

So, it wasn't all about the trouble at work. There were ongoing tensions with his ex, and Zack was the piggy-in-the-middle.

'You get to see him regularly?'

'Most weekends. He texts me a lot. He and Mark don't get on, so he finds life difficult, and I get the impression he's being bullied at school. He hasn't said much but reading between the lines…' Aaron frowned.

'Any chance I could see him one time you and he get together?'

'Don't see why not, but don't expect to get much notice, and Tanya often reneges on our arrangements.' He tapped the table with one finger. 'It's not what was agreed, but… it's that or nothing.'

'I'm sorry, son. I didn't realise.'

'You never liked her, did you?'

'I didn't think she was good enough for you. I may have said something to that effect at the time.'

'I know. I didn't listen. I was too besotted, then she got pregnant, and I did the right thing. Well, it didn't last. Zack is the best thing to come out of it and… Dammit, Dad, he's my son!' He thumped the table with his fist.

Ted had no response. He felt his son's despair. It hung over them like a cloak. They sat in silence, then Ted sighed. 'Finished?' He gestured to the egg which was congealing on Aaron's plate.

'Yeah. Guess I wasn't as hungry as I thought. When does this thing start? It'll at least keep me occupied, stop me thinking.'

'Good man.' Ted picked up the plates, patting Aaron's shoulder as he passed him on the way to the dishwasher. 'We should aim to get there around nine if we want to find a good spot and see the first heats.'

'Nine, that's…' Aaron looked at the clock on the kitchen wall which showed it was five to eight.

'Time for you to get a move on. A cool shower will make you feel better, and be sure to slather on the sunscreen. It's a hot one out there and will only get hotter. There's not much shade on the beach.'

'Okay, Dad.'

Ted smiled. Aaron was sounding better already. But the news about Zack was worrying. It didn't sound as if the boy was happy, and Aaron's words only reinforced the opinion Ted had formed from the photos on Tanya's Facebook page. He'd dearly love to bring the boy up here to show him some love and a different way of life. But how could it be done?

*

The beach was already crowded when Ted and Aaron arrived. Ted had anticipated this and suggested they walk down, avoiding the need to find a parking spot.

'Popular,' Aaron said, shading his eyes to stare across to where a group of contestants were receiving their final instructions.

'One of the highlights of the Bellbird Bay events calendar and remember it's Easter weekend and school holidays. There are a lot of out-of-towners here for the holiday. It's different to what it was in my day.' Ted thought back to his first surf carnival when he and his mates were in their teens. The town had changed since then. Transport had improved, and Bellbird Bay had become a tourist mecca for the rest of the state – and for many interstate tourists, too.

'Yeah, I'll bet. Back in the old days, eh?' Aaron chuckled as they were jostled by other spectators eager to obtain a better view.

'This way.' Ted led the way to an outcrop of higher ground from where they could see the entire beach. 'It helps to be a local.'

'This is great stuff, Dad,' Aaron enthused, when they had watched enthralled as the surfers demonstrated their skill in handling the waves which had strengthened since early morning. There were loud cheers when a local lad took out the honours in the male event.

'That's Will Rankin's son,' Ted said. 'Chip off the old block. His dad was a champion a few years after me. He now runs the surf school. Does pretty well, too, from what I hear.'

'I can't imagine you out there like that.' Aaron glanced at Ted.

'You wouldn't have recognised your old dad back then, sun-bleached hair to my shoulders, tanned skin. All that was missing was the tattoos that seem compulsory these days.'

'Tattoos, that'd be the day.' Aaron laughed at the thought of his conservative father with a tattoo.

'I wasn't always the conventional lawyer you know. I was young, too. They were good days, before I went off to uni, met your mum, you arrived on the scene and life became serious. Sometimes…' Ted gazed into space.

'You don't regret it?'

'No, but sometimes, when I look back…' Ted sighed. 'No, I wouldn't change a thing. What I would have done without your mum and without you to keep me on the straight and narrow, I dread to think.'

'But you're happy to be back now?'

'It's a good place to retire. And brings back good memories. There's something comforting about ending up where you began, closing the circle of life.'

'You're not…?' Aaron looked horrified.

'Hell, no. Got a few good years in me yet, and I intend to make the most of them. You're not going to get rid of me that easily.'

Aaron gave a mock sigh of relief. 'I've been thinking about what you said about Zack. You're right. I need to be more forceful, insist he spend more time with me. There's still a couple of weeks of school holiday. Maybe when Tanya and Mark get back from wherever, I can organise something.'

'That would be good, son.' Ted smiled. All Aaron had needed was a gentle nudge. Now, if he could only fix this matter with his work as effortlessly.

Eight

After Mel spent Good Friday swimming, lying on the beach, mooching around the house and complaining there was nothing to do here, Grace was glad when Saturday morning arrived, and the town would reopen. At least they could wander around the shops again, or maybe take one of the cruises she'd seen advertised. It was hard work keeping Mel amused. Grace had forgotten how difficult she could be.

'What's this surf thing?' Ben asked, looking up from the local newspaper. *The Bellbird Bugle* was published twice a week and delivered to the door, but Grace rarely bothered with it.

'What?' Mel asked lazily, looking up from her phone with the frown that was never far away.

'It says here, there's a surf carnival on this weekend. Sounds like a big deal. Mum?'

'Don't ask me. I don't surf. But I do believe it's a popular event. I've seen posters around town advertising it.'

'Maybe we should go. Could be interesting.'

'Watching a lot of stupid guys surf?' Mel scowled.

'Why not. Maybe we could have a go, too. There's always tomorrow and Monday. I may stay a few days longer, too, Mum.'

Grace smiled at Ben. 'That would be wonderful, honey. When do you have to be back to wherever you're working at the moment?'

Ben hesitated. 'The dig I was on is being closed. The funding has dried up.'

'So, what'll you do?' Grace's forehead creased. She absentmindedly stroked Tiger who had crept onto her lap, unsettled by the presence of two extra people in the house. Archaeology was Ben's life. It was something he'd been interested in since he was a small child, since he started digging in the paddocks around Brigadoon and unearthed an old horseshoe and some rusty nails. It was no surprise when he chose to study it at Sydney Uni and went on to work on digs all over Europe.

'I have an interview in Brisbane next Wednesday at the University of Queensland. They're looking for someone to head up a dig in the northern part of the state, working with the local indigenous people. It's a slim chance but it would be good to be closer to home, to you.'

'This isn't home,' Mel said. 'Brigadoon was home.' She rose to leave.

'That's not fair, Mel. Mum's doing her best. Home is where she is. Right, Mum?'

A warm glow filled Grace at her son's words, but Mel's reaction was still a worry. She decided to ignore it as her daughter flounced out. But her eyes followed Mel.

'Leave her, Mum. She's upset about something, can't take her eyes off her phone. She'll come round. This place is great. You've done well to settle in so quickly. The girls will have to get used to it.'

His words reminded Grace her other daughter still hadn't been in touch, apart from a brief text from the airport to say they were on their way to Bali. She supposed Lou and Greg were there now, enjoying breakfast by the pool or whatever they did there. Then what Ben said earlier sank home. 'You think you might get a job here in Queensland?'

'I thought that would please you. I've racketed around Europe for too long. This funding cut may be a godsend. There's still lots to discover right here in Australia. It may be time for me to spend more time in my native land, and I'd enjoy working with the indigenous leaders up there. I could learn a lot from them.'

'Oh, I hope you get it.' The thought of Ben being able to visit more often, perhaps even using her home as his base, was balm to her soul.

'Don't get your hopes up. I still have to pass muster at the interview. There'll be other well-qualified candidates, and they may prefer to appoint an Aboriginal to lead the dig. But I think I have a fair chance.' He gave Grace a hug. 'It'd be good to see more of you. Since Dad died... I worry about you.'

'I'm okay, but it would be nice to have you nearer.'

'The surf carnival?' he asked.

'Yes, a good idea. I'll clear up here, if you check with Mel again. I don't want to leave her here on her own. I know she's a grown woman, but you're right. Something is bothering her and if we leave her here, she'll only fret about it.'

After much grumbling on Mel's part, the three set off to walk down to the section of the beach where the carnival was taking place. It was much busier than Grace expected, and Mel soon became bored and wandered off, leaving Grace and Ben to enjoy the sight of the young men and women vying for honours in their sport. But Grace couldn't stop worrying about Mel and, after watching two heats of the men's competition, she left Ben and went in search of her daughter.

She found Mel sitting on one of the wooden benches close to the esplanade shopping plaza, staring at her phone, her face wet with tears.

'Mel, my darling. What's the matter?' She surely couldn't be worrying about work. It was a holiday weekend. The office would be closed. She couldn't have received a message from there.

Mel raised her eyes to meet Grace's. 'Mum!' She burst into tears, knuckling her already red eyes. 'I can't…'

'You can tell me.' Grace put an arm around Mel's shoulder. 'Is it a man?'

'How… how did you know?'

'I haven't lived this long without learning a thing or two. Your dad never gave me a moment's worry, but I have a few friends who suffered at the hands of men they thought they could trust.'

Mel wiped her eyes again and took a deep breath. 'I knew I shouldn't get involved with someone at work, but Jason was so persistent. He's one of the copywriters, the best and…' her eyes dropped, '…he's married.'

'Oh! And I suppose he promised to leave his wife?'

'How did… oh, I suppose it happens all the time. But I really thought… Oh, Mum, I've been so stupid and now… how can I go back and face him on Wednesday?'

'Is this why you've been checking your phone all weekend? The story about Graham was to distract me, wasn't it?'

'Yes… no… Graham did suggest I could try harder. I guess Jason distracted me at work and I wasn't doing my best. He promised to talk with his wife this weekend but…'

'He didn't?'

'His wife's pregnant, and he swore…'

'My baby.' Grace drew Mel into a hug.

'That's not all, Mum. I think I may be, too.'

Grace hadn't expected this but tried to hide her shock. Pregnant or not, what Mel needed right now was the comfort of knowing she was loved. 'Oh, my dear!' The pair hugged for a few moments longer, then Mel drew apart and wiped her eyes again.

'Sorry, Mum. I can't seem to stop crying.'

This wasn't the time to ask Mel if she wanted the baby, but the thought of a grandchild was a speck of light in this whole mess. 'Why don't you stay up here a few days longer? I presume you have sick leave you can take?'

Mel nodded. 'Could I, Mum? The thought of having to go into the office and pretend nothing has happened…'

'Of course you can. You must. Ben will be here for a few more days, too.'

'Here you are.' Ben appeared behind them. He gave Mel and Grace a searching look then said, 'There's a sausage sizzle down there a bit. Thought you might be hungry.'

'Tired of the carnival?' Grace asked.

'It's all much the same. There are some really skilful surfers taking part, but I think I've seen enough.'

'What do you think, Mel? Hungry?' Grace asked, only to see Mel shake her head. 'Let's see what's on offer,' she said, taking her by the arm as she rose to join Ben.

While Ben was standing in the queue for the inevitable sausages covered with fried onions, slathered with tomato sauce and wrapped in a slice of white bread, Grace said to Mel. 'You should eat something. I noticed you didn't have much for breakfast. Are you experiencing morning sickness?'

Mel shook her head. 'I'm not hungry.'

'You'll feel better with something in your stomach, even if it's a sausage and white bread. Then we'll go home, and I prescribe a long, hot bath and a nice rest. Remember we're having dinner with your Aunt Dot and Uncle Kev tonight.'

'Do I have to?' Mel's expression was miserable.

'Yes. They're looking forward to seeing you and Ben. It's been a while. They have no children of their own and have always looked on you three as the ones they never had. And it's better for you to go out, to keep busy. It'll stop you worrying.'

'I don't think anything will do that.'

'Hello again.'

Grace turned sharply to see a white-haired man who looked vaguely familiar. He was accompanied by a younger version of himself, a man of around forty with the dark blond hair the older man must once have had.

'Dinner at Kev Turner's a week ago.'

'Of course.' He was the man Dot had tried to set her up with. Today he looked more like an aging hippie, wearing jeans and a loose shirt, his hair blown by the wind. Despite her former aversion to the man, Grace felt an unexpected stirring in an area of her anatomy which had been numb to all feeling for some time. She quickly stifled it. She wasn't interested in forming a relationship with any man ever again, especially not this one.

'This is my son, Aaron. He's spending Easter with me.' The man raised an eyebrow in Mel's direction.

'My daughter, Mel, and my son's…'

Ben appeared as if by magic, carrying three steaming bundles wrapped in paper napkins. 'This is all they had. If you want something to drink…' He suddenly noticed their companions.

'This is my son, Ben,' Grace said. 'I'm sorry, I don't remember…'

'Ted, Ted Crawford.'

Ben handed sausages to Grace and Mel and shook Ted and Aaron's outstretched hands. 'Pleased to meet you.'

'Good to see you again. Guess we should let you eat in peace, and we should get into the queue,' Ted said.

They moved off.

'Who was that?' Ben asked, staring after the two men, his eyes turning back to Grace.

'No one, someone I met at your Aunt Dot's. I think he may be a neighbour of hers.' Grace was still trying to stifle the unexpected frisson she'd experienced seeing Ted Crawford again. She'd forgotten all about him, hadn't even remembered his name. How could his sudden appearance have this effect on her?

Nine

'You're a sly dog.' Aaron gazed at Ted in surprise. 'She's pretty.'

'What? Oh, no, you've got the wrong end of the stick. She's not… we're not… We met once. I think we were being set up. The woman didn't even remember my name.' But he remembered hers. Grace. He'd thought at the time how well it suited her. Despite the bright dress – or maybe because of it – she'd seemed graceful. She was slim, her silver hair in waves around her face, the high cheekbones, her eyes an unusual shade of deep blue. If the evening hadn't been such an obvious attempt to set them up, he might have been interested. Aaron was right. She did look pretty today, her hair windswept and dressed more casually in a tee-shirt and a pair of those culotte things that clung to her hips.

'You didn't introduce her.'

'I didn't?' There had been so many names being bandied about – his, Aaron's, her children Ben and Mel. Had he forgotten to introduce Grace to his son? 'Her name's Grace, Grace Winter. I think she's some relative of Kev Turner who I went to school with. He never left Bellbird Bay,' Ted continued, eager to move the conversation on from Grace. He needed time to digest what had just happened.

'Her daughter's pretty, too.'

Ted breathed a sigh of relief. Of course, Aaron would have noticed the younger woman. It was time he found a replacement for Tanya. He'd been on his own too long. Ted supposed there had been women in the past few years, but none his son wanted to share with him. 'You interested?' he asked.

'Always interested, but rarely do anything about it, Dad. Tanya left me with the impression any woman who wants me must be mad. It's taken me a long time to recover from her barbed comments.' His voice was bitter.

'Son!' Ted was lost for words. This was the first he'd heard this detail about their break-up. He knew it had been acrimonious, that Tanya had started a relationship with a man she'd met through work, had left and taken the then six-year-old Zack with her. At the time Ted thought Aaron had let him go too readily, but wasn't sure his son could cope with a young child as a permanent part of his newly single life. Their house had been sold, and Aaron moved to a small city apartment. If Ted thought about it at all, he'd assumed his son led an active social life.

'Maybe it's time.' Aaron was almost talking to himself. 'If you know this Grace woman, could we perhaps arrange to meet them again?'

Aaron was looking more cheerful than he had since he arrived. Ted didn't want to burst his bubble, but there was no way he could make any sort of arrangement with Grace Winter, even if he wanted to – and he didn't, did he?

*

When Grace and her two children arrived home, Ben decided to go for a swim, while Mel disappeared into the bathroom with Grace's precious supply of fragrant bath salts. Grace made herself a mug of fennel and cardamon tea and took it out to the deck. She dropped into a chair, put her feet on another one, and wrapped both hands around her mug, her thoughts travelling back to what had happened on the esplanade.

First there was Mel's bombshell. The poor baby. If only Grace had known. But what could she have done? Mel was old enough to make her own decisions – and look where it had landed her. A married man. Pregnant. While Grace loved the idea of becoming a grandmother, she didn't want Mel to become a single mother. How would she cope? Until now, she'd sailed through life. Everything had worked out for her. Even if Grace had not always agreed with her decisions, her choices,

Mel seemed to have an enviable way of avoiding the pitfalls which seemed to plague other people. Until now.

It would be difficult for her in the office, forced to work with the man with whom she'd had a relationship, the father of her child. But if anyone could cope, Mel could. Though this morning she'd shown a more vulnerable side of herself to Grace. Maybe she wasn't as tough, as invulnerable, as she pretended to be.

Grace took a sip of tea. She was too old to have to worry about her children. They should all be settled in their own lives by now, leaving her to get on with hers. It was at times like this she missed Russ even more. With his unflappable common sense, he'd have found a way to reassure her.

This brought her thoughts back to the man they'd run into. The image of Ted Crawford – she knew his name very well – rose up behind her eyes. She remembered the long-forgotten sensation triggered by his appearance. Had she been imagining it? Her gut clenched at the way her body had reacted even as her mind refused to acknowledge the attraction.

Grace laid her cup down on the wooden railing around the deck and closed her eyes, willing an image of Russ to replace the one of Ted Crawford's smiling face, his eyes twinkling with what looked like pleasure. As she dozed off, it was to imagine how it might feel to have him look at her like that again, to have his arms around her, to…

'Mum!'

Startled, Grace's eyes shot open. Ben was standing in front of her, a towel around his waist, his wet hair dripping onto his shoulders, his feet making wet footprints on the boards of the deck. He looked so like Russ, she felt guilty about the thoughts flitting through her mind in her dreamlike state.

'Ben, you're back. How was your swim?' Grace picked up her now cold cup of tea and drained it, hoping to quell her guilt.

'Brilliant. You should have joined me.'

'I prefer to swim in the early morning, before the sun gets too hot.' Though she hadn't been doing much swimming recently, taking long walks along the beach instead, before going to the library or settling down to her writing.

'What time did you say we were meeting Aunt Dot and Uncle Kev?'

'Six. They want to eat early. They've booked a table at *The Beach House*.'

'Good food?'

'Good reviews, but I haven't eaten there.'

'Time for a shower and a chance to check my emails, then.' With a grin, he headed off, leaving Grace alone again with her thoughts.

At a few minutes past six, Grace, Ben and a reluctant Mel arrived at *The Beach House*. It was a glass and timber structure built on an outcrop of rock and seeming to stand on top of the sea. The sun was beginning to set, casting a yellow and pink glow across the horizon, its dying rays reflected on the tall glass walls of the restaurant.

As they walked up to the entrance where Dot and Kev were waiting for them, a flock of rainbow lorikeets flew overhead, the sound of their wings and their screeching almost deafening.

'Wow,' Ben said, looking up at the sky. 'Now I know I'm really back in Australia.' He chuckled.

'Here you are.' Dot hugged Grace, then turned to greet Ben and Mel in the same way.

Kev shook Ben's hand, gave him a clap on the shoulder, and Grace and Mel a peck on the cheek.

'Look at you both,' Dot said to Ben and Mel. 'It's been too long. You should visit more often, and now your mum's living here there's nothing to stop you.'

'Let's go in,' Kev said, to interrupt what was sure to be a not-so-veiled criticism of Grace's children's failure to visit before now. 'It's lovely to see you all, and I'm sure your mum's pleased to see you two.'

Grace smiled her thanks to him as they made their way inside. She hoped Dot wasn't going to elaborate on her words once they were seated.

But the view, the extensive menu and the delicious food meant any criticisms Dot might have had, disappeared as they enjoyed their meals. It wasn't till they had finished eating and coffee was served, that she asked, 'What about you, Ben? I suppose you'll be off again in a day or so. I don't know why you couldn't find a job closer to home. Now your mother's on her own, she needs her children more than ever.'

Grace tightened her lips, wishing Dot would keep her opinions to herself. Her sister had always been inclined to call a spade a spade, as their mother would say, but sometimes a bit of tact would go a long way.

Ben didn't seem to mind. 'I might just do that, Aunt Dot. I have an interview in Brisbane next week which could lead to me working here in Queensland. If that happens, you might get tired of seeing me around.'

'We'd never do that,' Kev said.

'You're a good son,' Dot said, then turned to Mel. 'And what about you? Are you still working in Sydney? Advertising, isn't it? I don't know…' She broke off as Mel pushed back her chair.

'Sorry, I need to…' Mel rushed off in the direction of the ladies' toilet.

'Should we…?' Dot asked, starting to rise, too.

'No, she'll be right,' Grace said, hoping she was correct. She knew Mel had left to escape Dot's interrogation. She sympathised with her, knowing how insensitive her sister could be.

'We bumped into a friend of yours today, Uncle Kev,' Ben said, trying to change the subject.

Grace flinched. *Why did he have to bring this up?*

'Oh, who was that?'

'Not…?' Dot looked knowingly at Grace.

Grace flinched again. She hadn't met many of Dot and Kev's friends – only Ted Crawford and the other two couples who'd been at the dinner, people whose names she really didn't remember.

'A guy called Ted. Didn't catch his surname. We were at the Rotary sausage sizzle at the surfing carnival, and he appeared with his son. Seems like a nice guy. Neighbour of yours?'

'Ted Crawford,' Dot said, giving Grace another knowing look. 'Not a neighbour, no. He lives not far from your mum, in one of the renovated beach shacks along the boardwalk. I don't know why you couldn't have bought into *Bay Village*, Grace. We'd have been neighbours and there for you.'

For that exact reason. But Grace only smiled. She loved her sister, but living so close would drive her mad. 'I'm happy where I am, Dot.' Meanwhile her mind was going round in circles. *Ted Crawford lived near her? She could run into him any time she walked out from her back deck?* A warm sensation, whether of pleasure, anticipation or fear rushed through her.

She was glad when Kev asked, 'Did you enjoy the carnival?' then without waiting for an answer continued, 'We only caught the tail end of it this afternoon. I'm not surprised Ted was there. He was a champion surfer in his day. A sad loss to Bellbird Bay when he left to become a city lawyer.'

While Ben and Kev debated the merits of the surfing carnival, with the occasional interjection from Dot, Grace was left to her thoughts. Ted Crawford had been a lawyer. Not exactly the aging hippie type she'd taken him for. And a surfing champion. For a moment she pictured him like one of the young men they'd watched that morning, emerging from the ocean tanned and ripped, water cascading from his body, surfboard under his arm.

'Sorry.' Mel slid back into her seat.

Grace gave her daughter a searching glance. Her eyes were red. She'd been crying again. Grace hoped Dot wouldn't notice. She grasped Mel's hand under the table and squeezed it, receiving a look of gratitude.

The restaurant, which had been relatively empty when they arrived, was now filling up, and the buzz of chatter from the surrounding tables was making conversation difficult.

'Time to go,' Dot decided. 'Will we see you two again before you leave?'

Ben and Mel looked at each other. Neither spoke. Grace could sense their unwillingness to commit to another evening with their aunt and uncle.

'Their plans are a bit fluid at the moment, Dot. Why don't we wait and see?'

'If you think so.' Dot peered at Mel as if she wanted to say something more, then thought better of it. 'Well, it was good to see you tonight. Kev will get the bill,' she said, seeing Grace reach for her purse. 'Our treat.'

'Thanks.' Grace knew she now owed them a meal. It was the way things worked. Dot and Kev had had her to dinner, now they'd paid for this meal, it was her turn to host them next. Maybe she could wait till Ben and Mel had gone to invite them over to lunch or dinner. 'My turn next,' she said, as she hugged them goodbye, relieved to have avoided any further mention of Ted Crawford.

As Grace opened her back gate, she saw a figure standing further up the boardwalk. From this distance it was impossible to identify who it was, but from the size and shape, it looked like the man whose image kept returning to her thoughts. Was she imagining it, or was it really Ted Crawford? Had he been living so close by all this time?

Ten

Easter over, Ted's life fell back into something resembling his usual routine. He surfed early every morning before returning to have breakfast, then going to his study to open up his computer or heading out with his painting gear. He'd recently revived an earlier interest in art which had been set aside for decades and, after a short course with U3A – the University of the Third Age – had decided to work in pastels. Although they could be messy, he liked the speed with which he could work, the vibrant colours, and enjoyed portraying local landscapes. He had even managed to sell a few of his efforts in a local gallery.

The difference now was Aaron's presence, which forced him to make conversation at breakfast. And, instead of enjoying flipping through the daily papers and other news items on the internet, his time was spent researching ways to resolve Aaron's situation. He hadn't done any painting since his son arrived and was missing his solitary mornings seated on the headland or a rock outcrop with no one to bother him, the only sounds the roar of the sea and the seabirds calling to each other as they circled overhead.

Being unfamiliar with the particular nature of Aaron's culpability or otherwise, he was trawling through similar cases and had contacted a couple of former colleagues he thought might be able to help. One of them had referred him to a solicitor he knew in a small country town in New South Wales where he believed there had been a similar case.

Gordon Slater had been helpful. He only had a vague recollection of the case which had occurred some years earlier but promised to check out his notes and get back to Ted. When Ted mentioned he was living in Bellbird Bay, Slater had become chattier, mentioning a client of his had recently moved there, and wondering if Ted had come across her. The hair on the back of Ted's neck rose when Grace Winter's name was mentioned and, most inappropriately, Slater shared the information she was a widow who'd chosen to sell the family property after the death of her husband who had suffered from dementia for several years.

'I wasn't surprised she wanted to sell,' Slater said, 'but to move all that way… I think she has relatives up there, but it was a blow to the children.'

Ted ended the call before the country solicitor could reveal any more information about his client. It might be the informal way they did business in the town of Granite Springs and even though he relished learning about Grace Winter's background, Ted didn't want to be party to local gossip. But it reminded him he hadn't seen any sign of her since Easter Saturday, despite keeping an eye out whenever he went to the beach or into town. He wondered where she lived, perhaps in the lifestyle resort Kev and his wife had moved into. It wouldn't suit him – too many people – but Kev seemed happy enough there.

Meanwhile, having handed over his problem to Ted, Aaron seemed almost unconcerned about his future, spending his time on his phone or iPad, swimming and taking long walks. He might well have been on holiday without a care in the world.

Today, to Ted's surprise, when he emerged from the study, having spent another futile morning on the internet searching old cases, Aaron greeted him with a big grin. 'I had a text from Zack, Dad. He says Tanya has agreed he can come to visit. I can pick him up tomorrow.'

'That's great news, son. Have you spoken to Tanya?' Ted hoped the text was real and Tanya's agreement wasn't wishful thinking and a figment of the boy's imagination.

'Doing it now.' Aaron took his phone out to the deck while Ted put together a simple lunch consisting of a quiche he'd bought from the local patisserie and a green salad. He added a chunk of cheese and the remains of a loaf of sour dough bread and took two bottles of beer from the fridge.

Through the glass door, Ted could see Aaron striding back and forth, his phone held to his ear, his free hand waving wildly in the air. It didn't look good. Finally, Aaron finished his call and looked up to meet Ted's eyes.

Ted opened the sliding door. 'Well?'

'She agreed, but only after berating me for contacting Zack instead of her. He's my son, too. I have every right to contact him – and to tell him I want to see him, that you do, too. Anyway, the upshot is he can come for the rest of his school holiday – four days. He has to be back on Monday night. You were right, Dad. I need to be more forceful with her.'

It was another beautiful day, so Ted took lunch out to the deck and opened his beer, while Aaron texted his son to confirm the arrangement. Only a few minutes later, he joined his father.

'It's done, Dad. He'll be here tomorrow. I'll pick him up early and we'll be back in time for lunch. I texted him, too. Look at his reply.' Aaron held out his phone to let Ted see his grandson's reply: *Yay. Can't wait 2 see U and Grandpa Teddy. Zxx*

Ted smiled. Even at twelve, his grandson still called him by the name he'd coined when Ted bought him a special bear when he was only two. It had a heart sewn inside and when the boy learned his grandfather's name was Ted, he decided to call the bear Ted, and his grandfather Grandpa Teddy. The name had stuck.

'Great news,' he said. 'Now sit down and enjoy your lunch. Guess we should hit the shops this afternoon. I'm pretty sure my fridge and pantry don't contain the sort of food young Zack likes to eat.'

'His mother,' Aaron began. 'Damn his mother. She refuses to let him eat junk food or drink Coke. But when Zack's here, we don't need to follow her rules.' He chuckled.

'Right, sounds like Coke, chips and chocolate are on the agenda.' Ted raised his beer to Aaron who raised his in return.

*

Ted was looking forward to seeing Zack again. He still couldn't believe his daughter-in-law had agreed to permit him to visit. Not one of her favourite people having, as she saw it, sided with Aaron during the divorce proceedings, Ted had only seen her a couple of times since she and Aaron went their separate ways. It made communication with Zack difficult if not near impossible.

Now he was about to rectify matters and he couldn't wait. The pantry held all sorts of delightful and naughty items designed to tempt a young boy's palate and there was a carton of Coke sitting in the garage beside the beer for Aaron and him. They'd have a boy's own few days and, hopefully, Zack would come out of his shell. Ted still worried about the withdrawn images of the boy he'd seen on Facebook, and Aaron's suspicions of bullying were added cause for concern.

The sound of a car stopping broke into Ted's musings, and he headed to the door. The door of the BMW flew open and a lanky figure, his blond hair falling over his forehead, flew out and wrapped his arms around Ted's waist.

'Grandpa Teddy! I thought I was never going to see you again. Mum said…'

What his mother said was muffled by Zack burying his face in Ted's chest.

Aaron's eyes met Ted's over Zack's head. *What was Tanya up to?*

'Sorry. I didn't mean to behave like a baby. I'm just so glad to see you.' Zack rubbed his eyes and pushed an unruly lock of hair from his forehead.

'No worries. It's been a long time. You've done a lot of growing up since we last met. It must have been about three years ago.' Ted raised an eyebrow in Aaron's direction.

'Three years past at Christmas. It was when you came to visit and…'

Ted remembered. Zack had been spending a few days with his dad, and Ted had joined them. But, for some reason, Tanya had decided she needed to fetch Zack. Their last day together had been a fiasco with Zack crying he wanted to stay, and Tanya insisting he pack and leave right away. It had been the last time Ted saw Tanya, too.

'Well,' he said to his grandson. 'You're here now. We have four whole days together and we're going to have fun. I bet you'd like something to eat. A little bird told me you like Coke and chips. What about those for lunch with a meat pie from the freezer?'

'Yum.' Zack brightened at once. But he hung back before following the two men into the house. 'Wow!' he said when they entered the kitchen. 'We're so close to the ocean. Can we go for a swim after lunch, or… do we have to wait? Mum says…'

'Your mum's not here, Zack. While you're here we play by my rules. Of course we can go for a swim after lunch. Your mum need never know. Deal?'

'Deal, Grandpa Teddy. Wow! I'm so glad to be here.'

*

The four days with Zack passed in a flash. It had taken the first two for Zack to relax enough to really enjoy himself and come out of his shell. But when he did, he was a joy to be with, not unlike Aaron had been as that age. Ted watched him pack, promising he could visit again next holidays.

'I wish I could stay here,' Zack said when they hugged goodbye. 'I hate my school. They're only sending me there because it was Mark's old school. Can you talk to Mum?' he asked Aaron.

'I'll try.' Aaron looked down at his feet. 'It's a good school, Zack. Maybe…'

'It's because I don't play sport like most of the others. I'm no good at football and cricket. I like it here better, where I can swim and surf.'

'And you do both well.' Ted had spent a couple of mornings teaching Zack the rudiments of surfing, and the boy had cottoned on really fast. 'Maybe you could tell some of your classmates about your surfing experiences.'

'Mmm. Maybe.' But Zack sounded doubtful.

'We need to go, Zack.' Aaron checked his watch. 'Don't want to get in your mum's bad books.'

Ted watched the car drive off, then made his way back into the house. It felt empty after the past few days with Aaron and Zack filling it with their chatter, and the noise of the young boy who had quickly made himself at home.

*

'I feel sorry for him,' Aaron said a few days later, when he received a text from Zack to say he was back at school and nothing had changed. 'But it's up to Tanya. I had no say in what school he attends. And Mark insisted. It costs a bomb.'

'Well, at least we had a few days with him and maybe next school holidays he can stay for longer. You plan to be here again then?'

'I might still be here if we can't get my problem solved. You're no further forward?'

'I'm waiting to hear from a guy who was involved in a similar case. Don't worry, Aaron, I'm sure we can sort something out.' Ted patted his son on the shoulder. But he wasn't sure at all. The law had some strange twists, and it could be Aaron would be considered liable for the fault. 'What will you do if it goes against you?'

Aaron dragged a hand through his hair. 'I don't know. Find something else? What I don't understand is why it wasn't picked up by the engineers before the equipment was built.'

'Who knows? They need to take responsibility, too. Seems to me you're the fall guy. You're a good draftsman. There's always a demand for your type of skills.'

'Maybe.' Aaron gazed out the window. 'But my name will be mud in the industry.' He gave a sigh. 'I might need to relocate. But it would be harder to see Zack if I didn't live in Brisbane.'

'The boy needs you.'

'Yeah.'

'And you need to stand up to Tanya where Zack's concerned.' Ted's forehead creased. He wished he could force his son to be more proactive.

'Yeah, yeah.'

Ted sighed, and the two men were silent as each contemplated Aaron's options.

'I guess there are other industries,' Ted said, going back to Aaron's work issue. 'What about working in construction? It's a growing industry. You could do well there.'

'Hmm.'

Sometimes Ted wished his son had more ambition, more motivation. He seemed content to wait to see what his firm would decide instead of going out to find something else, something which might be more suited to his skills. It was much the same as the way he dealt with his ex.

'I think I'll go for a walk,' Aaron said, shrugging. 'I need to think.'

Ted watched Aaron walk out to the boardwalk, his hands in his pockets, his shoulders drooping in despair. He wished there was more he could do. But it was a long time since he'd been able to give him a hug and kiss to make things better.

Eleven

Two weeks had passed since the Easter weekend, and Mel was still in Bellbird Bay. Assuming Lou would have returned from Bali, Grace had called her older daughter, only to have a stilted conversation proving she still hadn't been forgiven for her move to Bellbird Bay. She'd sighed when the call ended, wondering how long Lou was going to hold the grudge. Grace would dearly like to be on good terms with Lou again and to show her daughter her new home.

Ben had duly attended his interview and was staying in Brisbane with an old mate from uni and mugging up on the area in North Queensland where the proposed dig was located. He was hopeful of being offered the job, while keeping his eye open for alternatives.

'I can afford to be out of work for a few months, Mum,' he said to Grace when she expressed worry about his lack of gainful employment. 'It's good to have a break. I've been flat out since I finished my degree. Don't worry, I'll pop up to see you before I go off anywhere else.'

With that, Grace had to be content. She didn't worry about Ben.

But the sight of Mel wandering around the house clutching her phone did concern her. Two days earlier, she'd taken a deep breath and asked Mel if she'd done a pregnancy test, only to be told it was none of her business and she'd do one when she was ready. From the way Mel clung to her phone and was secretive about her calls, Grace suspected she was still in touch with the man she only referred to as 'he' and 'him' when her mother dared to inquire.

Grace was finishing breakfast in preparation for her morning shift at the library when Mel appeared in the kitchen, her face white and drawn.

'I did the test,' she said, pouring herself a bowl of muesli and a glass of orange juice. 'I'm pregnant.' There was a touch of defiance in her tone. But as soon as she sat down, the tears began to flow. 'Oh, Mum! I can't believe it. Jason said…' She threw a wary glance at Grace. 'All right, I have been in touch with him. I've told him it's over, but he keeps calling. He says he can't live without me.' She smirked, then her mouth turned down again. 'But I can't face people at work. What if everyone knows – knows he and I… knows why I've taken sick leave, finds out I'm pregnant and it's Jason's baby?'

'Oh, my darling.' Grace's mind started working overtime. 'What do you intend to do? I agree. You can't go back to that office.' The thought of her baby girl becoming a single mother made her want to weep.

'I don't know. Maybe I can get another job, but what can I do? I've only ever worked in advertising, and I don't have any qualifications.'

'Will you go back to Sydney?'

'I suppose. Gwen and Marie will need my rent. But if I don't have a job, how will I pay it?'

'What have you told your flatmates?'

'The same as the office – I'm sick so am staying up here till I recover.' Mel picked up her spoon.

'Mmm. We'll find a solution. I'm here for you. I need to be off now, but I'll be back at lunchtime. Have a think about what you want to do. I'll have a think, too, and we can talk more then.'

*

On her way home from the library, Grace popped into the patisserie to pick up a cheese and onion flan and a loaf of sour dough bread for lunch, sure it wouldn't have occurred to Mel to think of making anything. On her own, Grace would have rustled up a sandwich or snacked on bread and cheese, but with Mel there, her mothering instincts kicked in and she felt the need to make a proper meal. Even more so now Mel was eating for two.

It had been difficult to concentrate on work, thoughts of Mel and her baby uppermost in her mind while Grace shelved books or helped young mothers to choose books for their toddlers. To think Mel would be a mother in less than nine months' time was earth-shattering. It forced Grace to regard those young women in a different light, to picture Mel as one of them. Mel could scarcely take care of herself, never mind a baby

She found Mel on the deck with her iPad, her eyes closed, her earbuds in. She looked up when Grace popped her head out the door.

'Lunch?'

'Oh, is it lunchtime already?'

'What did you do this morning?' Grace asked, when they were eating large slices of the flan accompanied by salad and thickly buttered bread. 'Did you go for a swim?'

'Didn't feel like a swim,' Mel said, taking a forkful of salad. 'I went for a walk up the boardwalk – to the headland. And you'll never guess?'

'I'm sure you're about to tell me.' Grace took a mouthful of the flan which was as delicious as she'd come to expect from the local patisserie. Her mind wasn't on what Mel was saying. She was still trying to get her head around what had happened in the library that morning just before she left. An elderly woman had suddenly collapsed. One minute she'd been chatting to her about choosing a book for her granddaughter, the next the woman had been lying on the floor gasping for breath.

The senior librarian had taken control, called an ambulance which had whisked the woman off to hospital. But the whole incident had shaken Grace. The woman hadn't been much older than her, maybe in her early seventies. It brought home how fleeting life can be, how one minute you can be going along as usual, when the next... Not everyone suffered the slow demise Russ had. Some get no warning of the end. The woman probably wouldn't die, but it left Grace feeling as if she needed to make the most of every day. And now she had a grandchild to look forward to, too.

She became aware Mel was still talking.

'And they live just a few doors up from here.'

'What? Who?'

'Haven't you been listening? I said I met one of those men again, the ones we met at Easter. The younger one. Aaron. He was out walking, too. He's staying with his dad temporarily while something at his work gets sorted out. We had a good chat. He's nice.'

A flicker of something indeterminable pulsated in the pit of Grace's stomach, only to disappear again in a flash. 'That's nice, darling.' Then what Mel had said sank in. She remembered Dot telling her Ted Crawford lived on the boardwalk. 'Only a few doors up?' she asked, recalling the figure she'd seen when they arrived home after dinner at *The Beach House.*

'Yes, it's amazing we haven't bumped into them before today. You didn't know?' Mel didn't wait for an answer. 'Anyway, we discovered we're both a bit bored and he invited me out for a drink tonight. I said *yes.*'

'Right.' Grace was finding it hard to take in the fact that, not only had Mel met the son of the man who now – much to her annoyance – she couldn't get out of her head, but she had agreed to go on a date with him. She seemed to have quickly recovered from her disastrous affair with the married Jason, and to have forgotten the result of the pregnancy test she'd done only that morning. Or was she just doing what Grace had decided to do and was making the most of every day?

'I've been thinking about your situation,' she said, seeing Mel's face drop. 'Those tests aren't always accurate. You need to see a doctor. I can make an appointment with my GP. You'll like Clare. She's not much older than you and very sympathetic. Once we know for sure, we can decide what to do. It's probably best if you stay here. I can help with the baby and… what?' she asked, seeing Mel's face turn red.

'It's my baby – if I am pregnant. And I'll decide what to do. I can go back to Sydney and…' Her words dried up. 'I'll manage somehow,' she said, wearing the mulish expression she'd used as a teenager when thwarted.

'I only want what's best for you, sweetheart. For you and your baby. How will you cope in Sydney on your own? Lou and Greg are busy. They have their own lives, and I don't suppose the father will help.'

'I don't want him to know.'

'Okay.' Grace agreed, though she wasn't sure it was a wise decision. Married or not, the man should take responsibility for his child. Though she did sympathise with Mel's point of view. 'But you will at least let me make an appointment with Clare?'

'I suppose.'

Satisfied to at least have agreement on one of her suggestions, Grace decided to let the other ride for now.

After lunch, while Mel disappeared for a rest, Grace called the doctor's surgery, pleased to be offered an appointment for the following morning. Then she took a book out to the deck with a cup of peppermint tea. But despite the novel being one Grace had been waiting to read, the lines of print blurred together as she tried to come to terms with how Mel's life was about to change, and to the news her daughter had befriended Ted Crawford's son.

Twelve

'I've been thinking about what you said. I might stay for a bit longer, get a job here.' Mel poured milk onto her cereal and looked at Grace through a curtain of hair.

'You will? I'm so glad.' This was such a turnaround from the girl who hated the idea of Grace leaving Granite Springs and moving to Bellbird Bay. 'What would you do?'

'Last night… Aaron…'

Grace had gone to bed early and hadn't heard Mel come home. She'd wanted to stay awake, but reasoned at thirty-one, Mel didn't need her mother waiting up for her.

'Oh, I meant to ask. Did you have a good time?'

'Mmm. He's interesting. Divorced, so not another married man. He has a son, too. At school in Brisbane. He misses him. But that's not it. We talked… about living in the city, about Bellbird Bay, and he said…'

Grace waited patiently, her morning cup of fennel and cardamon tea clasped in both hands.

Mel poked at her cereal with a spoon, slopping milk over the edge of the bowl. 'He said, why don't I look for work here in hospitality or something.' She looked up to meet Grace's eyes with an expression almost of defiance. 'So, what do you think?'

Grace took a sip of tea to hide her surprise. 'You'll stay here?'

'Not for good. It would be a stop-gap measure. Just till I get myself sorted out. Aaron said he was thinking of changing jobs, too. He has this problem with the firm he works in. I thought… It would save me going back to work for Graham, having to see Jason every day, everyone finding out. And if I stayed here, I wouldn't have to worry about paying rent. I could save some money.'

Grace gulped. Although she could see her peaceful existence disappearing, she was pleased Mel had seen sense, delighted her daughter would consider moving to Bellbird Bay, albeit temporarily. And, once she became used to the town, and her baby was born, perhaps she'd decide to stay.

'Sounds like a plan,' she said. 'Hospitality?'

'It was only a suggestion. Aaron said I could maybe find office work here, too. I plan to check out the local paper. You get a copy, don't you?'

'Last week's copies are in the laundry,' Grace said. 'Aaron seems to be full of good ideas. Are you sure about this, Mel? Won't you miss the city?' Now Mel had agreed to her suggestion, Grace wanted to be confident she'd made her decision for the right reasons. 'Does Aaron plan to move here too?' she asked, the idea suddenly occurring to her. *Was Mel about to become involved with Aaron Crawford on the rebound? If so, it spelt disaster.*

'I won't miss Jason begging me to see him again, but I will miss the buzz of the city, the cafes, the movies, the markets. It's not for ever, Mum, and Gwen and Marie will find another flatmate. I was getting tired of living there, anyway. I'll need to save some money for the baby, and I can find a place of my own later.' She grinned and rose to throw her arms around Grace. 'It'll be fine, you'll see. I won't get in your hair – not too much anyway. And, no, Aaron doesn't plan to stay here. He needs to be in Brisbane where his son lives. But he's here now.' She grinned wickedly.

Grace shook her head, unsure what to make of this sudden turnaround in Mel's mood. But it was good to see her looking happier.

'You're most welcome to stay as long as you want,' she said, mentally trying to work out how she'd cope with having Mel and her changeable moods around all the time. But it would be good to be able to spend more time with her younger daughter. Now it looked as if Ben might be moving closer, and with Mel living here in Bellbird Bay, it only left Lou to come round.

Grace bit her lip thinking of her elder daughter. There had been the brief phone call after she and Greg returned from Bali, but nothing since. Each time Grace had tried to contact her, the call had gone to voicemail and, while she left a message, there had been no return call. *Was Lou avoiding her? Was she so upset at the selling of Brigadoon and the move to Bellbird Bay, she'd decided to ignore Grace's calls?*

'Have you heard from Lou?' she asked Mel. The two had always been close, and Grace wouldn't be surprised if Mel had confided in her about Jason and her possible pregnancy before telling her mother.

'No, not since they got back.' Mel looked uncomfortable. 'She knew about Jason and didn't approve. And I couldn't tell her about my pregnancy fears. She and Greg have been trying for ages. She'd hate it if I managed to get pregnant when she couldn't – and I wasn't even trying.'

'Oh!' *Why hadn't Lou told her? Had Grace been too busy with her own life, too engrossed in taking care of Russ to provide a sympathetic ear for her daughter? No wonder Lou had lashed out at her on Christmas Day.*

'I didn't know.'

'No. She said she didn't want to worry you. You had enough on your plate with Dad. There wasn't anything you could do, anyway.'

'No, but…'

'I don't know how I'm going to tell Lou about the baby. Do you think you could tell her?' She gave Grace a pleading look.

'Let's wait to see what Clare says this morning. If she confirms what we suspect, then we can decide how to break the news to Lou. But she's your sister. I'm sure she won't allow her own disappointments to colour her feelings for you.'

'I hope not.' But Mel didn't appear convinced.

*

'Well, that's that.' Mel's mood was more upbeat than Grace had expected as they left the surgery. 'You're going to be a grandmother.'

'And you're going to be a mother. Oh, my dear!' Grace hugged Mel tightly, her eyes filling with tears. She wasn't sure if they were tears of joy or sadness. Although she and Russ had longed for their first grandchild, this wasn't how they'd imagined it happening. Grace was almost glad Russ wasn't here to see the situation his favourite daughter found herself in. 'How do you feel about it?'

'I'm not sure. I've never had to consider anyone but myself. I know some people thought I was selfish, but I always thought there was plenty of time to get serious and I should enjoy life while I could. I guess this is the time. You'll help me, Mum, won't you? I don't know anything about babies.'

'Of course I will, darling,' Grace said, hugging Mel again, while wondering how her daughter was going to cope with the responsibility a child would bring. But she was glad there was no talk of abortion. She was determined this grandchild of hers would be much loved and would never know he or she had been conceived by mistake. 'Now, how about we stop for coffee on the way home? I think what we both need is one of those delicious cakes from *The Pandanus Café* with a cup of Cleo's special brew.'

'Cleo?'

'She runs the café. You may not have seen her last time we were there. She likes to stay in the background.'

'Mmm. I remember. I liked it there. I wonder if she has any staff vacancies.'

'I doubt it. I always see the same girls when I drop in. You can check the papers when we get home. And don't worry if you can't find anything right away.'

'No, but I want to do something. I can't lie around for months waiting for the baby to be born.'

'You are happy about the baby?'

'I think so. It takes a bit of getting used to. I never imagined… I was on the pill, and I thought I was safe. Poor Lou. She and Greg have been trying madly for months, and I'm the one to get pregnant. It doesn't seem fair.'

'Sometimes life isn't fair, but we manage to make the best of it.'

'Sorry, Mum. It must have been hard for you when Dad got sick. And I wasn't much help.' It was Mel's turn to hug her mother.

Grace's eyes moistened. Mel was a good kid – not so much of a kid anymore, but her heart was in the right place. Maybe it had taken this shock to force her to think of others besides herself. The memory of something Ruby, the elderly woman who ran a B&B up towards the headland, once said to her came forcibly to mind. *There is always a silver lining. Sometimes you just have to look harder to find it.*

Thirteen

Now Aaron had returned to Brisbane, Ted's house seemed empty. It was amazing how, in the short time he'd been here, Aaron had managed to fill the place with his music and the papers he left lying around, scattered on the table and the floor.

Even though his work situation remained unresolved, Aaron was keen to get back to the city where he could try to keep an eye on Zack. He also told Ted he intended to look around for another job, in the construction business or even with an architect. He seemed to have found a new lease of life, and Ted wondered if his new friendship with Mel Winter had anything to do with it.

Aaron hadn't said much about the girl, only that she had her own challenges and planned to move up to Bellbird Bay for a time. Ted wondered how her mother felt about the move. Although he'd kept his eye out, he hadn't caught sight of Grace Winter since Easter. Maybe she was trying to avoid him. If so, she was doing a good job of it. But, he consoled himself, in a town this size, they couldn't avoid each other for long.

He was right.

Next morning, he was returning from his early morning surf, climbing the steps from the beach, when he cannoned into a woman coming in the other direction and almost hit her with his board.

They both spoke at once.

'Oh, I'm sorry.'

'I wasn't looking where I was going.'

Ted peered at the woman he'd almost knocked over. It was Grace Winter. This morning she was obviously on her way down for a swim, wearing a loose shirt and a wide-brimmed straw hat, her eyes hidden by a large pair of sunglasses.

'I'm sorry,' he said again.

'No harm done. I should have been more careful. My mind was elsewhere.'

'It's good to see you again.'

They stood gazing at each other as if unwilling to move away.

Ted was the first to regain his speech. 'You're going swimming.' He gestured to the towel she was carrying.

'Yes. I enjoy it at this time in the morning.'

'Me too, though I'm more of a surfer.' Ted gripped his board. 'It seems we're neighbours.' He pointed to the gate to his backyard several metres away. *This was awkward. He must sound like a fool.*

'Mmm.' Grace gripped her towel. She took two steps away.

Ted knew he had to act quickly, or she'd be gone. 'Let me buy you a meal. It's the least I can do.'

'There's no need. I was as much at fault as you were.'

'Granted, but I'd like to.'

'Now?' She gave him an amused look, her eyes twinkling.

'No, obviously not. How about lunch? We could walk down to the surf club.'

'Well…'

Ted could see she was considering it. 'I could pick you up at around twelve? Which one is yours?' He gestured to the row of renovated beach shacks bordering the boardwalk.

She pointed to the white-painted one with grey trim.

It was one Ted had often admired. He knew it had been sold in early January. *Why hadn't he put two and two together?*

'Twelve, then?'

Grace nodded.

*

'Is that you?' Grace pointed to the larger-than-life mural on the stairway.

'For my sins. Don't know why they haven't painted over it by now. It was a long time ago. There have been better surfers since. Will Rankin and Martin Cooper are two I could name.'

'Rankin? That name sounds familiar.'

'Will runs the surf school on the beach. Unlike me, he stayed around. Coop left, though he's back now. He's a hot shot photographer these days. His sister, Bev, owns *The Pandanus Garden Centre and Café*. She lives along here, too.'

'I haven't been here long enough to meet my neighbours,' Grace said, apologetically. 'I didn't know the owner of the garden centre lived nearby. I go there a lot. It's a great resource and I love the ambiance in the café.'

'Listen to you. You're almost a local.'

By this time, they'd reached the top of the stairs, and Ted steered Grace out to the deck. Being mid-week, it was fairly quiet out there apart from the roar of the surf in the background and the distant cry of the seabirds.

'Wine, beer, coffee?' Ted asked, when they were seated.

'Wine, I think. White. I don't normally drink at lunchtime, but…'

'Wine it is. I'll bring back a couple of menus.'

Ted was relieved to reach the bar and place his order. *What had possessed him to invite Grace Winter to lunch? What on earth would they find to talk about?* So far, he'd acted like a tongue-tied teenager. He was out of practice in talking with women. Apart from clients and the wives of friends, he hadn't made conversation with a woman for years. He took a deep breath, paid for the drinks, and carried his beer and Grace's wine out to the deck, picking up a couple of menus on the way.

'Thanks.' Grace accepted the wine and took a sip. 'Perfect. This is a lovely spot.'

'You haven't been here before?'

'No, but I believe my daughter has been here – with your son.' An amused pair of eyes met his over her glass.

Ted chuckled. 'I believe so. Aaron's gone back to Brisbane now.'

'You only have the one?'

'Yes.' Ted cleared his throat. 'My wife died when he was young. Since then, it's just been the two of us. I moved back here when I retired, but Aaron stayed in the city for work and his son. Zack's twelve now.' *Why was he telling her all this?* It wasn't like him to blurt out his life history to a stranger. But somehow, despite their awkward start, Grace Winter didn't seem like a stranger. 'You?'

'Three children. Mel is the one who met your son. She's my middle child and is staying with me at the moment. She normally lives in Sydney but…' Grace bit her lip, an indication to Ted there was something she wasn't willing to share. 'Lou, my oldest, lives there too with her husband. I'm afraid she disapproves of my move to Bellbird Bay.'

Seeing Grace's eyes cloud over, Ted was tempted to put his hand over hers, but restrained himself just in time. 'And the third?'

'Ben.' Grace smiled. 'You met him at Easter. He's never caused me any worry. He's an archaeologist and hoping to work on a dig in Northern Queensland. He's in Brisbane at the moment.'

'You only moved here recently, didn't you?'

'That's right. We – my husband and I – had a twenty-acre property in Granite Springs, in New South Wales. After he died, it was too much for me. I needed to get away.'

'Dot's your sister?'

'Yes. We'd visited her and Kev here when the children were little. It seemed like the obvious choice.'

'You don't regret it?'

'Not at all. I love the atmosphere here in Bellbird Bay. It's not so different from a country town. I just wish…' She gazed into space.

'I'm sure your daughter will come round.'

'I hope so.' Grace picked up one of the menus, as if feeling she'd revealed too much.

'What do you fancy?' Ted asked, picking up the other menu.

When they'd decided on their meals, Ted went back inside to order, leaving Grace gazing out at the beach.

She turned to greet him with a smile when he returned. 'I didn't mean to drop my family problem on you,' she said, apologetically.

'No worries. What are friends for? And I hope we will be friends,' Ted said.

'Thanks.' Grace stared down into her wine.

'There's something else?'

Grace hesitated, took a sip of wine, seemed about to say something, then shook her head. 'No.'

Then their meals arrived, a burger and chips for Ted and a Caesar salad for Grace, and conversation ceased while they ate.

'Thanks for lunch and for listening,' Grace said, when they had finished eating. 'I didn't intend to subject you to my family's shortcomings over lunch, but you're a good listener.'

'Comes from years of listening to clients' woes, I expect. Sometimes it helps to share your worries with someone completely uninvolved.'

'You're right.'

They sat in silence for a few moments, neither willing to spoil the mood. Then Ted said, 'I spoke to someone who knows you a short time ago. Gordon Slater from Granite Springs. I had reason to contact him about a legal issue, and he said a client of his had moved up here. It may not have been exactly professional of him to mention it, to give me your name.'

'Oh, Gordon. He's an old family friend. He and his wife – his first wife, Jo – were friends of Russ and me as well as him being our family solicitor. That's small towns for you – nothing's private. I'm sure he meant well. I don't think he approved of my move, either.' She chuckled. 'But I needed a fresh start. Sounds like you did, too.'

Ted considered. For him, coming to Bellbird Bay had been coming home, a return to where he'd grown up, but he could see how it might be viewed as a fresh start for him, too. He'd been lucky. Aaron had loved the idea of his dad having a place on the coast for him to retreat to when things in the city became too much for him. Grace hadn't been as fortunate. It sounded as if her decision to come to Bellbird Bay hadn't met with unqualified support from her children and, despite her trying to put a positive spin on it, Ted felt sure she wasn't entirely happy with her daughter moving in with her.

'I've enjoyed our lunch,' Ted said, when they were parting at Grace's back gate, having spent the walk up the boardwalk talking about the delights to be found in Bellbird Bay. 'Maybe we could do it again sometime?' He held his breath waiting for her reply.

Grace hesitated before meeting his eyes and smiling. 'Thanks, I'd like that,' she said.

Fourteen

Two weeks had passed since her lunch with Ted Crawford, and it hadn't been repeated, though Grace often thought of him with a smile on her face. He'd proven to be good company, a kindred spirit who understood her frustration with her daughters. There had still been no word from Lou who, Grace suspected, was in touch with Mel.

She sighed at the thought of her younger daughter. Mel hadn't been able to find employment in Bellbird Bay and was talking of returning to Sydney. To Grace's relief, she'd resigned from the advertising agency and had received a glowing reference from her boss there, but finding work in Bellbird Bay didn't appear to be as easy as she'd anticipated.

One bright spark was Ben's news. He'd arrived the previous Sunday with a bottle of champagne and the news he'd been successful in his interview.

'I start in a week's time, Mum,' he said with a grin. 'You're looking at the new leader of UQ's North Queensland archaeological dig.'

'Well done!' Grace hugged her son.

'Good for you.' Mel scowled at her brother, no doubt wishing she was the one who was announcing a new job.

'You'll find something soon, sweetheart.' Grace hugged Mel too, trying to stifle her concern.

But this morning the sun was shining, and, when Grace walked up the steps from the beach, she saw a man seated further up the boardwalk, a figure which looked like Ted Crawford, seated in front of a small easel. Tempted to see what he was painting, but conscious she was scantily dressed, with only a loose shirt covering her bathing suit, she continued to the gate which led to her back deck.

'Look at this, Mum!' Mel waved a copy of the local paper. 'There's an ad for a job I might have a chance at being considered for.'

'Just a minute.' Grace dropped her towel on the bench, removed her hat, and took off her sunglasses to replace them with her reading ones. 'Now, let me see.'

She took the paper from Mel and, with her daughter peering excitedly over her shoulder read, *Assistant wanted for small art gallery. Part time only, four days a week. Weekends essential. Must have good communication and organisational skills and be prepared to be flexible.*

'I don't know anything about an art gallery, but I worked with the art and design team in my last job. What do you think, Mum? It could be fun.' Mel sounded more positive than she had since arriving in Bellbird Bay.

Grace smiled and, laying down the paper, hugged her daughter. Fun? That was Mel all over. Life for her would never be the serious affair it was for her brother and sister. 'I think it sounds like an excellent opportunity,' she said. 'You are going to apply?'

'I've already drafted a letter of application. Can you have a look at it, see if it sounds okay?'

Suddenly Mel was like a small child again, seeking her mother's opinion of a school assignment.

'Let me have a shower and change first, then I'll read it for you. I think I've passed the gallery in town. It's near the newspaper office, next to a café.'

She left Mel making coffee while she took a quick shower. Then, dressed in a pair of knee-length shorts and one of the colourful shirts she'd purchased in *Birds of a Feather*, she went back to the kitchen.

'Coffee, Mum?' Mel asked. 'The letter's on my laptop.' She gestured to where the MacBook was sitting on the kitchen bench.

'Thanks, honey.' Grace picked up her glasses again, hoisted herself onto one of the high stools she'd bought when she moved in and, ignoring Tiger's pitiful cries, carefully read Mel's letter of application.

'It looks really good, sweetheart, but I wonder…'

'What?' Mel pouted.

'I think you're selling yourself short. You don't mention you studied art for your HSC. I know it was a long time ago, but it might just give you the edge over other applicants.'

'You think so?' Mel appeared doubtful.

'Well, it won't do any harm. Otherwise, I think it's an excellent letter of application. This John Baldwin would be lucky to get you.'

'Thanks, Mum.' Mel gave Grace a hug and a kiss on the cheek. 'I know I'm not always the easiest person to have around. But if I get this job, I promise to try harder. I'm grateful you're willing to have me to stay until I have the baby. I'll fix up the letter and send it off now.'

Grace sipped her coffee while she watched her daughter make the necessary alterations. Maybe there *was* a silver lining to Mel's pregnancy. Maybe her daughter was finally growing up.

'Done!' Mel closed her MacBook and swung around to face Grace, before picking up Tiger and hugging him. 'Tige slept on my bed last night, and I fed him earlier, but it seems he wants fed again. Don't you, puss?' she asked the squirming cat.

'He's greedy. I usually feed him night and morning and he knows it very well. He's taking advantage of your generosity.' But Grace was glad to see how Mel had bonded with the cat. She'd always loved animals when she was growing up, but Grace didn't think she had any in the city. 'What do you plan to do today?' she asked. 'I don't have to be at work, so we could do something together.'

'I'm good. I thought I might explore the town a bit more, maybe check out what this gallery looks like, and I want to get one of those wide-brimmed hats everyone seems to wear.'

'Good idea.' Grace had been dying to suggest Mel replace her cap with a hat which provided more protection from the Queensland sun but was afraid of her daughter's reaction. 'See you at lunchtime then.'

Once Mel had left and Grace had tidied the kitchen – and weakened to give Tiger a treat – she walked out to the deck and peered up the boardwalk. The man with the easel was still there. For a full minute, she debated with herself about the wisdom of walking up to see what he was doing, before pulling on her hat and sunglasses and closing the door behind her.

As she drew nearer, Grace could see it was indeed Ted Crawford totally engrossed in what he was doing. For a moment, she regretted the impulse which had led her to come, and was about to turn around when, as if sensing her presence, he turned to face her.

'Good morning, Grace. How lovely to see you. I think I may have seen you earlier coming back from your swim.'

Grace blushed. How did he know it was her? But how many other women lived along here and went for an early morning swim? 'I didn't know you were an artist,' she said to cover her confusion.

'Artist?' Ted chuckled. 'I dabble, but it keeps me busy, and I find it helps me relax.'

Grace moved closer and peered over his shoulder to see what was, to her eyes, an excellent depiction of the beach and ocean below. He'd caught the colour and atmosphere of the scene, and there was a figure emerging from the water who looked very like her. 'Is that me?' she asked, pointing.

'Afraid so,' Ted said apologetically. 'I didn't realise it was you until you reached the boardwalk and I saw which house you headed for.'

'It's very good.'

'I try, and I have sold a few of my daubs. An old school friend owns the gallery in town. He takes pity on me from time to time and displays my work.'

'*The Bay Gallery?*'

'That's the one. Know it?'

'I've seen it but haven't been in.' Grace made a mental note to visit the gallery next time she was in the neighbourhood. Not only was Mel applying for a job there, but she might get the opportunity to see more of Ted's work. She was intrigued to know what else he had painted. 'My daughter has just applied for a job there,' she admitted.

'She could do worse. John's a good guy. He's a great supporter of local talent. Went to town with an exhibition for the travel photographer, Martin Cooper, a few months ago. It was a great success.'

'Oh, I wish I'd gone.' Grace had a vague recollection of seeing the exhibition advertised, but had balked at the thought of being in a crowd of people and having to make small talk with strangers. Now she regretted her reluctance. 'I love his work. I think you mentioned him before, when we were in the surf club. He lives here?'

'Left as soon as he finished school but came back earlier this year. I get the feeling he may stay around this time. I'm about to finish up here. Why don't you come back with me? I can make us a cup of tea or coffee and if you're interested in seeing some of my other work…'

'Come up and see my etchings?' Grace asked with a chuckle. It was an old pick-up line they used to laugh about when she was a student.

'I guess so.' Ted laughed, too. 'But you will come?'

Grace nodded. Ted Crawford grew on one, she decided. There was a lot more to him than she imagined when they first met at Dot and Kev's. The man she dismissed as boring and an aging hippie was a lawyer turned artist. What other talents did he have hidden away?

Fifteen

Ted packed up his painting gear, surprised and pleased Grace Winter had appeared beside him on the boardwalk whether by chance or design. She looked good this morning, in another bright garment similar to the dress she'd worn when they first met. He was embarrassed to remember how he'd deliberately ignored her on that occasion, determined not to be caught in the trap he was sure Kev's wife was springing.

Now, he swung along beside her, chatting easily about how, on returning to Bellbird Bay, he'd decided to recapture an earlier interest in art, had enrolled in a course in U3A and chosen to work in pastels.

'What about you?' he asked, when they were seated on his deck with cups of the Earl Grey tea he kept for visitors, preferring coffee himself.

'Me?' Grace took a delicate sip of tea.

'What do you do to pass the time?'

'Oh! I work part-time in the library as the children's librarian and…' she appeared embarrassed, '…I write.'

'You do? How interesting. Fiction?' He couldn't imagine Grace turning out the sort of regency romances his wife had enjoyed reading and about which he had teased her mercilessly.

'Children's books. At least, I'm trying to write one. I haven't had anything published yet.' Blushing, she took another sip of her tea. 'No one else knows. You're the first person I've told.'

'I'm flattered you've confided in me. I suppose your work in the library lends itself to them.'

'I guess so. I love the challenge of writing for a young audience. They can be so critical, more so than some adults. And I can let my imagination run riot. I suppose I get the same sort of pleasure you do from your art. Speaking of which, where are those paintings you promised to show me? Or was it all a ploy to lure me here for tea?' She chuckled and lowered her eyes.

'Partly.'

They both laughed, suddenly more at ease with each other.

'If you've finished your tea, I can show you the room I've converted into a studio. I needed somewhere to work when the weather's not so conducive to sitting outside.'

Grace drained her cup. 'I'd love to see it.'

Ted led her into a small room with a picture window looking out to the ocean. Another easel was set up here and his work was stacked along one wall. 'Here it is.' He waved an arm to encompass the collection of paintings, some finished, some only partly done.

Grace walked across to examine the one featuring a group of surfers which was on the easel, then wandered over to where the others were stacked, peering at each carefully. 'I think this is my favourite,' she said, pointing to one in which a trail of turtles were making their way down the beach to the ocean. 'Do they really nest here in Bellbird Bay?'

'They sure do.' Ted came to stand close behind her. 'They come in to nest from November and we monitor them each day till they hatch late February and March. Both green and loggerhead turtles nest here every year. Sadly, only one in a thousand survive.'

'You say we?' Grace raised an eyebrow.

'I'm only one of the many TurtleCare volunteers who donate our time each year as soon as we hear reports of turtle tracks being sighted on the beaches. It's something I heard about when I came back here to live, and I remembered seeing the turtles hatching when I was a boy. We work under the auspices of the Queensland Government Turtle Conservation Project which provides training. Is it something you'd like to be involved in?'

'Perhaps. Your paintings are really awfully good. You were wasted as a lawyer,' she said.

'Hmph.' Ted frowned. While gratified with her admiration, he found it difficult to accept praise for his paintings. 'Now you've seen my work, I'd be happy to view yours.'

'Oh, I don't think so. It's nowhere near ready for another set of eyes, not yet.'

Getting the impression she didn't want to talk more about it, Ted decided to change the subject. 'Your daughter, the one who's applying for the job with the gallery. She's the one my son befriended? He talked about her a lot before he went back to Brisbane.'

'Yes, Mel's…' Grace bit her lip, as if she'd been about to say something she shouldn't. 'I think they're still in touch.'

'She plans to stay in Bellbird Bay?'

'For the moment. If she can find work here. She hasn't found it easy since Russ died. She was his favourite, and he spoiled her rotten.' She sighed. 'She took his death hard, didn't cope with it well and is still grieving. I think that's why she makes life difficult for the rest of us.'

Ted could see Grace was conflicted and sensed again there was something she didn't want to share. He understood. Children were the very devil. You thought when they grew up your duties as a parent were over. Sometimes it seemed they were just beginning.

'Thanks for the tea and for being kind enough to show me your work,' Grace said, suddenly becoming very polite.

Ted frowned again. What had happened? They'd been talking together quite amicably then the mood had changed. It was when they started talking about her daughter – and Aaron. There was something there, something she wanted to keep to herself. Well, he wasn't in the business of ferreting out people's secrets. He'd seen and heard enough of those in his career to know everyone had at least one thing which they wanted to keep to themselves.

'My pleasure. Perhaps we can have dinner some time?' Ted said as he showed Grace to the door.

She turned back towards him, her face lighting up with what he took to be pleasure. 'Oh, that would be lovely, thank you.'

There was a pause, during which Ted realised she was waiting for him to speak again. 'They do a special steak meal at *The Beach House* on a Friday. We could walk down. How about I pick you up around seven.'

He was rewarded with a warm smile.

'I'll see you then. Friday at seven.'

Ted watched Grace make her way back down the boardwalk, reflecting how his opinion of her had changed. She was just as reluctant as he was to form a new relationship. It was a long time since a woman had interested him. But Grace Winter certainly did. He was eager to know what made her tick, what her life had been like before she moved to Bellbird Bay, and what the secret was that made her eyes cloud and her lips tighten from time to time

*

After a quick lunch of bread with a chunk of his favourite sharp cheddar cheese and dill pickles, washed down with a beer, Ted retired to his studio aiming to finish the painting of the surfers on his easel. But his thoughts kept returning to his meeting with Grace. There was something troubling her. He wished he could remove the worry he saw reflected in her eyes, eyes in which a man could drown. He was willing to bet it had to do with her children. She had more than the one who was staying with her. There was also the son who'd been with her when they met on Australia Day, and an older daughter she'd mentioned when they had lunch. Which one was it who brought the hint of sadness to her eyes?

The ringing of his phone interrupted Ted's musings. He slid it from his pocket, sighing to see Aaron's number. What did his son want now? When Aaron went back to Brisbane, it was with the intention of trying to clear his name and perhaps seeking alternative employment. The information Ted had been able to glean from Gordon Slater had been inconclusive. The country solicitor had been of the opinion everyone involved could be deemed culpable, from the guy who designed the specs to the engineer who built the equipment. It didn't augur well for Aaron who'd taken the news badly.

To Ted's surprise, Aaron sounded excited.

'Hey, Dad. I'm coming back up the coast. I've been in touch with a guy I went to school with. Nick Armstrong. He's set up a boat building business along the coast from Bellbird Bay. There may be a place for me with his design team. He's keen to talk with me about what I've been working on.'

'That's great, son. Wasn't Nick the boy who took out his dad's boat without permission and almost got himself drowned?' Ted remembered the incident which had entailed local boat owners and the coast guard going out in a storm to rescue the teenager in distress. It had been madness for him to have taken the boat out with a storm brewing and he'd been lucky to survive, thanks to the bravery of those men who risked their own lives to save his.

'That was a long time ago, Dad. Nick's forty now. He's always loved boats, and his business is going from strength to strength. He builds yachts and motor launches for the idle rich, people with more money than sense.'

'Hmm. And you think you'd like it?'

'It would be a darn sight better than what I've been doing for the past few years. I'd have to move from Brisbane, but Zack could visit.'

'Sounds good. When did you say you were coming up?'

'I plan to drive up on Thursday. I'm meeting Nick on Friday and thought I might stay the weekend. Okay with you?'

'Sure.' But Ted couldn't help wishing his son had chosen a different weekend to visit. It wasn't that he wanted to keep his meeting with Grace secret, but he'd prefer to keep it to himself for the moment.

Realising he wasn't going to be able to concentrate on his painting any more today, he packed up again and went through to the kitchen where he took a beer from the fridge before going out to the deck.

Regardless of the interruption to his plans, Ted was glad Aaron was looking to the future. Working on the design of boats would be a lot different from what he'd been doing in Brisbane, the only downside, his inability to see as much of Zack. But it would be good to have him close by, even if it might cramp Ted's style with Grace Winter.

Ted chuckled at the thought, reminding himself he wasn't a callow youth, hadn't been for several decades. Surely by now, he should have learned how to handle himself with a woman. The trouble was he hadn't been in a relationship since Alison died all those years ago. Aaron had never known him to be interested in a woman. How would his son react to Ted's new friendship?

Sixteen

Friday came along too quickly for Grace, who was doubting the wisdom of agreeing to have dinner with Ted Crawford. Lunch had been fine, a way of smoothing the awkwardness when they'd bumped into each other. And she could persuade herself going to his house to see his paintings had been a neighbourly thing to do. But dinner at *The Beach House* couldn't be regarded as anything but a date.

She was debating what to wear, when Mel walked into her bedroom waving her phone in the air.

'I got it! John Baldwin just called me. He wants me to start the week after next.'

'Oh, darling, I'm so pleased for you. So, it means you won't be going back to Sydney?'

'I'll need to go back to get my things and to tell Gwen and Marie I definitely won't be back. Another girl has moved into my old room on a temporary basis so she can stay there if she wants to. I can fly down at the weekend, but I don't know how I'm going to get everything back up here. Do you think I can hire a car?'

'I'm sure you can,' Grace said, wondering exactly how much stuff Mel had accumulated in her Sydney flat.

'Oh, there's not much,' she said, seeing the expression in Grace's eyes. 'My clothes, books, a table lamp and a couple of other things. Where did you say you were going tonight?' she asked, suddenly changing the subject.

'*The Beach House*, where we had dinner with your Aunt Dot and

Uncle Kev. Remember?' Grace's forehead furrowed. She still owed her sister and brother-in-law dinner. 'I should return their hospitality.'

'Do it while I'm gone,' Mel said immediately. 'Aunt Dot's sure to be full of questions about why I'm moving here… and I'm going to begin to show soon.' She smoothed her dress over her still flat stomach. 'I can't bear to be subjected to her disapproval.'

'She's not so bad,' Grace remonstrated, but she knew her sister would be like a dog with a bone if she knew Mel was pregnant. She wouldn't stop till she got to the bottom of who the father was, when the baby was due and why she was staying with Grace. Grace knew she'd do everything she could to protect her daughter from the inquisition Dot would think was her right. She mentally decided to have her sister to dinner in the coming week. She'd invite her when they met at book club on Monday evening. 'You're fine,' she said, giving Mel a hug. 'I'll miss you next week.'

As she spoke, Grace realised it was true. She had grown accustomed to having Mel around. While, at first, she'd resented the disruption to her solitude and had often wanted to shake some sense into the moody presence in her life, as Mel had begun to change her attitude, so Grace had begun to enjoy her company.

'Aaron Crawford is in Bellbird Bay this weekend,' Mel said, trying unsuccessfully to sound nonchalant.

'Oh?' Ted hadn't mentioned his son was coming to visit – or was he coming to stay, too? Did this complicate matters? 'And are you going to be seeing him?'

'He texted me and asked to meet for a drink. Don't worry. I don't imagine we'll be going to anywhere as swanky as *The Beach House*.'

'It's not…' Grace caught the grin on her daughter's face. 'Okay, you got me there. His dad didn't mention he was coming up.'

'A job interview or something. Maybe he'll move here, too.'

Grace wasn't sure why this made her feel uncomfortable. There was no reason why Mel shouldn't make friends with Ted's son. They were both single, of a similar age. But Mel was pregnant and had just come out of an unpleasant relationship. She didn't know anything about Aaron Crawford. If he was anything like his father, he was one of the good guys. But he'd been married, too, had a son, and from what she'd gleaned from Ted, was in the habit of getting himself into scrapes. Grace didn't want Mel to make another poor choice.

'Are you sure it's a good idea to go out with him, to start something when…?'

'Mum! I don't intend to hibernate just because I'm pregnant and I messed up with the last man I was involved with. If you can date Aaron's father, what's wrong with me going out with him?'

'Nothing.' But Grace knew her expression gave her away. She didn't want Mel involved with Ted's son. It felt too… the word incestuous came to mind. But of course it wasn't. It was just odd.

'Wear the pink one.' Mel changed the subject again and picked up one of the dresses Grace had discarded and thrown on the bed. It was the fuchsia pink dress patterned with peacocks which she'd worn to dinner at Dot's the night she'd first met Ted. She hadn't worn it since.

'Do you think so?' Grace picked up the dress and held it against her. 'You don't think it's too bright?'

'You couldn't have worn something like that in Granite Springs. The Country Women's Association harpies would have thought you were a scarlet woman. But here in Bellbird Bay, it's like you have reinvented yourself. Maybe I can, too. I like the new you, Mum.' Mel put an arm around Grace's shoulder and gave her a peck on the cheek before drifting off.

Grace gazed at herself in the mirror. She was still holding the dress in front of her, and her face was wet with tears. Where had they come from? It was Mel's words which had prompted them, her suggestion she'd reinvented herself. It was true. It hadn't been deliberate, but here in this small coastal town, Grace had been able to become a different person from the dutiful wife who'd been a member of the Country Women's Association, always there when a helping hand was needed. Here, she wasn't dependent on anyone, she was free to make her own decisions, even to form a new relationship, if she felt so inclined.

*

'I hear you have your son staying with you.'

Grace and Ted were enjoying a glass of wine before their meal, seated by a window with a view of the ocean. They could see the distant gleam of lights from a ship at anchor on the horizon, and the night sky was ablaze with stars.

'Aaron? Yes, he arrived yesterday. He called just after you left on Tuesday. It was unexpected. He met with an old school friend today to discuss a job. How did you know?'

'My daughter. They kept in touch. They're meeting tonight, too.' Grace couldn't help frowning.

'You don't approve?' Ted appeared amused. 'I know he may not be the best bet in the romance stakes, but he's not a bad lad and he's a good father.'

'It's not that. It's…' Grace picked up her glass took a sip, then carefully placed it down on the table again. *Should she tell him?* It was Mel's secret, not hers. But she had an urge to share her concern with someone. She couldn't tell Dot and she didn't know anyone in Bellbird Bay well enough – other than Ted.

'It's not him, it's Mel.'

Ted's eyes mirrored her concern. 'Is there something wrong?'

'Not wrong, exactly.' Grace sighed and took another sip of wine before continuing. 'It's Mel,' Grace said again. She took another sip of wine, then met his eyes. 'She's pregnant.'

Ted's eyes widened.

'I can't deny it was a shock, but I'm getting used to it. I don't know why I'm telling you all this. But I have to tell someone, and Dot wouldn't understand. You have a child – and a grandchild. You know how things can happen.' Her voice trailed off.

Ted reached out to cover her hand with his. 'I'm sorry. It must be difficult for you – and for her.'

'Yes. My first grandchild,' she said with a note of wonder and delight. 'I just wish it wasn't this way. It won't be easy for Mel. Being a single mother never is, and she's always flitted through life with no thought of the future. I'm afraid this will bring her down to earth with a thump. I don't think she's quite realised the responsibility that comes with bringing a child into the world. Anyway,' she took a deep breath, 'she's agreed to move in with me at least till the baby's born. I know it's not the end of the world, but… the father's married. He was a work colleague. It's all a bit of a mess.' She sighed again, relieved to have shared the burden.

'She intends to have the child?'

'She does. It's why she's decided to stay in Bellbird Bay. I can help and I'm looking forward to being a grandmother, but…'

'I understand. It won't be easy for her.'

'No.'

'How does she feel about it?'

'I'm not really sure. Mel's always sailed through life. She's my youngest and her father spoiled her. We always believed she'd find her feet and decide what she wanted out of life. She's thirty-one, almost thirty-two, no longer a child, but she sometimes acts like one. This has been a shock. I think she's still coming to terms with it. I have no idea what sort of mother she'll make. She can scarcely look after herself.'

'I wonder if Aaron knows.' Ted looked thoughtful.

'I doubt it. My worry is she met him just as she discovered she was pregnant. I hope she hasn't latched onto your son on the rebound from her previous relationship.'

'I'm pretty sure Aaron can look after himself. I don't know much about his social life, but his marriage break-up seemed to undermine his self-confidence. It may be this friendship with your daughter will go some way to restoring it. He may need to associate with someone less fortunate than himself. He has a few problems of his own to deal with.'

Grace was curious to know what Aaron's problems were, but their meals arrived and the conversation slipped back into easier territory.

It wasn't till she arrived home to find Mel still out, that Grace wondered again about Ted's son. All she knew was he was divorced with a son, had some issues at work and was seeking alternative employment somewhere here on the coast. Despite Ted's assurances, Grace couldn't help worrying Mel was heading into another disastrous relationship and she was in no position to help her, even if her help would be welcome.

Seventeen

'Good night?' Ted asked Aaron when his son appeared at breakfast, somewhat bleary-eyed and dishevelled.

'It was okay. Yours?' Aaron winked. 'Mel said her mother was in a bit of a tizz. Seems like you've still got it, Dad.' Aaron helped himself to coffee, pulled out a chair and collapsed into it.

Deciding to ignore Aaron's remarks, Ted asked, 'Busy at the club?'

'Yeah. Friday night. They had a good group playing. Not bad for a town of this size. Mel's got a job here. She plans to move up from Sydney to stay with her mother.' Aaron grinned, clearly delighted at the news.

'Mmm. And what are your plans? You didn't say anything about your meeting with Nick.' Aaron had walked in just as Ted was about to leave, and there had been no time for questions about his interview.

'It went well, I think. He has a good set up there. Impressive. He'll let me know in a day or two. If I'm successful, can I stay here for a bit till I sort out some accommodation? Nick said there might be a townhouse going close to the yard.'

'Sure, son.' A bit like Grace's situation, Ted reflected. Neither of them had anticipated having their grown children move home to recharge their lives. It sounded like Mel hadn't confided in Aaron about her pregnancy. He hoped she did soon. He was beginning to understand Grace's concern and share it.

'Seeing her again, Dad?'

'Grace is a neighbour.'

'Not what I asked.' Aaron picked up a slice of toast and spread it generously with peanut butter before topping it with a sliced banana. 'I've never known you to be interested in a woman.' He took a bite of toast and grinned.

'She's a nice lady.' It was all Ted was willing to say. He enjoyed Grace's company. They had shared some confidences. But as to anything else, he was still undecided.

*

A somewhat similar conversation was taking place at Grace's, where Mel had arrived at the breakfast table fully dressed, her hair carefully styled.

'So,' Mel said, 'You and Aaron's dad? Isn't it a bit soon?'

Grace blushed.

'I mean, Dad's only been gone for…'

'Two years,' Grace finished for her. It had taken her two years to decide to make the move from the home they'd shared, two years of mourning the love of her life. She wasn't trying to replace him, no one could ever do that. But in Ted she'd found a kindred spirit, someone with whom she could share the challenges grown children could bring, someone who might be able to fill the void of loneliness, the ache she sometimes experienced.

'It's a bit weird,' Mel continued. 'I mean, last night. Me out with Aaron and you with his dad.' She grimaced.

'So, what is it with you and Aaron? Have you told him you're pregnant?'

Mel flinched as if she'd been struck. 'No, not yet. We're not… I'll tell him when I have to, *if* I have to.' She looked down at her stomach, as if hoping there wasn't a baby in there. It seemed to Grace Mel fluctuated between being pleased about the baby to wishing it would disappear.

'His dad says he's interested in a position here on the coast.' Grace looked across the table at her daughter hoping for some reaction, some indication of how she and Aaron were getting on together.

'Maybe. He has this old school friend with a boatbuilding yard. He seems excited about it. I guess it would mean we could see more of each other.' She shrugged.

'When is your flight to Sydney?' Grace asked, realising she wasn't going to get any further with Mel on this topic.

'Two o'clock. Can you give me a lift to the airport? If not, I can call a cab.'

'Of course.' Grace swallowed. She hadn't realised Mel was leaving so soon. 'Your friends are expecting you?'

'Yeah.'

'Will you see Lou when you're in Sydney?'

'I guess, but…' She bit her lip. 'What if she guesses I'm pregnant?'

'She'll find out sometime, so it's better if she hears it from you.'

'Mmm. I'd better go and pack.' Mel wandered out of the kitchen leaving Grace staring after her, her brow creasing. She wished there was more she could do to help her daughter, but there were some things Mel had to handle herself. Telling Lou about her pregnancy was one of them.

*

It was with a sense of loss that Grace waved Mel off at the airport. Despite the awkward start to her daughter's visit, she'd become used to having Mel's company and would miss having her around.

The younger woman had promised to return by the following weekend ready to begin work on the Monday. She had been vague when asked how she was going to travel back with her belongings, and Grace decided not to press her. But she couldn't help worrying.

She was driving home when she heard a text ping on her phone. She smiled, thinking it was Mel reminding her of something she'd forgotten to tell her. But when she reached home again and checked the message, it was from Ted.

My son tells me your daughter is leaving today. He has left, too. Join me for drinks around eight and we can commiserate or celebrate together? Ted.

Grace smiled, surprised to experience a frisson of pleasure and a quickening of her pulse. Without allowing herself time to think, she quickly typed, *Thanks, I'd love to. G*, before going inside with a smile on her face.

Tiger was waiting in the kitchen for her with a loud meowing, annoyed at having been abandoned yet again. Grace picked the cat up and gave him a cuddle. 'Just you and me again, puss,' she whispered into his warm coat. The cat purred loudly, then leapt down again, strutting across to stand over his food bowl, his tail in the air.

'Here you are, Tige,' she said, pouring in some cat food and ensuring his water bowl was filled to the brim. Then she poured herself a glass of water before heading to her study. It was too long since she'd spent time with her writing. Unsure of what Mel might think – or if she might demand to see her work – Grace had only been able to sneak odd moments while Mel was here. One plus of her daughter's brief return to Sydney was that Grace could write without fear of interruption. With the delightful anticipation of drinks with Ted later on, she settled down to immerse herself in her other life.

After what she considered to have been a successful few hours lost in a world of her own making, Grace fixed herself a plate of leftovers. Then she tidied her hair and checked herself in the bedroom mirror, wondering how she appeared to Ted Crawford. Tonight, she'd chosen to wear a pair of white wide-legged pants teamed with a colourful tunic top. It was so long since she'd worried what a man thought of her appearance, and she might be making too much of his invitation. It could be that, like her, his house seemed empty after his son left and he just wanted company. Or perhaps he was being kind, taking pity on her, knowing Mel had gone.

Being married for so long, Grace had got out of the habit of caring too much about her appearance. Russ had always assured her he'd love her in a sack with a bag over her head. They'd often laughed together about the fact they knew each other so well, they often didn't notice what the other wore or if Grace had remembered to apply her makeup.

But, somehow, Grace wanted to make a good impression on Ted. Each time they met, they discovered a little more about each other and, so far, she liked what she was finding out about him. He was an interesting, intelligent man and, when she'd shared the information about Mel with him, he'd proved to be empathetic too. When Russ died, it had never occurred to her she might meet another man who attracted her, but Ted Crawford had proved her wrong. How smug Dot would be to discover they were meeting. She'd be sure to take credit for introducing them.

Satisfied she looked reasonably presentable, Grace selected a bottle of shiraz from the wine rack, told Tiger to be good and, her heart in her mouth, made her way along the boardwalk to Ted's home.

*

It was a balmy evening, the sky gradually turning from golden to pink before the light faded altogether. Grace and Ted sat on his deck with a bottle of wine, a plate of biscuits and cheese and a bowl of stuffed olives.

'To us.' Ted raised his glass.

'To us,' Grace replied. It was peaceful sitting here in the twilight, the only sounds the waves breaking on the beach and the odd car in the distance. 'It's so quiet here. I thought I'd miss the tranquillity of my old place in Granite Springs, but this is a different sort of peace.'

'I love it. You don't regret making the move?'

'No. I love it here. I just wish Lou would come round.'

'Lou's your daughter?'

'My oldest. She refuses to accept I have a life and needed to move on. I'd love her to come here, to see my new home, to realise I haven't forgotten her dad, the memories. Mel took it badly at first too, but she's changed. Ben has always supported me. But Lou...' she sighed. 'Lou always thinks she knows best, knows what's best for me, for everyone. And she tends to keep things to herself. Until Mel told me, I didn't know she and Greg were trying for a baby and she was having trouble becoming pregnant. Maybe I could have helped... maybe not.' She sighed again and took a sip of wine.

'We think it's all going to get easier when they're grown, don't we? But I think I worry more about Aaron now than I did when he was a teenager. At least I had some control over him then – or thought I did.' Ted chuckled. 'More wine?' He picked up the bottle and gestured to Grace's empty glass.

'Thanks.' It was good to chat with someone who understood. Although Ted had only one child, he knew what it was like to feel helpless in the face of their problems, to wish you could wrap them up away from all harm. But once they left home, they had to face their own challenges, make their own decisions and deal with the consequences.

They sat in silence for a few minutes, letting the spell of the evening settle over them like a silken quilt, then Grace spoke. 'Your son… Mel said he was investigating a job on the coast. Does that mean he'll be moving in with you?'

'For a time. But I think he's anxious to find a place of his own, if he's successful, that is. The job's with an old friend of his. It's with a boatbuilding business up the coast from here. I'm pretty sure he'd prefer to live closer to work. But I expect he'll base himself here to start with.'

'So, your Aaron will be here and my Mel just down the way. I wonder…'

'They seem to get on pretty well. Does it bother you?'

'I'm not sure.' Grace hesitated. 'I don't want to think she's latching on to him because he's the first man she's met since…'

Ted put his hand gently on Grace's arm and patted it. 'We can't protect them from themselves. They're both old enough to make their own decisions. All we can do is be there when they need us – if they'll let us.'

'Your son – Aaron – he has a son, too, your grandson. Mel mentioned him.'

'Zack? Yes.' His brow furrowed.

'Is there a problem?'

'I don't think he's happy. His mother's part of the problem. She married again and Aaron didn't push for joint custody. He sees him most weekends, but not enough to make a difference to the boy. He was here in the Easter holidays, and it took a couple of days for him to open up and act more like you'd expect from a boy his age. His mother and stepfather have placed him in this school in which the currency is being good at sport. Zack's more like his dad and me. Surfing was the only sport I was ever any good at.'

'And you excelled there, I understand?' Grace remembered the mural in the surf club which commemorated Ted's achievements.

He reddened and drew a finger round the inside of his collar.

'Does your son surf, too?'

Ted shook his head. 'He grew up in the city. There was no opportunity for him to learn. But I gave Zack a few lessons when he was here. He's a natural.'

'There's no chance of him moving here with his dad?'

'I wish…' Ted shook his head. 'Tanya would never consider it. It's almost as if she holds the kid hostage just to spite Aaron.' He picked up his glass and took a gulp of wine. 'Sorry, I shouldn't be boring you with my family problems.'

'I asked, and I did start it with mine.' Grace smiled.

Suddenly realising it had become completely dark, Grace drained her glass. 'I've really enjoyed our chat, but I should get back. Tiger will be fretting.'

'Tiger?'

'My cat. I'm afraid I've become one of those women who is a slave to my pet. Tiger appeared on my doorstep soon after I moved in and adopted me. He's been good company.' She gave an apologetic smile.

'Well, I can't compete with that.' Ted chuckled. 'I've enjoyed tonight, too. It's been good to talk with someone my own age after having Aaron here. We should do it again.'

'Yes.'

'I'll call you.'

There was an awkward moment when Grace thought Ted was going to give her a peck on the cheek, then they shook hands and she left, feeling his eyes following her.

Grace's mind was in a whirl as she walked home along the boardwalk, her mouth dry, her pulse racing. *What had just happened back there? Had Ted almost kissed her? Had she wanted him to? Was her uppermost feeling one of relief or disappointment?*

Eighteen

Ted watched Grace leave, wishing he'd had the courage to take her in his arms. The evening had gone even better than he expected, as they shared the challenges both had with their adult children. It was strange how times changed. Who would have imagined he'd spend a date discussing the foibles of children who should have their own lives but who still posed a problem to their parents?

Grace Winter was a woman to be treasured. Ted couldn't believe how close he'd come to dismissing her as yet another middle-aged woman looking for a meal ticket. Far from it, she was an intelligent, independent woman, one he was lucky to count as a friend – even if he now knew he wanted more than friendship. From their brief acquaintance, he'd formed the opinion she was fiercely independent and wasn't looking for a relationship. But she did appear to welcome his company.

Sighing, Ted went inside, deciding to check his emails before going to bed. His eyes lit up to see one from Zack.

Hi Grandpa,

Missing you and Dad, but he says he's coming back to Brisbane so maybe we can meet. I told the guys at school about the surfing but they said it was weak and I should play a proper sport. I wish I could live with you and surf all the time. Maybe I could become a champion like you were. When can I come back to see you?

Love you, Grandpa Teddy,

Zack xx

Ted's eyes misted. The poor kid. It was all Tanya's fault, and the guy she'd married. And if Aaron got the job up here, Zack would be even more isolated. He shook his head. It was a conundrum. The job with his old friend could be the saving of Aaron, but with it came the challenge of his separation from Zack. The boy needed him. Twelve was an impressionable age. It was a time when Zack should be out with his mates having fun. Instead, he seemed to be retreating more and more into himself. It wasn't healthy.

Ted blinked away the incipient tears and typed a quick reply.

Hi Zack,

Great to hear from you. Sorry your friends don't appreciate the finer points of surfing. I'm sure your dad will make a point of seeing you this week. I miss you lots. Would love to have another surfing champion in the family. Hopefully we can persuade your mum to let you come up again next school holidays. And I might arrange a trip to Sydney. You can make a list of things you want to show me there.

Much love.

Grandpa Teddy xx

Ted sat back and stared at the screen before pressing *send*. It wasn't fair to keep Zack in a school where he was so unhappy. Ted suspected he was being bullied, too. His blood boiled when he remembered how the boy had blossomed when he was here in Bellbird Bay.

He poured himself a glass of scotch, then sent a text to Aaron.

Make sure you see Zack when you're in Brisbane. Had an email from him and he sounds down. Dad.

Satisfied he'd done what he could, Ted drained his glass, turned out the lights and headed for the bedroom.

*

A few doors along, Grace was still thinking about her evening with Ted, as she cuddled Tiger and made sure he was settled in the laundry for the night. Had she been mistaken, or had he been about to embrace her before he appeared to change his mind? How would she have reacted if he had taken her in his arms?

When Russ died, she'd never considered being attracted to another man, but there was something about Ted Crawford that made her wonder what it would be like to feel his arms around her, his lips on hers. She shivered. Was she too old for another relationship? She was only in her early sixties, and she supposed to some that would seem old. But she still had the same yearnings of her younger self and, though she'd been enjoying her solitary life here until Mel's arrival, she could see how she might get lonely after a while.

It had been good to share her worries about Mel and Lou with Ted but there were some things only a woman would understand. And Dot was no use. Much as she loved her sister, Dot was set in her ways. She'd never had children and had her own very definite ideas of how Grace should spend the rest of her life. But she may have been right about one thing. Grace admitted it would be good to have some women friends, women with whom she could share confidences and ask for advice.

Since coming to Bellbird Bay, Grace had tended to keep herself to herself, eschewing making friends with the women she met in the library or the book club, hurrying home from each to bury herself in her writing. That had changed while Mel was with her, but only meant she hurried home to her daughter instead.

She thought back to Granite Springs and how, as Russ's illness progressed, she had isolated herself there, too. Caring for him had taken up all her time and energy. Then after his death she had kept herself busy on the property, grieving in private and only going into town for essential shopping.

Only one friend had continued to keep in touch. Jo Ford had refused to accept Grace's excuses and had insisted on keeping in contact and, while it was sometimes difficult to maintain a conversation, Grace always enjoyed the other woman's company.

The pair had met at the school gate when Lou started primary school. Grace had been a nervous new mother, while Jo was farewelling her third child. Her youngest, Rob, was in the same class as Lou, and although the two children had never become friends, Jo and Grace had.

Back then, Jo had been married to Gordon Slater who'd become their family solicitor, and Grace and Russ had become friends with the other couple, spending many enjoyable times together. But, several years earlier, Gordon had formed a relationship with a younger woman. Now Jo was married to his former business partner and her old friend, Col Ford. It put an end to the foursome's regular get-togethers, but Grace and Jo had kept in touch, albeit less frequently.

Now, Grace regretted not being in touch with Jo after leaving Granite Springs. She hadn't spoken to her since the two had tea together the week before Grace left to start her new life. Jo had always been ready to listen and had been there with comfort and advice. Her three children were now grown and still living in Granite Springs, but Grace was sure they hadn't been without their problems, And Jo knew what it was like to form a relationship later in life.

How she'd love to sit down with her old friend and pour her heart out to her over a cup of tea. She couldn't do that, but she could call her. Grace checked the time. It was too late to call now. She'd do it in the morning.

Nineteen

For a moment, when Grace woke up, she couldn't remember what she'd decided the previous night. Then the image of Ted Crawford swam before her eyes, and she recalled her decision to call Jo Ford.

She rose, showered and dressed, then made sure Tiger was fed and watered before fixing her own breakfast of fruit and yoghurt and taking it and her cup of fennel and cardamon tea out to the deck.

It was still early, only a few brave souls on the beach at this time of the morning. Grace wondered if Ted was out there with his surfboard, blushing at the memory of her confused feelings the previous evening.

Knowing Jo and Col were early risers, Grace was about to pick up her phone when, to her surprise, Ted appeared outside her gate carrying a white paper bag.

'I went into town to get an almond croissant for breakfast and thought you might enjoy one too,' he said, waving the bag in the air. 'I can leave one with you, if you don't want company.'

Surprised to feel a flutter in her stomach, Grace smiled. 'Sounds lovely. Why don't you join me in a cup of tea – or would you prefer coffee?'

'Tea's fine, thanks.' He came through the gate and sat down on one of the cane chairs on the deck. 'I'm not interrupting?' he asked, nodding to Grace's now empty bowl.

'Not at all.' Grace blushed recalling how she had been thinking of him just before he arrived. She was glad to be able to go into the kitchen to hide her embarrassment.

By the time she re-emerged with tea for Ted, her own replenished cup and a couple of plates, she was feeling calmer and was accompanied by Tiger.

'Who's this?' Ted asked, as the cat wound himself around Ted's ankles, meowing loudly. 'Is this the young man you deserted me for last night?'

'Tiger,' Grace said needlessly.

'He's a handsome fellow.' Ted bent down to scratch the cat's ears and was rewarded with a loud purring.

'He'll let you do that all day,' Grace laughed, delighted to see Ted make friends with her pet. 'You like cats?'

'I'm probably more of a dog person. We always had one when I was growing up, but it was more difficult in the city when the house was empty all day. It's been a long time since I cared for an animal.'

Catching sight of movement in the garden, Tiger bounded away. Ted laughed. 'Young Zack would love him,' he said, sadly.

'Your grandson?'

Ted nodded. 'I had an email from him last night. I wish there was something I could do for him.' He picked up his cup and stared into it before taking a sip. 'Sorry, I didn't come here to bore you with my problems. You got enough of them last night. I wondered if you were free today, if you'd like to take a drive into the hinterland, perhaps have lunch somewhere?'

'Oh!' For a moment Grace didn't know what to say. She'd planned to spend the day with her writing, but the prospect of seeing more of the surrounding area plus the opportunity to get to know Ted better was appealing.

'I'll understand if you're busy.'

'No. I did have plans, but… I'd love to. I'm not familiar with the area outside Bellbird Bay. It's a kind thought. Thank you.'

'I need to get changed.' Ted looked down at the scruffy tee-shirt and shorts he was wearing. 'I went straight to town after my surf. How about I pick you up around ten-thirty?'

'Sounds good.' It would give Grace time to call Jo and change into something more suited to going out to lunch. Expecting to spend the day alone in her study, Grace had simply pulled on a pair of track pants and a long-sleeved shirt.

'Thanks for the croissant,' Grace said with a smile as Ted rose to leave. It wasn't often she indulged in a sweet breakfast, but she had thoroughly enjoyed the buttery almond treat.

'No worries.' Ted's face creased into the grin with which Grace was becoming familiar.

Alone again, Grace smiled to herself as she took out her phone and keyed in Jo's number.

'Jo, I'm so sorry I haven't been in touch before now,' she said when her friend answered.

'I'm sure you've been busy settling in. I've been wondering how you were. I'm guilty of not calling, too. How are you enjoying living on the coast?'

'Very much. It's different, peaceful in a different way.'

'Do you miss your Brigadoon?'

'I do and I don't. I don't miss all the work.'

'Too right. If Col and I hadn't got together, I might have given in to Danny's pleas by now.' She chuckled, but Grace knew how annoyed Jo had been when her son tried to persuade her to move into a new development in town.

'And your girls. Have they accepted your move by now?'

Grace remembered telling Jo about Lou and Mel's reaction to her plans.

'Lou is still being difficult, but Mel…' she hesitated, then decided to confide in Jo. After all, wasn't that why she was calling her? 'Jo, Mel's pregnant.'

There was a stunned silence, then, 'Is she in a relationship?'

'That's the trouble. The father's married, a work colleague. But she's decided to keep the baby and move in with me for a bit.'

'Sounds like a good plan. How do you feel about it?'

Grace felt a release of a tension she hadn't been aware of at the opportunity to share her concern with someone who'd understand. 'Oh, Jo. I'm really not sure. I'm excited about becoming a grandmother, but I know how difficult it'll be for her. As you know, Mel has always sailed through life without a care, and expected everything to go her way. This has been a shock for her. Though, I have to admit she seems to be taking it in her stride. She's resigned from her job in Sydney, found one up here and…' Grace hesitated again, '…in typical Mel fashion she seems to have latched on to a guy she met here in Bellbird Bay.'

'You don't approve of him?'

'It's not a case of approving or disapproving. He's a nice enough guy. He's actually the son of a friend of mine.'

'And why is that a problem?'

Trust Jo to get to the heart of the matter. She identified Grace's problem before Grace had figured it out herself.

When she didn't immediately reply, Jo continued. 'I'm glad you're making friends there. You did tend to isolate yourself when Russ became sick, and I worried you might continue to do that when you moved. This friend, is she someone you met through your sister? Does she disapprove of Mel's friendship with her son?'

'It's a man. The friend. That's another thing I'm concerned about. Oh, Jo, what am I going to do?'

Jo chuckled. 'Sounds like a good problem to have. I assume he's attractive and available?'

'Ye…es, but… You've been there, Jo. You and Col. How did… ?' Grace wasn't sure exactly what she wanted to ask, but she suddenly felt awkward.

Jo chuckled again. 'How did we get together, you mean? I think it was a case of convenience, alcohol and hot chocolate. You haven't…?'

'No!' Grace was horrified, even though she had imagined what it might feel like to be in Ted's arms, to have his lips on hers. 'We've had a few meals together, talked about our children, and we're going for a drive today. I'm not sure where it's all leading.'

'Where do you want it to lead?'

Grace chewed on the inside of her cheek. 'I'm not sure. Ted's good company. He's been on his own for a lot longer than I have. I get the sense that while he's pretty self-sufficient, he can be lonely too.'

'And your sister?'

Grace was surprised at the change of subject, but realised what Jo meant. 'It was Dot who actually introduced us, but the introduction was a disaster. She doesn't know we've been seeing each other. She'd turn it into some big thing.'

'And it's not?'

'No.' *But it could be.*

'Well, all I can suggest is you go for it. Life's too short to waste it wondering if you're doing the right thing. And about Mel and this guy – she's old enough to make her own mistakes. It sounds as if life has finally caught up with her. Maybe she's learned her lesson. But regardless, Grace. You can't live her life for her. You and Russ spoiled her. It's about time she found out what it's like to stand on her own two feet. And don't let Mel's opinion get in the way of *your* decisions and *your* life.'

'Wow! You don't mince your words.'

'Sorry if I hit a hot button, but I know what it's like to worry about your children – and to have them try to run your life for you. It wasn't all roses with my lot when Col and I got together, but we weathered the storm and couldn't be happier. Russ has been gone for over two years now, and I know he wasn't the Russ you knew for some time before that. He wouldn't want you to spend the rest of your life alone if an opportunity arose for you to find love again. Don't beat yourself up if you're developing feelings for this man you've met.'

How did Jo know? But love was a pretty strong word to use.

'Sorry if I sound harsh, Grace.'

'No, it's okay. I think I needed you to knock some sense into me. I have been beating myself up, wondering if I was doing the right thing, if it was too soon after Russ's death. Heck, listen to me. It's not as if he's even made any move to kiss me.' Grace thought of the moment when she imagined Ted might be about to, when she'd quickly stuck out her hand, of how she'd imagined being in his arms.

'If it's to happen, it will. The best I can say is to advise you to be open to possibilities. Tell me a bit about him.'

'Ted?' Grace pictured Ted Crawford, his thatch of thick white hair, his kind eyes, the way his face crinkled when he smiled, his wide shoulders, strong hands. But that wasn't what Jo meant. 'He's interesting, was a lawyer in Brisbane, his wife died young, and he brought up his son on his own. Now he's retired and returned to Bellbird Bay where he grew up. He surfs, paints beautiful landscapes and volunteers with turtles.'

'Wow! Sounds like an all-round good guy. And is his son a paragon, too?'

'I'm not sure about Aaron. He seems to have had some issues at work and is looking at finding a job up here. He's divorced with a son who lives with his mother and stepfather in Brisbane.'

'And this is the guy Mel is becoming involved with?'

'They seem to have become friends. I don't know if there's more to it. She's kept her pregnancy to herself.' As she spoke, Grace remembered Lou and wondered if Mel had told her sister yet. She could imagine Lou's reaction if, as Mel said, she and Greg had been trying for a baby. She wished her older daughter had confided in her, but it was so like Lou to keep something like this to herself. She could almost hear her say, 'I didn't want to worry you, Mum.' As if Grace didn't worry about all three of them all the time.

The two women chatted a little more, Jo filling Grace in on the Granite Springs gossip which failed to interest her as much as it used to. When the call ended, Grace gave a deep sigh. It had been good to talk with her old friend, to get her worries off her chest and to listen to Jo's advice. Now she just needed to take it.

'But it's not easy, puss,' she said to Tiger, who was lying at her feet.

Twenty

Ted was feeling good. It had been a stroke of genius to buy an extra croissant from the patisserie and drop by Grace's on the way home. He hadn't been sure what his reception might be and had been delighted to join her, delighted too when she agreed to go for a drive and have lunch with him.

If anyone had suggested, when Kev invited him to dinner, that he'd be enthusiastic about having a woman in his life, he'd have rubbished them. Yet, here he was, getting excited about spending his Sunday – the day he normally enjoyed spending with his landscapes – driving into the hinterland with Grace Winter for lunch.

In the years since returning to Bellbird Bay, Ted had managed to keep loneliness at bay. He'd filled his time with his painting, the TurtleCare in season, surfing, and reading the authors he hadn't taken time to enjoy while running a busy legal practice. But all of those activities had been designed to hide the fact he was alone, that he missed the day-to-day buzz of the office, missed seeing Aaron regularly, missed being busy. No matter how often he told himself he enjoyed his own company, enjoyed the solitary life, he knew there was an emptiness in it, a space which couldn't be filled.

Meeting Grace Winter had shown him how the company of a sympathetic woman could ease the pain of his loneliness. Kev was a good mate, but there were some things he couldn't understand. Not having children himself, he had no inkling of how Ted felt responsible for Aaron, even though he was grown up and perfectly able to look after himself. But the boy had taken the break-up of his marriage badly, and the loss of Zack on top of Tanya's betrayal had taken away his self-confidence and sent him into a spiral of despair. This last setback at work had only compounded that.

Grace understood. A parent herself, she knew how difficult it was to let go, to allow children to make their own mistakes, but to be there to pick up the pieces when things went awry. And, for the first time in decades, Ted felt the stirrings of desire.

He whistled as he dressed in a pair of pressed jeans and a blue and white striped shirt. Then he checked himself in the mirror before deciding he didn't look too bad for someone in his sixties. He still had a full head of hair which was something not too many men of his age could lay claim to and, although the lines on his face seemed to increase every year, surely they were a sign of a life well-lived.

By the time he drove down to Grace's front door, Ted had almost convinced himself he hadn't strayed far from the young man who had wooed and won Alison back when they were both twenty-one. There was something about Grace that made him feel young again.

'Hello.' Grace appeared at her door wearing another of those bright outfits she seemed to favour. She looked like a tropical bird in the orange and green top, her hair waving around her face like two wings. For the first time, he was tempted to attempt a portrait instead of his customary landscapes.

'Hi there. You're looking lovely. Those bright colours really suit you,' he greeted her.

'Do you think so?' Grace appeared uncertain. 'I splurged in one of the local shops when I arrived in Bellbird Bay. When I lived in Granite Springs, I dressed much more conservatively. You don't think it's too much?'

'Not at all. I noticed your outfit at Dot and Kev's.'

'Oh!'

Had it been a mistake to remind her of the evening when they first met?

'I'm afraid I wasn't very communicative that night,' he said with a wry grin.

'Me neither. My sister... I knew she was trying to set us up and I was determined to avoid you. Sorry.'

'It was the same for me. When Kev invited me to dinner, I suspected

Dot wanted to match me with one of her cronies. And there you were… the only single woman in the room.'

'It was so obvious, wasn't it?'

They laughed.

'Yet here we are.'

'We managed to meet again without Dot's help.' Grace smiled.

'Shall we go?'

'Let me just get my bag.'

Half an hour later, they had left Bellbird Bay behind and were driving up a winding road to the Sunshine Coast hinterland. On either side of the road the scenery had changed, from the seascape of which Ted was so fond, to rolling hills and pasture with cows or horses grazing contentedly.

'This reminds me of Granite Springs,' Grace said, gazing out of the window, 'but it's not as flat.'

'You kept animals?'

'We had a couple of horses when the children were little, and dogs and cats over the years. In more recent years, after Russ became ill, we leased part of the acreage to a neighbour. It meant we could still enjoy watching the animals without the bother of taking care of them.'

'You miss it?'

'Sometimes. But I'm glad I made the move. The place was too big for me to take care of on my own… and there were too many memories.'

'You didn't consider moving into the town?' Ted recalled what Gordon Slater had said.

'It was what everyone expected.' Grace gave a sigh. 'But no. Russ and I had always talked about moving here, closer to Dot and Kev. Before he got sick.' Her eyes clouded over.

*

'Tell me about your husband,' Ted said. They had finished lunch and were enjoying coffee in a small café with views over the valley.

'Russ?' Grace smiled in reminiscence. 'He was a lovely man. We met at university and there was never anyone else for either of us. When we moved to Granite Springs and bought an acreage outside of town, we were so happy. It was a wonderful spot to bring up children. We were both from the city but found it easy to settle into life in the country and make friends. I joined the Country Women's Association and Russ the local Lions Club. We became pillars of the community. The children loved it there, but they all moved away once they grew up. Lou and Mel found jobs in the city and Ben's work took him overseas. But they always came back for Christmas and special celebrations. It was an idyllic life until…'

Grace's eyes clouded over, and she put a clenched fist to her mouth. 'What happened?'

'Russ. He was considering early retirement when everything began to go wrong. It was only little things at first, then it became more noticeable. The tests showed he was suffering from dementia. As time went on, he needed more care and I found myself isolating at home. I didn't like to leave him. The man I knew and loved disappeared. He became a stranger.' Grace's eyes misted and she wiped them with a tissue. 'Sorry.'

'No need to be. It must have been difficult for you.'

Grace nodded. 'But life went on. The children still came home for visits. But there wasn't much they could do, and they had their own lives. When he passed away it was almost a relief. I'd lost my soulmate, but I really lost the man I loved long before that.'

They sat in silence for a few moments, then Grace roused herself. 'And what about you? You lost your wife a long time ago?'

'Yes. Alison was diagnosed with breast cancer when Aaron was in primary school. It was an aggressive cancer, and she went quickly. It was a shock.' He exhaled. 'It was just Aaron and me, but we coped. It became easier as he grew older. I always intended to come back to Bellbird Bay, but work got in the way; Aaron had his friends in the city. It wasn't till I retired that I made the move. Now, I wonder why I left it so long.'

'You never considered remarrying?'

'No, there was never anyone else.' Ted looked across the table to where Grace had now regained her composure. *Not till now.*

'Perhaps we should leave.' Grace looked around the café which was emptying. The staff were beginning to clear the tables and pack up the chairs.

'I guess you're right. Sorry for the morbid turn of conversation.' Ted coughed. It had been good to learn more about Grace's life, but he had the impression her loss was still raw. It wasn't the time to make any advances, but he was willing to wait till she was ready. Grace Winter was worth waiting for.

Twenty-one

It was late afternoon when Ted dropped Grace off at her door. While tempted to invite him in for a cup of tea, Grace decided against it. They had already spent most of the day together, and she needed time to reflect on their friendship.

As soon as she walked in, Tiger leapt down from his spot on the sofa to rub himself around her ankles, purring. Grace picked up the little creature and cuddled him. 'What am I doing, puss?' she asked, carrying her pet into the kitchen before putting him down by his food bowl and filling it with cat food.

Once Tiger was satisfied, Grace slipped off her shoes and put on the kettle, making herself a cup of peppermint tea and taking it through to the living room. For once, she didn't want to sit out on the deck, preferring the security of her house with four walls around her, rather than being exposed to the boardwalk and anyone who might choose to walk along it.

By anyone, she supposed she was referring to Ted, though she had no reason to imagine he'd be walking there.

As she drank her tea, Grace thought about Ted and the time they'd spent together. He was good company, a perfect gentleman, never overstepping the mark, only taking her elbow when they entered the café for lunch. But, underneath his respectful behaviour, Grace sensed a simmering yearning for something more intimate – and she wasn't sure she was ready for it. Despite Jo's sage advice, something still held Grace back, even if she couldn't ignore the flutter in her stomach when his hand did take her elbow and when their knees accidentally touched under the table.

She drained her cup and reached for her phone. She'd turned it off while she was with Ted, not wanting their afternoon together to be disturbed. Now she saw she had two missed calls – both from Lou.

Grace's heart plummeted. *Had Mel told her she was pregnant? Was she calling Grace to sound off about her sister's irresponsible behaviour?*

She pressed to return the call.

Lou answered immediately. She must have been waiting for Grace's call.

'Mum! How could you?'

Grace blanched. *What had she done to upset Lou now?* 'Hello to you, too, darling. Lovely to hear from you, Sorry I missed your calls.'

'I suppose you were out with that man.'

Grace swallowed. *By that man, did she mean Ted? Who else could she mean? But how did she know and what was there for her to know?* 'I don't know what you're talking about, honey,' she said to gain time.

'Mel told me all about it, how you started seeing this man who's the father of a new friend of hers, how embarrassing it is for her. How could you, Mum, with Dad scarcely cold in his grave?'

Grace took a deep breath before replying. 'I suppose Mel is talking about Ted Crawford. He's a neighbour. We met at dinner at your Aunt Dot's. He's been kind enough to buy me lunch on a couple of occasions. And, yes, Mel has formed a friendship with his son.' She waited.

'But Dad…' Lou wailed.

'Your dad's been gone for over two years now, sweetheart, and even before that, as you know, he had changed so much.'

'But…'

'Surely you wouldn't want to prevent me from making new friends?'

'New friends? No, of course not, but women friends, people with whom you'd have something in common, like… those women you knew in Granite Springs.'

Those women who, apart from Jo Ford, she'd allowed to disappear into the woodwork when Russ became ill, doing nothing to retain their friendship and refusing invitations till they ceased to be extended. 'I have your Aunt Dot. That's why I came to Bellbird Bay. Remember?'

'I suppose.' There was a pause. 'And Mel's pregnant!' Lou's tone was accusatory, as if Grace had conspired with her younger daughter to give her the child Lou longed for.

'Yes.' Grace bit her lip, realising she wasn't supposed to know Lou and Greg had been trying for a baby and how much this must upset them. 'It won't be easy for her, but she seems to be handling it well. Your little sister is having to grow up fast. She's told you she plans to move here to have the baby?'

'Yes, and I'm not sure it's such a good idea. There are better facilities in the city. If she…'

'Lou, darling. It's Mel's choice, and I have to say I'm impressed with the way she's handling things.' Grace stifled the reminder Mel was forming what might be an unsuitable relationship with Aaron Crawford. Despite – or perhaps because of – his being Ted's son, and all she'd heard about him from his father; Grace wasn't sure how reliable he was.

'Well, that's as may be. Anyway, I'm taking some time off to drive her up. You say she's handling things well, but she had no idea how she was going to get all her stuff up to Bellbird Bay. And it's about time I saw this place where you decided to move to.'

A curl of anticipation combined with fear whipped around Grace's stomach causing the hair on the back of her neck to rise. She wanted to see Lou, to show her around Bellbird Bay, to share her new life with her. But there was something in Lou's tone that sounded almost like a threat. Grace was reminded of the teenage Lou when she didn't get her own way. While it had been Mel's habit to pout and whinge, Lou had always chosen to go on the offensive.

'We'll be there some time on Thursday. See you and talk then.' Lou finished the call without saying goodbye.

Grace sighed and put her phone down. 'Oh dear, Tige,' she said to the cat who, having finished eating, had decided to join her and leapt onto her lap. 'My Lou is not happy. What do you think she is more upset about – my friendship with Ted or Mel's pregnancy?' Knowing her daughter, they'd come close to equal in her mind.

*

Thursday arrived before Grace was ready to face Lou. She'd had a busy couple of days at the library, and had joined Ted for coffee one day when they'd bumped into each other in town. She'd also managed to stock up on provisions and ensure there were beds made up and ready for both Lou and Mel.

Lou hadn't given any indication of how long she intended to stay, but Grace didn't anticipate she'd be in Bellbird Bay for long. Her older daughter's life was in Sydney. It was where her husband and job were, and where she'd lived since leaving Granite Springs for university.

Grace was taking a break and enjoying a welcome cup of peppermint tea, having just taken a batch of scones from the oven, when she heard the sound of a car stop outside. Hurrying to the door, Grace flung it open to see Mel ease herself out of the car, Lou not far behind her. The car looked as if it was packed with boxes, no doubt all of Mel's belongings.

Mel moved toward her with a hug and a kiss on the cheek, then Grace turned towards her older daughter. Lou was standing, her hands on her hips, staring at the house.

'So this is where you're living.' Lou's tone was disdainful. 'It's a lot different to Brigadoon. Mel *said* it was a renovated beach shack.' She scowled.

Grace took a deep breath. 'Lovely to see you, darling. How was your trip?' She gave her older daughter a hug, flinching when Lou stiffened in her arms. 'I bet you'd love a cup of tea, and I have some scones fresh from the oven.'

'Yummy, Mum. I'm starving. I always seem to be these days,' Mel said, leading the way into the house.

Lou followed half-heartedly, staring around as if ready to find fault.

'Hi, Tiger. Did you miss me?' Mel bent down to fondle the cat who appeared in the hallway to greet them.

'A cat?' Lou asked, skirting around the animal and grimacing. 'Mel didn't say you had a cat.'

Grace remembered Lou had never been very fond of cats, always choosing to ignore the strays Ben brought home to Brigadoon. 'Tiger has been good company for me here in Bellbird Bay. Now, why don't you both go out onto the deck while I make the tea? It's pleasant out there today and the view's lovely.' Grace knew she was babbling but was somewhat shocked by Lou's reaction. She'd hoped, by choosing to drive Mel to Bellbird Bay, Lou was softening towards her and her move, even though her daughter's comments on the phone had indicated otherwise.

'It's good to be back.' Mel threw her arms wide as Grace came out to the deck carrying a tray on which were three cups of tea, three plates, another of scones and dishes of jam and cream. 'Wow, Mum. This is just like afternoon tea at Brigadoon. Isn't it, Lou?' she asked, turning to her sister. 'And isn't this a marvellous view?'

'I suppose,' Lou said reluctantly. 'The scones look nice, Mum.' She took a seat and picked up a cup of tea. 'But I don't know why you wanted to move so far away. If you had to move, you could have had a nicer place than this in Granite Springs.'

'But not with this view.' Grace stood still for a moment gazing out at the sight of the ocean she'd come to love. Then she sat down with the two girls. 'I love it here, Lou, and I hope you'll be able to see what I like about it. Your Aunt Dot's here too.'

Mel grimaced.

'Mel! Dot's harmless. Her heart's in the right place and she is my sister. She wasn't always so…' Grace searched for the word, '… interfering.' She chuckled. 'You should have seen her in her twenties. It was a disappointment to her and Kev that they never had a family, so they sort of adopted the three of you instead.'

As she spoke, Grace saw Lou look down with a frown. Damn! She'd been so busy trying to explain away Dot's sometimes unfortunate attitude. For the moment she'd forgotten Lou's own disappointment in that regard. She wanted to apologise but to do so would reveal Mel had shared her sister's secret. How Grace hoped Lou would confide in her, but by her expression, Lou had no intention of sharing any confidences with her mother.

'Your Aunt Dot will love to see you, Lou. She always asks about you. I've invited her and your Uncle Kev to dinner tomorrow night.'

'Mum, you haven't!' The outburst came from Mel. 'You said you'd have them over when I wasn't here.'

It seemed Grace couldn't please either of her daughters. 'I know,' she sighed, 'but you were only gone for a few days, and Dot and Kev chose that time to try out their new motorhome. They plan to become grey nomads and travel around Australia with another couple from *Bay Village*. They drove up to Yeppoon to try it out last weekend and stayed a few days.'

Both Lou and Mel's eyes widened at the thought of Dot and Kev traipsing around the country. 'But…' Mel began.

'They're not too old, if that's what you were about to say, Mel. Dot's only a couple of years older than me. Evidently, it's something they've always wanted to do but until this other couple suggested it, had never thought they really would. Good for them, I say.'

As soon as she spoke, Grace remembered Jo's words to her. Maybe she was being overly cautious. If Dot and Kev could follow their dreams, maybe she could, too. But what *was* her dream these days? She'd made the move to Bellbird Bay. Was that enough – or was she willing to take an extra step and allow Ted Crawford into her life – and her bed?

Twenty-two

There had been no word from Aaron, and Ted was beginning to think the meeting with his old schoolfriend hadn't come to anything. Nothing from Zack either. Ted hoped Aaron had managed to see his son. The boy was desperately in need of more affection than he appeared to be getting from Tanya and Mark. It was a great pity Aaron couldn't gain custody. But what was done couldn't be undone without a lot of legal hassles. Ted sighed. At least he intended to ensure Zack visited again next holidays, even if he had to go down and pick him up himself.

He was enjoying a mug of coffee on his deck and considering whether to start a new painting or continue with the latest Jeffrey Archer book he'd started reading last night, when a familiar figure stopped outside his gate.

'Kev, old mate. What are you doing here? Thought you and Dot were up north somewhere testing out that new rig of yours.'

'Got back last night and needed a break from the wife. Thought I'd drop by to see what you were up to.'

'Not much, as you see. Join me?'

'Sure.'

Pleased at the arrival of his old friend, who he hadn't seen for over a week, Ted made another coffee for him and refreshed his own cup before joining him on the deck.

'You have a nice place here. It's a good spot,' Kev said, leaning back in one of the stained Adirondack chairs Ted had purchased when he returned to Bellbird Bay. They'd seemed a fitting addition to the house and provided a comfortable place to sit and enjoy the view.

'I like it,' Ted said, wondering why Kev was here. It wasn't like him to drop in unannounced and he hadn't come to admire the view. Despite what he might say, Ted knew Kev preferred the security of his own home in *Bay Village*. The pair had often argued about the pros and cons of each. 'How was your trip?' he asked.

'Good. This motorhome we bought is a tad bigger than a campervan, you know, quite roomy, really. And we liked Yeppoon. We plan to spend a few more days there when we start our big trip, might go out to the reef. Geoff and Carol had been there before and were full of ideas. They're the couple we plan to travel with.'

'Sounds good.' It wasn't something that appealed to Ted. But he was aware of the attraction travelling around Australia held for some.

'And what have you been up to?' Kev asked, with a wary glance along the boardwalk.

'Much the same as usual. Young Aaron was up from Brisbane for a few days. He's hoping to find work here with an old school friend – Nick Armstrong. Nick moved up from Brisbane a few years ago and set up a boatbuilding business – *Coastal Boats*. You may have heard of them.'

'I think so.' But Kev's mind was clearly elsewhere. 'Ted…' Kev cleared his throat. 'Dot wanted… she asked me… Hell, this is difficult.' He drew a hand along the inside of his shirt collar. 'That night you came to dinner. Dot's sister, Grace. Dot was hoping… The woman's pretty new in town. She doesn't have many friends. You didn't seem to take to her, but Dot wondered…'

Ted almost laughed at his friend's discomfort. 'You can tell Dot I don't like being set up,' he said. 'But I'm sorry if I seemed rude. It was kind of you and Dot to invite me and it was a lovely dinner. Your sister-in-law is a lovely woman, but that night…' he shook his head, '…I wouldn't have been interested in anyone.'

'Oh!' Kev seemed deflated.

'But you can tell Dot we've met since.'

'You have?' Kev's face brightened. 'Grace didn't say.'

'I don't suppose Grace enjoys being set up any more than I do. But you can report we bumped into each other at the surf carnival and have met a couple of times since.' Ted decided not to disclose how many times, and to keep his attraction to Grace to himself.

'Thanks, Ted. It's a load off my mind. Dot worries about Grace. She always has, and now she's a widow. You know what it's like.'

Ted smiled. He had no idea what it was like to worry about a younger sister who was a widow and was sure, from what he knew of Grace, she'd hate to be the subject of Dot's concern. It made him want to protect her from her sister.

'Well then,' Kev said as if something had been settled.

'When do you head off again?' Ted asked, keen to get back to their previous topic of conversation.

Kev appeared relieved, too. 'In a few weeks. We want to spend most of the winter up north, come back for the spring and summer then head off again next year. Thought we'd do the red centre next time. It's a great life and we can lock up our place at *Bay Village* and know everything will be safe and waiting for us when we return. There were quite a few others like us where we parked near the beach at Yeppoon. We had some good evenings around the campfire with a few beers. Geoff says it's always like that. Dot loved it too. She'll be glad you'll be here to keep an eye on Grace while we're gone.'

'That's not…'

But Kev had already risen to leave. 'Thanks, Ted. It's a weight off my mind. I'll let Dot know you and Grace…' He winked.

Ted watched Kev walk jauntily along the boardwalk. He had no doubt his friend had put two and two together and made a damn sight more than five. But was he really so wrong? Hadn't Ted been having thoughts about Grace since their first lunch together? The only difference between Kev's impression and Ted's reality was that Ted hadn't shared any of his thoughts with Grace. The poor woman had no idea of either Ted's feelings or her sister's ambitions for her.

Twenty-three

'I think that's all.' Grace examined the table setting carefully, knowing Dot was a perfectionist who would take every opportunity to find fault. It was crazy to be so concerned. She was a grown woman, had kept her own home for well over thirty years, been married and raised three children and she still cared about her big sister's opinion. She smoothed the tablecloth for the umpteenth time.

'Leave it, Mum. It all looks lovely,' Mel said. 'I don't know why you're even bothering to have them to dinner, never mind fussing so much.'

'Mel's right, Mum,' Lou said. 'It's only Aunt Dot and Uncle Kev. Surely we could have even eaten in the kitchen.'

'No, your Aunt Dot always likes things to be done properly. It's how we were brought up. Your dad and I… we didn't always keep to the sort of standards Mum and Dad expected when Dot and I were growing up. But she did.' Grace thought back to the evening with Dot and Kev. Dot had pulled out all the stops to impress – the starched linen tablecloth, her best china, the silver cutlery – and the meal had been a triumph. She hoped the beef wellington, now cooking slowly in the oven to be served along with the baby potatoes, broccoli and carrots, would pass muster.

'You're a good cook and a brilliant housewife. I know what big sisters can be like.' Mel sent a pained look in Lou's direction. 'We're here for you, aren't we, Lou?'

'Of course,' Lou responded, smiling for the first time since she arrived.

It had been a difficult day. Grace had wanted to show Lou Bellbird Bay, and the three had made their way down the boardwalk to the esplanade in the morning to enjoy lunch at *The Bay Café*. It was too cold for the beach, so in the afternoon they'd all stayed home while Grace prepared dinner.

There had been an awkward few moments when Lou had cornered Grace in the kitchen to ask what she thought about Mel being pregnant. Grace had tried her best to be diplomatic. Until Lou confided her own worries to her, there wasn't much else she could do or say.

*

Dinner went smoothly. Dot was delighted to see Mel again and to meet Lou after so long. Most of the conversation during the meal was taken up by Dot and Kev reliving their recent trip and encouraging the others to sample the delights of the northern part of the state.

To Grace and Mel's relief, there were no barbed comments about Mel's lifestyle or obvious gain in weight. Grace knew she'd have to confide in Dot sometime soon, but wanted to give Mel more time to adjust to her situation.

Dot raised her eyebrows when Grace mentioned Mel was starting work in the gallery the following week, but only said, 'She'll be company for you, Grace.'

Grace was caught unprepared when, towards the end of the evening, Kev said, 'I was speaking to Ted Crawford this morning.'

Dot looked surprised. 'You didn't tell me.'

'I didn't get the chance,' Kev said, 'but it seems your sister has been holding out on us.'

A shiver ran down Grace's spine. She began to tremble.

Dot's eyes swivelled to where Grace was sitting, beads of sweat forming on her forehead despite the cool of the evening, then back to Kev. 'What do you mean?'

'Ted Crawford and I have met.' Grace forestalled him. 'We discovered we're neighbours. I didn't tell you because there was nothing to tell.'

'Hmph. Not what I heard,' Kev said.

Dot's eyes moved from one to the other and back again.

'Well, Kev, what did you hear?' Grace asked. Surely Ted wouldn't have been indiscreet, not even with Kev?

'Well,' he blustered. 'Ted only said you'd met a few times, but I got the impression there was more to it. I've never known him to be interested in a woman.' He gave Grace an apologetic look.

Dot peered at Grace as if she could find the truth of the situation written on her forehead and, despite her sister's scrutiny, a warm glow suffused Grace at the indication Ted might be interested in her.

Recognising her mother's confusion, Mel stepped in to ask, 'When do you set off again, Aunt Dot?' and the conversation moved to Dot and Kev's forthcoming trip.

Grace sighed inwardly. An awkward moment had been avoided. And all went well, till Dot and Kev were about to leave. As Mel was helping her aunt with her coat, Dot scrutinised her before saying, 'I hope this work at the gallery will have you moving around more. Seems to me you're putting on weight lying around at home doing nothing.'

Too shocked to reply, Mel threw an anxious glance at her mother.

'She's…' Lou began.

Grace glared at her.

'…eating a lot,' Lou concluded, much to Grace and Mel's relief.

'I can see that for myself,' was Dot's acerbic reply. 'Thanks for a lovely dinner, Grace, though not before time. And it was nice to see your two girls again.' She looked around but both Lou and Mel had disappeared. Dot sniffed. 'I don't know what the younger generation are coming to. They didn't even stay around to say goodbye.'

'I think they're clearing up.' Grace attempted to excuse them, while knowing quite well they couldn't bear another moment of Dot's criticisms. She wished her sister could be more accommodating, more understanding of Lou and Mel, and more willing to accept them as they were.

'I told you what it would be like,' Mel expostulated when Grace joined her and Lou in the kitchen. 'And you almost told her,' she said to Lou.

Lou shrugged. 'She'll have to know sometime. It's not as if you can keep your pregnancy a secret for ever. I wish…' She broke into tears. 'I'm sorry, I…' She turned and ran out of the kitchen, the bedroom door slamming behind her.

'Mum?'

'It's not your fault, Mel. Although I do agree with Lou that your Aunt Dot will need to know sometime. Though tonight wasn't the time. There was enough going on without your pregnancy adding to it. Come here,' she said, seeing Mel's bottom lip tremble. She hugged her daughter, but her mind was on Lou. 'I need to talk to your sister,' she said. 'Will you be okay?'

Mel nodded. 'It's time Lou told you. I'm not the only one keeping secrets around here.'

Grace went to the closed bedroom door and tapped gently. 'It's me, Lou. Can I come in?'

There was a muffled sound which Grace took to be agreement. She pushed open the door and went in, closing it behind her.

Lou was sitting on the bed, her eyes red, shredding a crumpled tissue in her hands.

Grace sat down beside her and took one of Lou's hands in hers. 'What's the matter, sweetheart? What's upsetting you so much?'

At first, Grace thought Lou wasn't going to reply, then the words poured out.

'It's Mel. It's not fair. How can she just get pregnant with no effort, when she doesn't even want a baby? Greg and I have been trying for years.' She began to cry again. 'So many months, so many disappointments. I'm so tired.' She dropped her head onto Grace's shoulder. 'Oh, Mum, what am I going to do? I want a child so much, but it never happens. Greg wants us to see a doctor, to talk about IVF and…'

'What do *you* want?' Grace swept a strand of hair from Lou's forehead, wishing she could wave a wand and make everything better for her.

'I don't know. I don't know how I can bear seeing Mel become bigger and bigger, then with a child, the child that should be mine.'

Grace took a deep breath. 'Not exactly. But I can see how it would upset you to see your sister pregnant. I'm sorry, I had no idea you and Greg were trying for a baby.'

'I wanted to confide in you, but I didn't want to worry you when Dad was so sick. I thought you'd be there at Brigadoon to help with the baby when it was born. Dad's death devastated me, then you moved up here and so far away.' She sniffed.

Grace felt guilty, but how could she have known? 'You know I'm always here if you need me. And you know Mel didn't fall pregnant deliberately to annoy you.'

'I know. It's just so unfair,' she said again.

'Life's not fair.' Grace found herself repeating what she'd once said to Mel. 'But we go on living. Maybe you should talk with a doctor or discuss IVF with Greg. If it's a case of the money, maybe I can help.'

'Thanks, Mum. It's not that. I've read so much about the process I'm not sure if it's something I want to go through, even if there's a baby at the end of it – and there may not be.'

Grace hugged Lou feeling helpless. She wished there was something she could do, but Lou and Greg needed to resolve this by themselves.

'Thanks, Mum,' Lou said when they drew apart. 'It helps you know. Greg said I should talk with you. I'm sorry I didn't tell you earlier, and I'm sorry for the way I feel about Mel, but I can't help it.'

'Oh, I think you can. Just imagine yourself in her position. No Greg, no secure job, no home of her own. It must be a frightening prospect to find herself pregnant. I'm only glad she decided to come to stay with me at least until the baby is born.'

'What will she do then?'

'I have no idea. I don't expect she's thought so far ahead.'

'At least no one knows her here,' Lou said after a few moments. 'It would have been more difficult for her if you'd stayed in Granite Springs.'

'So there is a silver lining to my move to Bellbird Bay?'

'Maybe.' Lou managed a weak grin.

'Now, why don't you come out and join us? Mel's been left to do the clearing up on her own. It's lovely out on the deck at this time of night. We can have another glass of wine, listen to the roar of the ocean and gaze up at the stars.' She put out a hand to pull Lou up.

'Thanks, Mum.' Lou gave Grace a hug. 'I feel better already.'

Twenty-four

Invigorated from his early morning surf, Ted was settling down to a day of painting. The stiff wind which had provided excellent waves, wasn't conducive to sitting on the headland, so he'd decided to work inside today and to try his hand at the portrait of Grace which he'd been thinking about since they last met. He'd never painted a portrait before and he'd be painting from memory, but the image of her face was so clear in his head, he was sure he could do it.

He'd been working solidly for several hours, totally engrossed in the attempt to transform his thoughts onto canvas when he was interrupted by a loud knocking at the door. Covering the partly finished painting with an old piece of sheeting, he went to open it.

'Hi, Dad.' Aaron stood there with a grin on his face. 'I got it!'

It took Ted a moment to realise to what Aaron was referring, then he matched his son's grin. 'The job with Nick? Well done!' He clapped his son on the shoulder and drew him into a warm hug.

'Thanks, Dad. I was on edge till Nick called me. I'll put in my resignation at work on Monday. I'll be glad to get shot of the place. They still haven't made any decision about my status. Guess they'll be glad to see the back of me, too. At least they don't seem to be about to charge me with anything.' His mouth turned down for a moment, before he grinned again. 'Come on. Let's go out to lunch to celebrate.'

Thirty minutes later, Ted and Aaron were climbing the stairs into the surf club. 'My shout,' Ted insisted when they reached the bar.

Aaron held up both hands with a laugh. 'Okay, Dad.'

They ordered two beers and a couple of burgers with chips and found a table by the window, Aaron agreeing with Ted they'd be blown away on the deck today.

'Now,' Ted said, once they were seated, 'Tell me all about this new job.'

As Aaron proceeded to explain about Nick's business and what his role was to be. Ted felt a glow of satisfaction to see his son so passionate. It was a long time since Aaron had shown such enthusiasm for anything. There was only one fly in the ointment.

'I worry about Zack,' Aaron said, reading Ted's mind. But I can make sure I go down to Brisbane regularly and he can come up here. I've been speaking to Tanya.'

'What did she have to say?'

Aaron picked up a beermat and twirled it on its end. 'Not a lot, but she didn't outright refuse. I think Zack's unhappiness is getting to her, and Mark…' Aaron frowned. '…I don't think he's ever really accepted him.'

'But he's lived with them for years.' Ted couldn't believe what he was hearing. No wonder the boy was unhappy.

'Tanya said they're trying for another baby. Mark wants a child of his own.' He shook his head. 'Don't know how that'll affect Zack.'

Ted frowned. This wasn't good news, though it wasn't a surprise. The only surprise was it hadn't happened earlier. Tanya and Mark had been together now for six years. It was only natural he'd want a child of his own. But it would make things even more difficult for Zack. 'They didn't try before now?'

'Tanya always said she didn't want any more children. She had a difficult time with Zack, and he wasn't an easy baby. It must have taken Mark all this time to get her to change her mind.'

'Does Zack know?'

'I'm not sure. But he was even more subdued than usual when I took him out on Wednesday. I picked him up after school and we went for a smoothie on South Bank. I think he knows something is in the wind.'

Ted was about to speak when Aaron pointed to a group of women who were seated several tables away.

'There's Mel Winter,' he said, 'with her mother and another woman. Should we go over to say hello?'

Ted looked across to where Aaron was pointing, to where three women were clearly enjoying their lunch, though a closer examination seemed to indicate they were engaged in some sort of dispute. 'This may not be the best time,' he said, 'perhaps later.' He wondered about the third woman. Had Grace's older daughter come to visit? He hoped for her sake, she had. Families needed to be together.

*

Out of the corner of her eye, Grace noticed Ted and his son arrive and take their seats only a few tables away. He was facing in the other direction so did not see her. To her surprise, Lou seemed to have reconciled to the idea of Mel's pregnancy and had even made a complimentary remark about the surf club.

They were partway through their meal, and she was beginning to relax, when Lou looked across the table at Mel. 'Did you tell Mum what you did in Sydney?'

Grace looked at Mel with a questioning expression. *What was Lou talking about?*

Mel shifted uncomfortably in her seat. 'It was nothing, Mum.'

'Don't say that. You vowed never to see him again.'

'Who?' Grace asked, her skin tingling.

'I didn't intend to. I had to go into the office to pick up my things and Jason saw me. He… we… I went for coffee with him.' Mel adopted the belligerent expression she always did when she knew she was in the wrong but wasn't going to admit it.

'You what? Oh, Mel!' Grace couldn't hide her shock.

'I told her he was no good. He's been cheating on his wife, made Mel pregnant. There's no telling how many other susceptible young women he's been running around with.' Lou smirked.

'Stop it! You make me sound like a… a… I was in love with him. I thought he loved me, too. And I didn't intend to get pregnant. We were taking precautions.'

Mel's words fell into a well of silence as she realised she had just antagonised her sister even more. 'Sorry Lou. But I didn't. I can't help it if you and Greg are having problems. I have a problem, too.' She looked down at her stomach.

'Girls,' Grace said, glancing around to see if anyone was watching this altercation, 'it's not the time or place for this discussion. I agree with Lou, Mel. It was unwise to meet Jason again. But I can also see your difficulty. Did you at least resolve things with him? Finish it for good? Did you tell him about the baby?'

'I told him we were finished but not about the baby.' She cradled the small bump now beginning to appear on her previously flat stomach. 'He's not going to find out about it from me.'

Lou snorted. 'And how long's that going to last? It seems to me…'

'That's enough, Lou. If you two can't behave in a civilised fashion, we'll have to leave. You're acting like three-year-olds instead of grown women.'

'Sorry, Mum,' Mel said.

'Sorry,' Lou repeated.

'But you know, Mel, you really should tell Jason. He *is* the baby's father.'

Mel scowled.

Grace sighed, but she hoped Mel would consider what she had said even though she hated the idea of her meeting with him again or even communicating with him. 'Now, let's try to enjoy the rest of our meal without any more disagreements. It's so lovely for me to have you both with me. Please don't spoil it with your arguing. It's a pity Ben can't be here, too.' Grace thought longingly of her son who'd no doubt have managed to calm his sisters if he'd been here.

'How is Ben?' Lou asked. 'Last I heard, he was off to far North Queensland on some dig or other. At least it's better than being on the other side of the world.'

The rest of the meal was spent more pleasantly with Grace filling Lou in on Ben's exploits, and Lou recounting her latest coup at work. She appeared so keen on her job, Grace wondered how she'd make time for a child.

They were about to leave when she became aware of two men walking towards their table.

Mel immediately perked up and smiled as Aaron Crawford greeted her with a grin. 'Hey, Mel. Saw you and your mother having lunch.

Is this your sister?' he turned to face Lou who was gazing at him in surprise. 'Aaron Crawford,' he said, holding out his hand. 'And this is my dad.'

Twenty-five

'Is that the old man you've been seeing?' Lou hissed, as they made their way down the stairs to the door of the club.

Old? Grace grinned to herself. She supposed both she and Ted appeared old to Lou, whereas to her they were in their prime. It had been a surprise when he and his son had come over to speak to them. To be correct, when Aaron had dragged his dad over so he could speak with Mel. Ted had looked embarrassed.

'He's not old,' she objected, to buy time. Was she "seeing" Ted as Lou put it? 'Ted Crawford is the neighbour I've become friendly with.'

'And this Aaron,' Lou turned to Mel. 'What's with him?'

Sometimes Grace wanted to slap some sense into her older daughter. This was one of those times. Not content with harassing Mel about the father of her child, now she wanted to ruin this new friendship with her barbed comments.

'We're friends, that's all. And it's none of your business, Lou.' Mel pushed her way out the door ahead of Lou and set off, striding up the hill to the boardwalk.

'No, Lou.' Grace put a hand on Lou's arm to stop her from following. 'Leave her be. You've done enough damage.'

'Me? What about her?'

Grace sighed. Mel and Lou had never been close, but this latest fracas seemed destined to beat all others. 'She's your sister. Family should stick together. What would your dad think to hear the pair of you having a slanging match – just because Mel has been unfortunate enough to become pregnant when you can't?'

Grace bit her lip. She knew it was unfair to bring Russ into it, but she was at her wits' end how to resolve the impasse which seemed to have arisen between the two sisters.

'Dad? Dad would…' Lou's voice trembled as she no doubt realised what her dad would say. He'd hated it when his girls, as he liked to call them, disagreed. As a result, they'd rarely fought in his presence, choosing to keep their quarrels to themselves. He and Grace had often discussed how difficult it was for the two to stay at peace for long and had hoped as they grew older, they'd become closer.

By this time, they'd reached the house, and Tiger greeted them as if they'd been gone for weeks. As usual, Lou skirted around him, and with a baleful glance, he scuttled away to curl up in a corner. There was no sign of Mel.

'I think we could all do with a cup of tea,' Grace said, filling the electric jug and switching it on before choosing three camomile teabags from the pantry and taking three cups from the cupboard. They needed something calming.

'Whatever.' Lou sat down on the nearest chair. 'I didn't mean to cause a fuss, Mum,' she said, picking at an invisible thread on her spotless linen pants. 'But you have to admit, Mel asks for it. First, she gets pregnant by this married guy in Sydney, then she latches onto the first guy she meets up here. It's time she grew up and learnt life isn't all fun and games.'

'I think she's realised that, honey. It's no fun for her to find herself about to become a single mother. I know you'd rather it was you, but I wish you could feel some sympathy for her. Mel needs all our love and support right now.'

'Hmph.'

'Here's your tea.' Grace handed Lou a cup. 'I'll see if I can persuade Mel to join us. Please try to be kind to her.'

When Grace entered the bedroom, Mel was lying on her bed, her face to the wall. 'Mel?' she said, going across to her daughter and putting a hand on her shoulder. 'Come and have a cup of tea with us. I think Lou's sorry for what she said.'

'Why does she have to try to spoil everything?' Mel turned to face Grace, her face wet with tears. 'Aaron is the only friend I have up here. That's all he is. He's not what Lou suggests. He has his own issues to deal with. He doesn't know about the baby. He accepts me as I am… as I was before all this. And I saw how Lou looked at his dad, too.' She sat up and rubbed her eyes.

'Well, I think she regrets it now.' Grace mentally crossed her fingers. She wasn't too sure Lou had reversed her view about Ted. But Lou's opinion was the least of her worries right now. It was more important she make peace between her daughters. Lou would be gone back to Sydney soon, and Grace was determined the two would have resolved their differences before she left.

Reluctantly, Mel slid from the bed and scrubbed her eyes with a tissue. 'Tea might be nice,' she said, trying to smile. 'Thanks, Mum.'

Back in the kitchen, Lou managed to restrain herself while they drank their tea. But, when Grace was loading the dirty cups into the dishwasher and Mel had disappeared into the other part of the house cuddling a purring Tiger, she came to stand behind her mother.

'That man,' she said. 'This Aaron guy's father. He's the one you've been seeing, isn't he?'

Grace sighed and turned to face her daughter. She thought Lou had forgotten about her earlier comment. She should have known better. Lou never forgot anything, and once she got her teeth into something, she'd worry away at it till she was satisfied.

'Ted's a neighbour. We met at your Aunt Dot's. I told you all that, and you heard what your Uncle Kev said about him at dinner last night. They went to school together and renewed their old friendship when Ted came back to Bellbird Bay to retire.' Hoping this would satisfy Lou, Grace was about to move away, when she saw her daughter's eyes were filling with tears.

'You wouldn't ever think of marrying again, would you? I'd hate it. No one could replace Dad. Surely you're too old for that sort of thing.' She wrinkled her nose in disgust.

'I'm only sixty-one, Lou. I could live at least another twenty years. I'm not contemplating marriage to Ted Crawford or anyone else, but do you really expect me to pass up a chance of happiness if it comes along? Your dad and I had over thirty happy years together. I'll always love him. But that doesn't mean I can never love anyone else. We love everyone in a different way. At the moment, Ted is just a friend. He may become a good friend, even something more. Time will tell. He lost his wife a long time ago when Aaron was only a child. He's been on his own longer than I have. But I know what it's like to be lonely, to miss having someone to talk to at the end of the day, to share things with.' *And to hold me in their arms, and snuggle up to in bed.*

'But you have us. If you'd come to live in Sydney, Greg and I would have been there for you, but you had to prove something by coming up here, to this… this…' She swept an arm to encompass the view through the kitchen window.

'…to this beautiful spot,' Grace finished for her. 'And Mel will be with me till her baby's born. But children provide a different sort of companionship. As you get older, it's good to spend time with people who share your memories, who remember the same music, who lived through the same history. Dot and I have that. But sometimes, it may not be enough. And your Aunt Dot and I are very different people.' Grace chuckled.

'What would Dad think?'

'Your dad would be the first to encourage me to be happy. It's something we used to talk about… before he became too disoriented to make sense. But, as I said, it's not something I'm contemplating right now. You wouldn't want to prevent my making friends with people, would you?'

'People, no, but…' Lou folded her arms and gazed out blindly at the view. 'You will tell me, won't you, if… if you and this Ted guy…'

'You'll be the first to know. Now,' Grace put an arm around Lou's shoulders, 'I'd really like to show you more of Bellbird Bay to give you some idea of what I like about it. Why don't we go for a wander tomorrow, go up the boardwalk to the headland, check out the town and perhaps take in a visit to *The Pandanus Garden Centre and Café?* It's one of my favourite spots to relax over a cup of tea or coffee and they have the most divine cakes.'

Grace held her breath as she waited for Lou's response, hoping she wouldn't shake off her arm or reject her suggestion. To her delight, Lou turned to hug her. 'Sorry if I'm being a pain, Mum. I only want what's best for you. I want you to be happy.'

'I know you do, sweetheart. You just have to let me decide what will make me happy.'

*

After an early breakfast during which Lou managed to be pleasant to both Grace and Mel, her earlier annoyance seemingly forgotten, the three set off up the boardwalk. It was lovely if a trifle cool, and deserted at this time in the morning. When they reached the topmost point and gazed out to the ocean where some early surfers were riding the waves – mere specs in the distance – even Lou was impressed.

'It's not bad,' she said. 'I can see what you like about it.' High praise from one who sought to disparage everything about Bellbird Bay.

They were about to turn for the walk back down, when an elderly woman rode up on a pale green bicycle with a large basket attached behind the seat. A pair of sharp eyes peered out from the weather-beaten face under a floppy, wide-brimmed hat. 'Hello there,' she called, dismounting and smiling at the three women.

'Hello.' The woman was a stranger to Grace. Although she'd heard about the old woman who ran a B&B up here on the headland and supplied the delicious cakes to *The Pandanus Café,* she'd never met her.

'I'm Ruby,' the stranger said, 'and you must be the person who moved into the old Jarrett shack in January. I haven't seen you up here before. Are these your daughters?'

'Yes. I'm Grace Winter and this is Mel and Lou.'

Both Mel and Lou smiled at the woman.

Ruby regarded them in silence for several moments, during which Grace wondered if it would be rude to leave. Then she spoke. 'You are all troubled in different ways, but your wishes will be granted, though perhaps not exactly as you imagine. You need to be patient. Good to meet you. Enjoy your day and be kind to each other.' She wheeled her bike through the gate and went into the house, leaving Grace and her daughters staring after her.

Lou was the first to find her voice. 'What was that about?' she asked.

Grace shook her head. 'I've heard about her. She's lived here for ever. The house is a B&B and she's the one who makes the cakes I was telling you about for *The Pandanus Café.*

'How old *is* she?' Mel asked with a shiver. 'She looks like a witch… but a kindly one. What she said didn't make any sense.'

'Apart from her suggestion to have a good day and be kind to each other,' Grace said with a laugh. 'Good advice at any time.'

Putting the woman's strange appearance behind them, the three spent a pleasant morning wandering around the shops along the esplanade, where Lou bought a couple of summer tops, and Mel purchased a toy penguin which she hugged to her chest.

'It's beginning to feel real,' she said with a smile and an apologetic glance in Lou's direction.

'I think it's time for lunch,' Grace said, before Lou could make any comment. They'd driven down to the esplanade, so now they all piled into Grace's car and drove to the garden centre.

'This is quite a place,' Lou said in surprise when they had parked and were walking through the arched entrance under the sign which proclaimed it was *The Pandanus Garden Centre and Café.*

Grace smiled. 'Not such a backwater. I understand the woman who owns it built it up from nothing. Wait till you see the café.'

They walked through the busy garden centre until they came to a gap in a carefully trimmed plumbago hedge where the café was situated. Once inside they took their seats at an empty table close to the large pandanus tree which gave the café and garden centre its name.

'It's quite pleasant,' Lou said, gazing around. Almost all of the other tables were filled with chattering groups of women. She picked up a menu.

Grace gave a small smile. Lou was beginning to thaw to Bellbird Bay. It was a pity she was leaving next day, but maybe she'd visit again and bring Greg next time.

Grace ordered an open sandwich on rye with her usual lemon and ginger tea, while both Lou and Mel chose the café's salad of the day along with coffee.

'You must try one of the cakes,' Grace said when they had finished eating, and the waitress came to remove their plates. 'What do you recommend today?' she asked.

The young girl reeled off a list of cakes, all of which sounded delectable, the group finally deciding on the pear frangipani.

'And you said the woman we met this morning bakes these cakes?' Lou asked. 'How amazing!'

'Isn't it? Last time we were here, Mel and I had the strawberry cheesecake. It's divine, too. I often buy a couple of slices to take home.'

'I can see why. But you always used to do a lot of baking, Mum. I remember when we were growing up…'

'I got out of the habit when your dad was sick. He lost his appetite for sweet things. And there's not as much point baking for myself, honey, especially when I can buy Ruby's masterpieces when I feel like a sweet treat. I can't compete with her cakes.'

'I suppose. Maybe now you have Mel staying with you, you can start again.'

'Maybe.' But Grace didn't imagine she would. It had been different when the children were little, when everyone was at home, when she spent an entire day baking. Now she made the odd batch of scones or muffins but drew the line at anything more complicated or time consuming, preferring to spend her time on her writing.

They were walking back through the garden centre, Lou carrying a box containing slices of the strawberry cheesecake Grace had spoken about, when they had to sidestep to avoid a group of women discussing the merits of two varieties of lemon tree.

'Sorry,' Grace said, as she almost cannoned into a trolley filled with a variety of plants and bags of potting mix.

'No worries.'

The voice sounded familiar. Grace looked up into Ted Crawford's amuscd cycs.

Twenty-six

Ted was enjoying a pleasant afternoon wandering around the garden centre. He had persuaded Aaron to join him and, having decided on a selection of plants, they were on their way to the checkout when a woman almost fell over their trolley.

'Hello there.' He grinned at Grace Winter in amusement at her confusion. 'Fancy meeting you here.' He was aware of Aaron greeting Grace's daughter, and of the other daughter staring at him with an expression he couldn't fathom.

'We've been having lunch,' Grace said. 'Looks like you plan to be busy.' She nodded towards the overflowing trolley.

'Yeah.' Ted pulled on his ear, aware of waves of disapproval radiating from Grace's older daughter. *What had he done to earn her censure?* 'We do seem to have got carried away. Good lunch?'

'Yes, thanks.'

They stood indecisively for several moments, Aaron and Mel whispering to each other, while the other daughter scowled in his direction, before wandering off.

'Your daughter doesn't seem to approve of me,' Ted said with a wry grin.

'No, she… she's a bit overprotective, I'm afraid. I must apologise for her rudeness. She appears to be reading too much into our friendship.' Grace's eyes followed the young woman as she affected interest in a row of native plants, glancing back towards them from time to time.

'Ah!' Ted understood. Grace's daughter was afraid he might have designs on her mother. It took Ted back to his teenage years when the parents of a potential girlfriend were concerned about his intentions towards their daughter.

'She's leaving tomorrow. She only came to drive Mel up with her belongings, and I think she may have been curious to see where I was living. It's been a difficult few days, but I think she is finally accepting my decision to move here – and Mel's situation.'

Ted would like to have asked more, but was aware of Grace's daughter's impatience – and Aaron and Mel had stopped whispering and moved within earshot.

'You're back with your dad again?' Grace asked Aaron with a smile.

'Got a job here, so will be moving up permanently in a week or so,' Aaron replied. 'Just been telling Mel about it.'

'In a boatyard, Mum,' Mel said, tossing her hair back coquettishly, making Ted wonder about Aaron's assurance that he and Mel were nothing more than friends.

He would be willing to bet the young woman had other ideas, and while Ted would welcome another woman in his son's life, this one had problems of her own to deal with. And how would Zack react if his dad became involved with a woman who was pregnant? He was going to find it difficult enough if Tanya and Mark had a child.

'We should be going,' he said, more gruffly than he intended. 'Good to see you again.'

'Good to see you, too. Maybe…'

But whatever Grace was going to say was lost as her older daughter reappeared and, putting a hand on her mother's arm, led her off.

'What was that about?' Aaron asked, staring at the three women walking away. 'I was going to suggest we invite them for drinks.'

'I don't think the older one, Lou, approves of either of us. Drinks are probably not a good idea. She's leaving tomorrow. Best let them enjoy their family time together. I understand Mel is starting work at *The Bay Gallery*.'

'Is that the one that sells your paintings?'

'It is.' Ted wheeled the trolley into the checkout queue.

'Wait a minute. If you know that, you must have been talking to her mother while I was in Brisbane.'

'Is it so strange? We're neighbours. And, yes, we have met on a couple of occasions.'

'I've never known you to be interested in a woman before.' Aaron winked.

Ted was glad the couple in front of them in the queue moved off at this point and he was able to unload the trolley and pay for his purchases.

But Aaron hadn't finished. 'She seems like a nice lady, Dad. I wouldn't mind if you and she got together. It must be lonely for you at times. I know you have your old mate, Kev, the other old surfers, and the volunteers at the turtle thing, but I'd like to think you could find some happiness in your old age.'

Ted chuckled at Aaron's notion he was old, but was pleased his son didn't think he was past it. *Unlike Grace's daughter.* 'Thanks, son. Glad I have your permission,' he said, tongue-in-cheek.

'No worries, Dad.' Aaron had no idea his dad was amused.

Back home they unloaded the car, and Aaron helped Ted plant the flowering shrubs along the pathway before they went inside for a well-earned beer.

'Thought I'd invite Mel out to dinner tomorrow night,' Aaron said, when they were relaxing with cans of Corona. 'Her sister's going back to Sydney. You don't mind if I leave you on your own?'

'Not at all.' *Had Aaron forgotten that's how Ted spent most of his time?* 'You becoming interested in Mel Winter?'

'Would it bother you? I know you and her mother…' Aaron tapped the side of his nose with his finger.

'None of my business how you spend your time, but you don't know much about her, do you?'

'What do you mean? I know her mother is a friend of yours, which should be recommendation enough, that she had a challenge with her job in Sydney and has come up here to be with her mother. I know how it feels to have to change jobs and move house. We have that in common. She's attractive, good company. What else is there to know?'

Ted bit his tongue. He couldn't reveal Grace's confidence. He only hoped Mel would tell Aaron before they became too involved. 'I don't want to see you get hurt again. I remember what you told me, how Tanya's defection affected you.'

'Mel's not like Tanya, Dad. She hasn't said, but I get the feeling she's been hurt, too.'

Ted frowned. It was true what he'd said to Grace. No matter how old your child was, a parent still worried. He wished he could wrap Aaron up and protect him, but he was old enough to make his own decisions and reap the consequences. All Ted could do was be there for him when he was needed to pick up the pieces.

Twenty-seven

As soon as they arrived home, Lou disappeared, ostensibly to pack but Grace knew her daughter. Lou was no doubt stewing about their meeting with Ted and Aaron in the garden centre. As if Grace could have avoided it.

Seeing Ted's packed trolley had reminded her how she hadn't done much with her own garden since moving in. From his collection of plants, it looked as if Ted knew what he was doing, and while she had enjoyed pottering about in the garden at Brigadoon, Grace wasn't familiar with what would grow here in Queensland. She'd wait till Lou had left, then ask Ted for advice.

'When are we going to eat the strawberry cheesecake, Mum?' Mel called from the deck where she had settled into a chair with Tiger on her lap.

'We've only just had lunch. You can't be hungry again.' But Grace remembered how when she was pregnant, she'd always been hungry.

'It's not me, it's the sinker.' Mel stared down at her baby bump. She had taken to calling her baby this, something which worried Grace a little, but not enough for her to object.

'Let's wait till Lou joins us again.'

'What's up with her now? I thought she'd got over my being pregnant. It's not as if I can do anything about it, not now.'

'I think it's me she's annoyed with, and meeting Ted and Aaron after lunch didn't help matters.'

'Oh! But you and Aaron's dad aren't…' her eyes widened, '…are you? I know you've been seeing each other, but you're both…'

'Too old?' Grace chuckled.

'Well…'

'Wait till you're my age and see how you feel.'

'Gross.' Mel scratched Tiger's ears. 'Shall I go and tell Lou to hurry up?'

'Better not. She'll come out in her own good time. Let's try to make her last evening with us as uncontentious as possible, shall we?'

'Okay by me. As long as she doesn't decide to have another go at me.'

Grace didn't reply. She hoped so, too. And she hoped by the time Lou did emerge she'd have got over her dummy spit about Ted.

*

'I'm sorry I've been such a pain.' Lou hugged Grace and Mel. 'I worry about both of you stuck up here, so far away.'

'We're fine, darling. We have your Aunt Dot and Uncle Kev, and we have friends here, too.'

Lou's forehead creased.

It had been the wrong thing to say. 'The ladies I work with at the library are lovely,' Grace said quickly. 'It's a pity you didn't get to meet any of them.' She tried to infuse a sense of regret into her voice, knowing quite well how she'd never made any effort to make friends with her fellow librarians.

'Hmm. Well, let me know how you get on, Mel,' she said to her sister, looking pointedly at her burgeoning baby bump, 'and take care, Mum,' she added to Grace. 'It would be wonderful if you could come to visit us in Sydney. Though I suppose you won't want to leave Mel.'

'We'll see. Promise you'll speak with Greg and come to some resolution. And let me know. I worry about you, all three of you, even though you're all grown.'

'I don't expect Ben gives you much to worry about,' Lou said. 'He's always been your favourite.'

Where had that come from? Why did Lou always manage to sound resentful of her siblings? Grace took a deep breath before replying. 'Ben's the youngest so always needed more care and attention when you were all little. But he's led an independent life for some years now. I'm glad he's back in Australia – in Queensland. It means I may see more of him. But, like any parent, I don't have favourites. I love you all with your different quirks – some good, some not so good.' She gave Lou a kiss on the cheek. 'Now, drive safely and have a good trip home. Give my love to Greg. I'll be thinking about you.'

Grace and Mel stood waving as Lou drove off, then walked into the house together arm-in-arm.

'Phew, she's hard work,' Mel said. 'Why can't she be happy? She has everything she wants – a husband who loves her, a good job…'

'But not a baby.'

'She told you?'

'Mmm.'

'It's like when we were little. Lou always had to get what she wanted. She'd claim because she was the oldest, it was her right, whereas…'

'Whereas you always did. You used to wind your dad round your little finger, while Lou had to work at it.'

Mel grinned. 'I did, didn't I?' Then her grin faded. 'I'm glad Dad doesn't know about this.' She patted her stomach.

'Oh, my darling.' Grace hugged Mel. 'He'd be surprised, but just as happy as I am to be a grandparent.'

Mel cheered up immediately. 'He would, wouldn't he? Aaron told me how proud his dad is of Zack. That's his son's name. He says I might get to meet him in the next school holidays. We could do some things together. Though I suppose I'll be really fat by then. Sometimes I wish…' she grimaced, '…then I'm glad I'm having this baby. It's the one thing I've managed to do that Lou hasn't.'

'Mel!' Grace was horrified.

'Well, it's true, Mum. All my life she's gone on about how she's been better than me at everything. She can't do that now.'

'But…'

'I know. I'm not being fair to her. And I'm sorry she and Greg are having trouble. It's not as if I set out to have this baby to beat her to it. But now I am, I feel sort of glad… in a way.'

Grace had no words to express her dismay.

'Well, maybe she'll get pregnant now, too, and our babies can grow up together,' Mel said, seeing her mother's distress.

'Maybe,' was all Grace could think to say.

'Do you mind if I go out tonight?' Mel asked, checking her phone. 'Aaron has invited me to dinner.'

'I'm sure you don't need my permission.' Grace was suddenly tired of dealing with her daughters and the thought of an evening by herself sounded wonderful. She could curl up with Tiger, a glass of wine and a good book.

'No need to be like that, Mum.' But Mel had a smile on her face as she disappeared into her room.

*

Grace had fixed herself a toasted sandwich for dinner and was settling down for the relaxing evening she'd promised herself, when there was a knock on the glass door leading out to the deck. Tiger immediately leapt down from her lap and went to the door to stand there meowling.

Muttering to herself about inconsiderate visitors, Grace laid her book aside and went to the door, surprised to see Ted Crawford standing there, a bottle of wine in his hand.

'Ted, this is a surprise,' she said.

'I saw your older daughter leave earlier and I know Mel has gone to dinner with Aaron, so I thought you might like some grown-up company and to share this.' He waved the bottle of Wolf Blass Yellow Label Shiraz. 'It's been languishing in my wine rack for some time and needs to be drunk.' He gave a lopsided grin.

Immediately, any annoyance Grace felt melted away. 'Come in,' she said. 'I know the very thing to go along with it.' She pulled a couple of glasses from the cupboard and, while Ted took them and the wine through to the living room, ferreted in the pantry to find a packet of fig and black olive crackers and took a round of brie from the fridge.

'I'm sorry. Did I interrupt your evening?' Ted asked when she returned. He gestured to the copy of *The Nightingale* she'd cast aside to answer his knock, and the half-empty glass of wine.

Grace blushed. 'I was only planning a quiet evening alone after a few hectic days with my two daughters. It's lovely to see you.' She meant it. Her heart had leapt at the sight of his familiar face at her door.

'Your older daughter, would I be right in assuming she doesn't approve of our friendship?' They were seated together on the sofa. Ted had poured the wine and the brie was gradually coming to room temperature.

'No.' Grace took a sip of wine. 'This is delicious, Ted.' She put her glass down again. 'Lou is of the opinion I need women friends, that I should be satisfied to live with the memory of Russ, that I shouldn't need anyone else in my life.'

'And Mel?'

Grace chuckled. 'She just thinks we're too old to be anything other than friends. Oh!' She put a hand up to her mouth wishing she could take back her words.

But Ted only laughed. 'And what do you think?' he asked, picking up a cracker, loading it with a sliver of brie and popping it into his mouth, as if his question hadn't sent shivers up her spine.

'I… I…' Grace looked down at her hands which were shaking. She wanted to take another sip – even a gulp – of wine but was afraid she'd drop the glass.

Ted took Grace's hands in his. 'Definitely not too old,' he said with a smile, his face moving closer, so close she could see the wrinkles around his eyes, the small hairs on his cheeks his razor had missed.

As Ted took Grace in his arms, a tumult of desire swept through her making her want to cry out, but before she could utter one sound, Ted's lips were on hers.

Twenty-eight

Ted couldn't believe it. He had come to Grace's to share a bottle of wine, with no thought of anything more. Even though he wanted to hold her in his arms, to feel his lips on hers, he was wary of being too hasty, conscious of her vulnerability.

But when she opened up to him about her daughters, the temptation to kiss her had been too great. It could have gone wrong, but it hadn't.

They snuggled up together, kissing and hugging like a pair of teenagers. She felt so good in his arms. It had been too long since he'd held a woman like this – since he'd held a woman at all.

Grace was lying in his arms, his lips in her hair. He was breathing in the flowery scent that always surrounded her, when there was the sound of laughter and a door opening.

They jumped apart and Grace put a hand up to tidy her hair, while Ted picked up his glass again.

By the time Aaron and Mel walked into the room, Ted and Grace were seated several centimetres apart, each holding a glass of wine.

'Mum!'

'Dad!'

Aaron and Mel spoke at once.

'You didn't tell me you were coming to visit Mel's mum,' Aaron said.

'Mum?' Mel said again.

'You're not privy to all my comings and goings. I knew Grace would be on her own, so I brought down a bottle of wine to share.' Ted gestured to the empty bottle with his glass.

'It was kind of your dad to think of me,' Grace said blushing. 'Now you two are back, why don't I make some coffee?'

'I can do it, Mum.' Mel disappeared into the kitchen, while Aaron took a seat in one of the armchairs facing the sofa. He gave Ted a penetrating look.

Ted cleared his throat. 'Did you have a nice meal? You're back early.'

'Mel didn't feel too good.'

'I should check on her.' Grace started to rise.

'No, I will.' Aaron went out of the room.

Ted and Grace looked at each other and burst out laughing.

'Do you think they guessed?' Grace asked in a low voice.

'Aaron may have,' Ted said, 'but I doubt your daughter did. Is it just me or do you feel like a teenager caught out by your parents?'

Grace giggled, the sound making Ted want to hug her again.

'Here we are.' Aaron and Mel returned carrying two mugs each.

'I thought you'd prefer tea, Mum,' Mel said, handing her mother a mug of a peppermint-smelling beverage.

'Coffee for you, Dad.' Aaron handed a mug to Ted.

'Mel's been telling me about her new job,' Aaron said, leaning back in his chair. 'It sounds good. Maybe she can help sell some of your daubs, Dad.'

'Your dad is very talented,' Grace said. 'I've seen some of his work and I was impressed.'

Aaron shrugged. 'Not to my taste, but they do seem to sell to the tourists. Now, the photographic exhibition the gallery had was something else.' He turned to Mel. 'This local guy who's a world-renowned travel photographer held an exhibition. Was in all the papers, even on the local television. You should have seen it. People came from all over Australia. He had these editions of his work, and now there are books of his photos. It's hot stuff.'

Glad to have the focus taken off him, Ted let Aaron enthuse about the exhibition, till Mel said, 'I might have read about it. Do you know the photographer? Does he live here?'

'Martin Cooper? Yes, he grew up in Bellbird Bay, and like me, has come back here to live. There seems to be something about the place that draws people to come home, though I think it's more than the place that's kept Coop from going off again.' Ted could see Grace was curious, but chose not to continue. 'You should enjoy working at the gallery, Mel. John Baldwin's a good guy and he's made a success of it in the few years since it opened. He's another native son who returned to Bellbird Bay.'

Ted could see Aaron and Mel were becoming bored with the conversation, and Grace was looking tired. He was sorry their evening had been interrupted, but perhaps it was just as well. There was no hurry. Unlike the teenagers they'd sought to emulate, they were of an age to take their time, rather than rush madly into a passionate relationship which might be doomed to fail.

He liked Grace a lot and was sure she felt the same about him, but it was too soon to tell whether or not their friendship would blossom into something more. For now, it was enough to have held her, kissed her, felt a resurge of a passion he'd thought never to feel again.

'I should be getting home,' he said, rising.

'I'll see you out, then I think it's bed for me, too.' Grace picked up their empty mugs and, with Ted carrying the empty glasses and wine bottle, they made their way to the kitchen, leaving the two youngsters alone.

At the door to the deck, they stopped. Ted took Grace's face in his hands. 'Thanks for tonight,' he said, before kissing her gently on the lips. 'You've made me feel young again. It's been a long time…'

'I'm glad you dropped round.' Grace put a hand up to the back of Ted's head, her fingers entangling themselves in the short hairs at the nape of his neck, making him shiver. 'It's been a while for me, too. I never thought to feel this way again.'

Ted's heart lifted. *Could his feelings be reciprocated? Could Grace be feeling the same surge of desire?* He looked into her eyes to see his own yearning mirrored there. 'Oh, my dear,' he murmured, pulling her to him and kissing her again, before regretfully taking his leave.

Twenty-nine

The next few weeks passed uneventfully for Grace, apart from a trip to accompany Mel to her second trimester ultrasound where they discovered the baby was a girl. Both Grace and Mel were overjoyed but decided to keep the news to themselves for the time being.

Grace was delighted that now Mel had started work at the gallery, she found she enjoyed talking with customers about the paintings on display, and John Baldwin appeared pleased with her. It made life easier when Mel was happy, and Grace found time to spend on her writing when she wasn't at the library.

She'd thought a lot about Ted since the evening he'd taken her in his arms but, now Aaron had returned to Brisbane to sell his unit in preparation for moving to the coast, there had been few opportunities to repeat it. Mel was home every evening and expected Grace to be there, too. They spent the time in knitting for the baby, and in Mel selecting and discarding possible names. She and Ted were only able to meet for lunch and the occasional walk along the beach, and he'd come to dinner on a few occasions. They'd kissed again, when they managed a few moments alone, but Grace sometimes wondered if she'd imagined those stolen moments of pleasure when their bodies strained against each other in mutual longing.

But all that was about to change.

Yesterday over lunch, Ted had mentioned Aaron was about to return and would be starting at the boatyard next week, and Grace had received a mysterious call from Ben.

After several weeks of no communication, Ben had called to say he had a few days leave and was coming to visit with a surprise. He refused to be drawn on what the surprise was, leaving Grace and Mel to speculate. Mel thought he was bringing a girl to meet them, but Grace dismissed that idea. Ben had always been open about his relationships in the past, none of which had come to anything.

This morning, as she prepared for another day at the library, Grace was buoyed up with the prospect of seeing Ben again. When he took up the position with the dig in North Queensland, she'd expected to see him more often, but this would be the first time since he began his new job.

The library was busy with story time for mums and bubs and a pre-school group arriving unexpectedly and causing chaos in the children's section. Grace was glad when her shift ended and she was able to leave. Her heart was singing at the thought of Ben arriving in a few hours. She'd stocked up with his favourite foods and made up a bed for him. She planned to introduce him to Ted and hoped the two would get on well, and that Ben would accept her need to move on with her life.

On her way to the car, Grace peered in through the window of *The Bay Gallery* to see Mel busy at work. She seemed happier knowing Aaron was coming back, though by this time, she wouldn't be able to hide her pregnancy from him. She hadn't revealed to Grace whether or not she'd already told him, and Grace wasn't game to ask. There were some things Mel was very touchy about and her relationship with Aaron was one of them.

On the spur of the moment, Grace stopped in at *The Pandanus Café* to pick up one of Ruby's strawberry cheesecakes, knowing how much Ben enjoyed sweet treats. She was surprised to be stopped on the way out by a tall slim woman, her faded blonde hair pulled back in a ponytail and wearing a green pandanus apron.

'You're Grace Winter, aren't you?' she asked, 'Dot's sister? I believe we're neighbours. I've been somewhat remiss. I should have introduced myself before now. I'm Bev Cooper, I…'

'You own all this,' Grace said. Ted had told her about this woman, the twin sister of the photographer whose exhibition had caused such a stir. She remembered Ted saying she was a neighbour too.

'Yes.' Bev looked around as if surprised at the extent of her domain.

'I live on the end of the row of beach shacks. You may have noticed the white-painted one with the wild garden. It's been a busy year for me so far, but it's easing off a bit now. I'm having a few people round for drinks on Friday – some neighbours, my brother and his partner and a few friends. You'd be most welcome.'

Grace was surprised. At first glance, Bev Cooper appeared to be around ten years younger, but there was something about the woman that resonated with her. She reminded her of Jo Ford. Grace thought of Lou's telling her she needed more woman friends. Maybe this was where she could start.

'I'm not sure,' she said. 'At the moment, things are a bit hectic. I have my daughter staying with me, and my son is arriving today for a visit. It's kind of you to invite me, but…'

'Bring them along. I've actually been meaning to do this for ages. I've allowed myself to become caught up with the garden centre to the exclusion of everything else. It took the arrival of my brother in town and his hooking up with an old friend of mine to make me realise how isolated I'd become. Have you met any of the other neighbours?'

'I've met Ted Crawford. He's an old friend of my brother-in-law.'

'Another surfing legend,' Bev chuckled. 'My brother's one of those, too. This town's full of them. Do come along. We need some fresh blood in the place. Seven o'clock Friday. No need to bring anything.'

'Thanks,' Grace said, but Bev had already turned away to deal with a waiting customer.

Grace was still thinking about the encounter when she arrived home to find Ben and a tall dark-haired woman waiting for her on the porch. The meeting with Bev immediately forgotten, she sprang out of the car.

'Ben! I wasn't expecting you so early. And this is…?' She gazed at his companion expectantly. Mel had been right. This was Ben's surprise.

'Hi, Mum.' Ben came across to hug her, leaving the girl standing awkwardly by the door. Then he held out a hand to draw her towards them. 'This is Gemma. She teaches in a school close to where the dig is located.'

Gemma moved forward to accept a hug from Grace.

'Welcome to Bellbird Bay, Gemma. What a lovely surprise. This son of mine didn't tell me about you.' She gave Ben an accusatory glance.

'We wanted to surprise you.'

'You succeeded.' Grace smiled at the pair. 'Come along inside and I'll make us some tea or coffee. You must be thirsty after your trip.'

Once in the kitchen, Grace filled the coffee machine and the electric jug, mentally trying to work out how to reorganise the sleeping arrangements.

Seeing her concern, Ben put a hand on her shoulder and kissed her on the forehead. He was so like his dad, Grace thought, as her son towered over her, his dark hair flopping over his forehead. 'It's okay, Mum. I know you don't have room for us both. I've booked us into the B&B on the headland I saw when I was here at Easter.'

'Thanks, Mrs Winter.' Gemma accepted a mug of tea, visibly relaxing. She'd appeared a little tense earlier, not surprising, Grace thought, given this was her first meeting with her boyfriend's mother.

'Call me Grace,' she said automatically.

Gemma smiled, sat down on the edge of a chair, and sipped her tea.

Ben was wandering around, mug in one hand. 'This is new,' he said, stopping in front of the painting of turtles on the beach. It was the one she had admired in Ted's studio. He had arrived with it one evening before Lou brought Mel up from Sydney. Neither had noticed it, but she should have known Ben would.

'It's by a local artist,' she said, going to stand beside him. 'Good, isn't it?'

'I like the way he's captured the movement of the little creatures. Must be difficult to do in pastels. What do you think, Gemma?' Ben put an arm around her waist.

'Mmm.' Gemma tilted her head from side to side as she examined the painting. 'It's good. A local painter?' She peered at the signature.

'Ted Crawford. He's actually a neighbour.' Grace wondered why she persisted in referring to Ted as a neighbour rather than a friend – a close friend. 'Mel is friendly with his son.'

Ben turned to face her. 'Mel?'

'She should be home soon. Ben's sister,' she said to Gemma, who had been listening to their conversation.

'I've told Gemma about Mel.' He glanced across at the girl with a secretive smile.

Grace followed his glance. She couldn't be... No, it was too soon. She was imagining things.

'How is my sister? Lou called me to say she'd driven her up from Sydney. She had a few things to say about her – about you, too, Mum.' He grinned. 'What have you been getting up to?' He looked from Grace to the painting and back again. 'It's the man who did this, isn't it? He's the one Lou is banging on about.' He chuckled. 'You should have heard what she said. Your ears must have been burning.'

'I don't expect she said anything to you she hadn't already said to me. But I'm sure Gemma doesn't want to hear all our family gossip. Mel should be home soon. I was planning to roast a chicken for dinner, but perhaps you'd prefer to go out somewhere?'

'Gemma?' Ben asked the girl who was sitting very still and listening avidly.

'I don't mind. Whatever you and your mum think.'

Grace wondered if she was always so compliant. Somehow, she doubted it. Ben wouldn't be attracted to anyone who didn't have a mind of her own. She determined to get to know Gemma better. She had the impression she'd like what she found out.

'How about the place we went with Aunt Dot and Uncle Kev? Or is it a bit fancy? Maybe the surf club would be better. What do you think?'

Grace wasn't sure which of them he was asking but since Gemma didn't reply, she did. 'Maybe the surf club,' she said. Perhaps Ted would be there. Mel would like it, too. 'Do you need to check into Ruby's before then?'

'Ruby?'

'The B&B. It's run by a woman called Ruby. She's a local character as you'll soon discover – and she bakes delicious cakes.'

'Right. Perhaps we should. Gemma?'

'Sure.' Gemma rose with her cup. 'Where should I put this, Mrs… Grace?'

'Don't worry about it. I'll see the two of you back here around…?'

'Five or six. Do we need to book at the surf club?'

'I don't think so. Mel will know. She should be back soon.'

Just then, Grace heard footsteps and Tiger ran towards the front door ahead of Ben and Gemma who were preparing to leave.

The door opened and a flushed Mel appeared, stopping in surprise at the sight of her brother and the dark-haired woman.

'Hey Ben, and who's this?' Mel grinned and winked.

'Gemma, she's… Wow, sis! Look at you.' Ben's eyes widened.

Mel glanced down at her baby bump which was now very obvious. 'Lovely to meet you, Gemma,' she said, ignoring her brother. 'I told you he'd be bringing a girl home,' she said to Grace.

'Ben and Gemma are about to leave. They're staying at the B&B on the headland, and we've decided to have dinner at the surf club. Okay with you?'

'Oh!' Mel's lips turned down. 'I'd sort of made an arrangement to…' Then she smiled. 'But we were probably going to end up at the surf club, anyway, so it'll be fine. See you later, guys. I'm dying to have a shower and put my feet up for a bit.' She disappeared inside the house, leaving Grace to farewell Ben and Gemma.

'What arrangement do you have? You knew this was to be Ben's first night home,' Grace buttonholed Mel as she stepped out of the bathroom wrapped in a towel.

'It's Aaron. He arrived back today, too. He texted me this afternoon and I agreed to see him tonight, I didn't think you'd mind. It's only Ben, and I haven't been out for ages.'

Grace mentally counted to ten before she replied, thinking of all the evenings she'd stayed home to keep Mel company when she could have been… *Don't go there*, she told herself. 'It's Ben and Gemma,' she said. 'This is the first time Ben has brought a girl home. It must be serious. We should have dinner together as a family.'

Mel tossed her wet hair over her shoulder. 'Well, if Ben can have Gemma there, I can have Aaron. And what about you?' she asked with a cheeky grin. 'Why not invite Aaron's dad, too?'

'I don't think…' Grace began. But Mel wasn't listening. She stalked into her bedroom and closed the door.

Left alone, Grace didn't know what to do. Ted would be pleased to have Aaron back and would no doubt be just as annoyed as she was to discover he and Mel had arranged to spend his first night in Bellbird Bay together. But they were young and didn't consider anyone other than themselves.

What should she do? She hated to think of the five of them enjoying dinner at the club while Ted sat at home alone, when she could be enjoying his company, too.

She picked up the phone.

Thirty

Ted was feeling nervous as he and Aaron climbed the stairs into the surf club's restaurant. The call from Grace had come as a surprise. Only that afternoon, Aaron had arrived, his car filled with boxes and cases containing more clothes, books and sports equipment than he'd thought it possible for any young man to possess.

'I've put the rest in storage till I get a place of my own, Dad,' he said, when Ted asked sarcastically where the kitchen sink was.

Assuring Ted he'd be no trouble, Aaron proceeded to say he'd be out for the evening, and Ted was preparing to spend the evening alone, perhaps catching up with the series of Nordic Noir he'd been watching on SBS.

But the call from Grace put paid to his plans. It seemed her son had arrived with an unexpected companion, and they were all having dinner at the surf club. Since Aaron and Mel had already made an arrangement to meet, they were to be part of the group and Grace invited Ted to join them.

Ted had already met Ben, Grace reminded him, and he had a vague recollection of the tall young man who was with Grace and Mel at Easter. But that was before they'd become friends, before there was any hint of a relationship. Aware of Grace's older daughter's antipathy towards him and her disapproval of her mother's involvement, Ted was concerned Ben may take a similar view.

'There they are.' Aaron pointed to a table by the window where Grace was sitting along with Mel, Ben and a dark-haired girl.

Ted took a deep breath.

When they reached the table, Grace's welcoming smile settled the fluttering in his gut. Ben stood to shake Ted and Aaron's hands and introduced the girl whose name was Gemma. She smiled a welcome, and they all sat down, Ted between Grace and Ben and Aaron next to Mel and Gemma.

As soon as he sat down, Grace took Ted's hand under the table. 'I'm glad you came,' she whispered.

'Me, too,' he whispered back, squeezing her hand, before replying to Ben who was asking him about his painting.

They chatted about Ted's painting and Ben's work on the dig while waiting for their meals to arrive, then the conversation turned to Mel and her work at the gallery.

'John is planning to mount another exhibition soon,' she said. 'It's really interesting to work with local artists. This one will focus on portraits of local identities – a bit like a local Archibald,' she said, referring to the annual portrait painting competition which had been held in Sydney for over eighty years, 'though it's not a competition, and the subjects don't have to be famous, only local.'

'You should show the one you're working on, Dad,' Aaron said.

Everyone looked at Ted, and he looked at his son in surprise. When had Aaron seen the portrait he was working on?

'I peeked into your studio when you were in the shower. Was looking for somewhere to stow my skis. It's good, but different to what you normally do.' He looked across the table to where Grace was sitting. 'It's a good likeness.'

Everyone gazed at Grace except Ted who dropped his eyes, a flush creeping across his cheeks. This wasn't how he wanted her to find out. He'd planned to unveil her portrait in private with a glass of wine. Damn Aaron. But he should have known better than to have left the uncovered – and unfinished – portrait on his easel.

Grace's eyes widened in disbelief, then she turned to him. 'You didn't.'

'It was meant to be a surprise.'

'But how…?'

'I painted it from memory.'

'Oh!'

Ted couldn't work out whether Grace was pleased or annoyed but suspected the latter.

Their meals arrived, Mel asked Gemma about how she and Ben met, and no more was said about the portrait, but Ted could feel Grace's irritation building up. He waited till they had finished eating and the two young couples excused themselves to join others on the small dance floor at the far end of the club's restaurant – a local group was providing music.

'When did you intend to tell me? I assume you did mean for me to know.' Grace met his eyes with a look he was unable to interpret.

'I'm sorry. I didn't mean you to find out like this. It was to be a surprise – I'd hoped it would be a nice one.' He dragged a hand through his hair. 'I didn't expect Aaron to go into the studio. He never usually does. I wanted to wait till it was finished before showing it to you. If I'd known you'd be upset, I'd never have…' But would he? The temptation to reproduce her face had been so great, the challenge of doing a portrait in soft pastels so exciting, could he have resisted? As soon as he drew Grace's head and shoulders on the sheet of mottled grey-pink pastel paper with a charcoal pencil, he knew he couldn't stop till he had faithfully reproduced the face of the woman he was coming to love. He also knew it was one of his best pieces of work.

'I don't know I'm upset exactly. It just feels a bit odd. I never imagined…' She gave a half smile.

'I'm sorry,' Ted said again, wondering how he could retrieve the situation.

'I'd like to see it.'

'Now?'

Grace looked across to where the four young people were busy moving to the music. 'Why not? I don't imagine they'll miss us.'

It was a lovely balmy evening, the stars bright in the deep blue sky and the moon almost full. Ted reached over to take Grace's hand as they made their way up the boardwalk, enjoying the feel of her fingers, her skin soft against his.

'I love the evenings here,' Grace said, breathing in the sea air, the roar of the waves echoing in their ears.

'You don't miss the country?'

'Sometimes.' Grace sighed. 'But Bellbird Bay has its own special magic.'

'Spoken like a true convert,' Ted chuckled.

Once inside the house, Ted delayed revealing the portrait. He wanted to capture the atmosphere he'd planned. 'I want to do this properly,' he said, taking a bottle of prosecco from the fridge and filling two flutes with the sparkling wine. 'To us.' He lifted his glass in a toast.

'To us,' Grace repeated, following his example with an amused expression.

'Now, close your eyes.' Taking Grace's hand again, he led her into the studio where the portrait of her was sitting on the easel in the middle of the room. It wasn't exactly as he'd left it. Now there was a pair of skis and a couple of boxes vying for position, and, with the moonlight coming through the window, the picture had a ghostly appearance.

Ted switched on the light. 'You can look now,' he said.

'Oh!'

Ted glanced at Grace warily. *Didn't she like it? Had he offended her in some way?*

'That's not me. She's beautiful.' Grace turned to face Ted, a tear forming in the corner of her eye.

'It's you. You're beautiful to me.'

Grace was silent, examining the portrait again. She moved closer to it.

Ted stood looking at the portrait and Grace together, pleased he'd caught the essence of this woman who had arrived in his life so unexpectedly and turned it around. 'Do you like it?' he asked, his stomach churning.

'Like it? I love it, but I can't believe it's me.' She turned to face him again.

'It's how I see you.'

'Oh, Ted!' Her eyes glowed.

Was now the time to tell her he loved her, or was it still too soon?

There was a commotion and the door burst open. 'Dad, thought this was where you'd be.' Aaron appeared, followed by Mel and Ben, Gemma hanging back.

*

Grace was lost in a cloud of wonder. *This* was how Ted saw her? The woman in the painting had an ethereal quality, not something she'd ever imagined she possessed. She was beautiful. She had the impression Ted was about to say something, something important that would change everything, when suddenly they were surrounded by a noisy group. It took her a few seconds to recognise Aaron, Mel and Ben. Gemma was there, too, standing in the background.

'So, this is the famous portrait,' Ben said. 'It looks a bit like you, Mum, but…' he moved his head from side to side as if to examine it more carefully, '…younger somehow.'

'No,' Mel said, 'it's an illusion. It's the way Ted has used the soft pastels in layers. That's it, isn't it?' she asked Ted, who was watching and listening with amusement.

'I think that's enough,' he said, ushering them out of the room. 'It was meant to be a secret, but you've all seen it now. I hope you're satisfied.'

Ted was managing to hide his annoyance pretty well, Grace thought. She was annoyed too, annoyed at the interruption of what had been a special moment.

They all filed into the kitchen. Ted stood behind the bench, hands on hips. 'Coffee or something stronger? I'm having a whisky. Grace?'

'I'll have one, too.' She was still recovering from the shock of seeing herself portrayed so… so… She couldn't find the word to describe the way Ted had depicted her.

Aaron and Ben opted for beer, and Mel and Gemma for coffee. Grace gave Gemma a concerned glance, but the girl didn't appear perturbed. 'I don't like alcohol much,' she said. Grace tried to remember if she'd had wine at the club but couldn't. What did it matter? But she felt there was something the pair weren't telling her. She glanced over at Ben again, but he was chatting to Aaron. She sighed and tried to relax.

'Here, you look as if you need this.' Ted handed her a glass of whisky.

'Thanks.' Grace took a sip, the fiery liquid burning her throat and settling in her stomach, doing nothing to allay her qualms. Though she had no idea what was worrying her.

The younger members of the party drifted out to the deck. Grace and Ted could hear the sound of their voices from the kitchen, where Ted was leaning against the benchtop, Grace seated on a high stool.

'I'm sorry we were interrupted. Can I see you on Friday?' Ted asked.

Grace was about to agree when she remembered. 'Sorry. I've been invited for drinks by Bev Cooper.'

'Damn. I have, too. I'd forgotten. Bev's a good sort. She gave up her career to come home and care for her aging parents, then set up the garden centre which has gone from strength to strength. Well, I guess I'll see you there.'

'I guess.' Grace took another sip of her drink, this one going down more smoothly. Maybe she'd swallowed the first one too quickly. She looked out through the glass door to where her two children and their partners – was Aaron Mel's new partner? – were enjoying each other's company. They were almost like one big happy family.

But Grace couldn't help thinking about Lou, the one family member who was missing. *What would she make of this gathering?*

Thirty-one

It was only two more days, but by the time Friday arrived, Grace was feeling frazzled. Despite spending time with Ben and Gemma, she still hadn't worked out her misgivings about their relationship. Gemma was perfectly pleasant, and Ben seemed infatuated with her. Perhaps that was the reason. Her baby had fallen in love. His world no longer revolved around his mother. Not that it had for years – those years when he'd been gone overseas. But he'd always returned for special family occasions. She hoped she wasn't going to become one of those clingy mothers she'd always despised, who made their daughter-in-law's lives a misery.

Determining to make an attempt to get to know Gemma better, Grace fed Tiger and fixed breakfast for herself and Mel. She didn't have to be at the library today, so planned to spend the morning with Ben and Gemma. They were leaving again on Sunday, so there wasn't much time left for her to spend with them as she didn't want to monopolise them, though she did wish she could have time with Ben on his own. They'd always enjoyed such a special relationship, ever since he was a small child. Perhaps that was the root of her discomfort.

'Hey, Mum!' Ben's head appeared at the door from the deck, Gemma's silent figure behind him. She was like a wraith, the way she seemed to always appear so noiselessly.

'Morning, Ben, Gemma. You're early birds. Have you had breakfast?'

'Have we ever. Ruby served up a feast of pancakes with fruit, bacon and maple syrup. I feel as if I don't want to eat again for a week. But I'll have a coffee if you're making it,' he said, seeing the packet of ground coffee sitting on the benchtop.

'Of course you will.' Grace had never known Ben to turn down a coffee. 'Gemma?'

'Just water, thanks.'

Grace filled the coffee machine and poured a glass of water which she handed to Gemma.

'So, what's this thing tonight?' Ben asked, once Mel had appeared, yawning, her eyes half-closed. 'Aaron said we've all been invited.'

'Bev Cooper is another neighbour and has invited all of us, along with several others, I expect, for drinks. I don't really know her, but I often visit the garden centre and café she established in town.'

'Is that the one you said Ruby bakes for?'

'Yes, Mel and I have been there a few times since she's been here.'

'Didn't think you were the garden centre type, Mel,' Ben said with a grin.

Mel made a face and helped herself to coffee before joining the others at the table and pouring muesli into a bowl. 'I have to be at the gallery this morning. I almost overslept. Thanks for wakening me, Mum.'

Mel had left by the time Grace had cleared up and was ready to go. 'I thought we'd wander down the boardwalk to the esplanade to let you get the sense of the town. Last time Ben was here,' she said to Gemma, 'it was Easter, and he didn't see much of the place.'

'Can we go to the gallery where Mel's working?' Ben asked. 'Gemma would be interested in seeing it.'

'Sure. Anywhere else?'

'We'll leave it to you, but we'd like to check out the local museum while we're here. Gemma has read about it. It claims to have a replica of one of the old fishing boats and a history both of the local fishing industry and of the original inhabitants, the people who lived here before the white man came.'

'We can do that too, perhaps after lunch? I haven't been there yet, either. I thought we could have lunch out. There are a couple of nice cafés in town.'

'Sounds good.'

At the gallery, Mel was busy talking to a customer, and they were greeted by a man of around Grace's age. He had greying hair and wore a pair of the sort of half-moon glasses Grace thought had gone out of fashion years earlier.

'Good morning, how can I help you?' he said with a welcoming smile.

'Oh,' Grace said, flustered, 'I'm Mel's mum and this is her brother. We wanted to see where she worked. I'm ashamed to say I've been living in Bellbird Bay since the beginning of the year and haven't made it here till now.'

'It's never too late. I'm John Baldwin.'

'Grace Winter and this is Ben… and Gemma.' She looked across to where Gemma had wandered off to examine a wall of paintings.

John walked across to the display which had attracted Gemma's interest.

Grace and Ben followed to inspect the collection of flower paintings which were hung there.

'I love this one.' Grace pointed to a watercolour of a red flowering gum. 'It looks so real.' She caught Gemma staring at her. 'I don't claim to be an art critic,' she said. 'I'm one of those cretins who know what I like but have no idea of the finer points. Do you paint, Gemma?'

'I've tried my hand at landscapes, in water colour like these floral ones, but I'm not very good, nothing like those or the ones by your friend, Ted.' She gestured to another wall which contained several landscapes, a couple of which Grace recognised as being Ted's.

'You know Ted Crawford?' John Baldwin smiled. 'He's another of our local success stories. Came back here to retire and discovered his vocation. He was wasted as a city solicitor. Happens a lot. People come home to Bellbird Bay to retire and find a whole new life.'

Was that what had happened to her, Grace wondered. Coming to Bellbird Bay hadn't been coming home, but it sometimes felt that way, as if the town had been waiting for her to arrive, to enfold her in its clutches. And it was where she started to write.

After lunch at *The Greedy Gecko* next to the gallery, and before heading to the museum, Gemma wandered into a bookshop, giving Grace her longed-for opportunity to spend time alone with Ben.

'Gemma seems a nice girl. She's very quiet,' she said, hesitant about interrogating her son but curious to know more about their relationship.

'She's special, Mum. I knew as soon as I saw her.' He gave a shy grin. 'She's only quiet because she was nervous about meeting you. I've told her so much about you and Dad. But she's really passionate about her job, about helping underprivileged young people. It's one of the things that attracted me to her, that and her caring nature.'

Hearing the strong emotion in Ben's voice gave Grace a momentary qualm. It made her want to protect him, but he was too old to need his mother's protection, even if she was able to give it.

Before they could say much more, Gemma reappeared carrying two carrier bags. 'This is for you,' she said, handing one to Grace. 'Thank you for being so welcoming.'

'Oh, thank you, Gemma.' Grace gave the girl a kiss on the cheek, before peeping into the bag to see a copy of the latest novel by Nicole Alexander, a favourite author of hers, who wrote beautifully about the Australian countryside. 'How did you know?'

Gemma glanced at Ben who grinned at his mother. 'I've seen all her books on the bookshelf in your study and I didn't think you'd have this one yet.'

'Thanks, Gemma,' Grace repeated, 'it's very thoughtful of you.' Maybe things would work out for the pair of them. Grace hoped so.

*

Bev Cooper's house was, as she'd said, at the end of the group of what had been beach shacks but were now renovated beach homes. The garden, far from being the wilderness she'd described, was a profusion of winter blooms, an excellent advertisement for her business.

The sound of loud voices and laughter greeted Grace and her family as they made their way up the path to the front door which stood wide open.

'Should we just go in?' Grace wondered aloud, as they heard voices behind them signalling the arrival of Ted and Aaron.

'Saw you ahead of us but couldn't catch up,' Aaron said, taking Mel's arm, and the group all walked in together.

Once inside, they were swept up in a crowd of people, most of whom seemed to know Ted. Grace and he were soon separated from the others, and he took her by the elbow as they pushed their way through the crush to a door which led outside to where there was a table of drinks.

Bev was nowhere to be seen, but by the time they had glasses of wine, she appeared, a couple following her. 'This is my brother, Martin, and his partner and my old friend, Ailsa,' Bev said, drawing forward a masculine version of herself accompanied by a thin woman, her dark brown hair showing flecks of grey.

When the usual greetings had been observed, the woman called Ailsa said to Grace, 'Bev tells me you're from Granite Springs. My sister lives there.'

Grace was tempted to say that a lot of people did, and it was unlikely she knew the woman's sister, when Ailsa said, 'Liz has a bookshop called *The Reading Corner*. You may know it.'

'I do indeed. A lovely place to browse. I often went there.' Grace recalled the auburn-haired woman who owned the shop, along with the ginger cat who always accompanied her. She had a vague memory of a new relationship with… the editor of the local paper, that was it. It had been a topic of local gossip for a few days combined with the demise of a development plan which would have seen the bookshop and its neighbours being demolished for one of those dreadful shopping arcades.

It transpired Ailsa had visited Granite Springs several times, so Grace and she chatted about the town, while Ted talked with Martin who he already knew. Bev soon disappeared to mingle with her other guests.

After a while the conversation flagged, and Grace looked around for Mel and Ben. Seeing them in a distant corner, she made her excuses and headed towards them, only to be waylaid by Ruby Sullivan.

'Here you are,' Ruby said, as if she'd been searching for Grace. 'Not with Ted tonight?' She peered over Grace's shoulder, making Grace want to turn to follow her gaze. 'It'll work out for you in the end,' she said, 'and for your daughter, too. But your son has heartache ahead and your other daughter…' She frowned.

A shiver ran down Grace's spine. It was just like when she had met Ruby with Mel and Lou. The woman said some weird things then too. How could Ben and Gemma stay in this woman's B&B? She was either mad or a witch.

Bev appeared at that moment and, seeing Grace's face, spoke to Ruby. 'You haven't been frightening Grace with your stories, have you?' she asked.

Ruby only gave an enigmatic smile and drifted off.

'What's she been saying to you? You look as if you've seen a ghost.'

Grace shivered and took a gulp of wine which made her feel fractionally better. 'What is it with her? She makes these weird pronouncements. It's as if she has some way of seeing the future.'

'Or seeing what you're thinking? She's lived a long time, seen a lot, and does seem to have the knack of seeing right into your inner thoughts and worries. It can be a bit disconcerting. I suppose we've all become used to it over the years. The thing is… she can be strangely accurate. She didn't predict anything dreadful, did she?' Bev's forehead creased.

'Not really. It was just a shock to hear her…' Grace shook her head. 'I'm fine. Thanks for your concern.'

'Cleo is bringing out some food now.' Bev nodded to where a couple of the staff Grace recognised from *The Pandanus Café* were placing platters of food on a long table. 'Something to eat would probably help.'

'Thanks.'

'Are you okay? Did something happen?' Ted was at Grace's side, a concerned expression marring his normally cheerful countenance.

'I'm fine. It was just something Ruby Sullivan said.'

'The old witch. That's what we called her when I was in my teens. She seemed old even then, though she probably wasn't as old as we are now. She was always a bit strange, but her B&B is popular, and her cakes are delicious.'

'Ben and Gemma are staying there. They seem happy enough with it.'

'What did she say to upset you?'

Grace shook her head again. 'Nothing really.' She had no intention of sharing the old woman's words.

'Let's get something to eat, then.' Ted led her across to the table where the array of dishes was a sight to behold, a wonderful advertisement for Bev's café. There were even several of Ruby's cakes interspersed with a variety of dishes which had obviously been made by Cleo.

When Grace had filled a plate with tasty bite-sized delights, she and Ted found a spot to sit on the deck overlooking the ocean. 'It's interesting to see the view from this aspect,' she said, Ruby's words fading in Ted's comforting company, but not completely disappearing. 'I'm sorry I let Ruby upset me. It was foolish.'

'All good now?'

Grace nodded.

When they had finished eating, a blast of music started up inside the house and people began to sing. Ted grimaced. 'Not my thing. How about we walk home along the beach? It's a glorious evening.' He looked up into the clear sky where the stars were twinkling.

Grace's eyes followed his. A walk along the beach sounded wonderful, exactly what she needed to blow away the shreds of worry left by Ruby's words, though they hadn't all been bad, had they? Hadn't she said things would work out? Was she referring to Grace and Ted when she said that? Grace's heart felt lighter as she slipped off her shoes and joined Ted on the steps leading down to the beach.

Thirty-two

'It's school holidays next week,' Aaron said over breakfast one morning. It was two weeks since he'd arrived on the coast to start his new job, and Ted and he had fallen into a routine of sorts.

Each morning, Aaron would join his dad on the beach in the early morning. He would swim while Ted surfed before they returned home to eat breakfast together. Then Aaron would head off to work, leaving Ted to his own devices. He'd spend the morning painting, then on the days she wasn't working in the library, he and Grace would enjoy lunch together. Sometimes he would walk down to her house, on others, she'd walk up to join him, but more often, they'd wander into town together to eat in one of the cafés which proliferated there to cater for the tourists.

The portrait of Grace was finished and ready to be part of the display in *The Bay Gallery*, then Ted planned to give it to Grace on her birthday which he'd managed to find out was in early November.

Until Aaron mentioned them, he'd completely forgotten about the approaching school holidays, the holidays in which he'd promised Zack would visit. 'Have you made arrangements with Tanya for Zack to come up?' he asked.

Aaron shuffled his feet. 'It's not easy, Dad. You know what she's like.'

Ted did. He also knew his son well, knew how easily he could be deterred from a difficult course of action.

'I promised the boy. You did, too. You can't let him down. Do you want me to contact her?'

'No, Dad. I'll do it. I just need to find the right time.'

Ted's blood boiled. *Right time?* This was Zack they were talking about. Ted hadn't seen him since Easter, and Aaron had barely seen him since he moved up here – only on weekends when, according to him, Tanya had put up all sorts of barriers and objections. 'And when will that be? I can…'

'Don't bug me, Dad. I'll do it. Okay? I need to get to work. I may be late tonight. The townhouse Nick mentioned is becoming available. I'm going to check it out after work.'

'Right.'

But Ted was far from satisfied. He waited till Aaron had left, then sent a text to Zack.

Looking forward to seeing you in the holidays. Grandpa Teddy x

Before long, there was a reply. *Can't wait* with a thumbs-up emoji.

Ted grinned. He was looking forward to seeing Zack again. The boy was growing up fast and would soon be too involved with his mates and other activities to want to spend time with his old grandad. He needed to make the most of the next few years. As he carried his painting gear up to the headland where he intended to spend the morning, Ted wondered how Zack was coping, both with school and his home situation.

There had been no more reports of Zack being bullied at school, but would he or Aaron find out if he was? And what was happening with Tanya and Mark's plan for another child? Although Aaron had seen his ex-wife and her partner on the occasions he'd picked Zack up, he was remarkably short on information. And, while Ted could understand his son's reluctance to spend any more time than necessary with Tanya, he did wish Aaron would be more communicative.

The morning passed peacefully, the light perfect for the scene Ted wanted to portray. He was humming to himself as he packed up, looking forward to seeing Grace. Today they were aiming to try out a new café which had opened in the Botanic Gardens on the outskirts of town, and he couldn't wait.

Ted sang in the shower, his voice echoing in the enclosed space as the water cascaded down his body. It was something he'd only begun to do again recently – since he met Grace Winter. She'd had such an influence on him, on his life. It was difficult to imagine how he'd survived all those years without female companionship. When Alison died, he'd never made a conscious decision to shun women, but it always seemed easier to avoid entanglements, especially when Aaron was young and required all of his time and attention.

Then it had become a habit. And he'd taken pains to steer clear of any situations in which he might be forced into the sort of evening in which he'd found himself at Kev and Dot's. He chuckled. It hadn't turned out too bad, after all, even if the night itself had been a disaster.

Dressed in a pair of chinos and a blue and white striped shirt, a dark blue sweater knotted casually around his shoulders, Ted drove around to where he could see Grace waiting for him at her gate. Today she was wearing a pair of smart black pants topped with a jacket in the same shade of deep blue as her eyes. She looked so lovely, he wanted to take her in his arms and kiss her. He settled for a quick hug and peck on the cheek, when she got into the car.

'You're looking very smart,' he said with a grin, as she fastened her seatbelt and they drove off.

Grace blushed. 'You look pretty good yourself.'

Ted grinned again. 'Good morning?'

'Yes. I finished the first draft of my book. There's still a long way to go and I don't know if any publisher will be interested, but…'

'Well done! What's next?'

'I plan to let it sit for a while to percolate, then I'll need to edit it, then…'

'Then?'

'I thought I might try it out on some of the children who come to the library, get their opinion before I do anything else.'

'Good idea.'

'How was your morning? Did your painting go well?'

'Yes, thanks. And…' he remembered, '…Aaron's going to look at a townhouse after work.'

'He's moving out?'

'He never intended to stay with me permanently. He has a lot of stuff in storage, and this place is closer to his work.'

'So, you'll be on your own again.'

'Yeah.' Ted risked a glance at her out of the corner of his eye. *Did she understand what that meant?* It meant they'd have the opportunity to spend time together at his place without any danger of being disturbed.

Grace blushed. *She did understand.*

'I wonder if Mel knows.'

'She's told him she's pregnant?'

'She says so. He'd have guessed anyway. But she still insists they're only friends. I suppose she may be right, but…'

'They'd make a good couple. Aaron needs someone who'll treat him better than that bitch, Tanya. Sorry, it just slipped out, but she managed to take away all his self-confidence. He's only now getting over it and still has difficulty coping with her. I worry about Zack.'

'Your grandson.' Grace nodded. 'A few months ago, I wouldn't have agreed Mel would be a good influence, but she's changed, become more responsible, grown up. I think she's going to make a good mother.'

'I'm sure she will. But I'm like you, I have no idea about her and Aaron. It's a pity we can't arrange their lives for them.'

'Like Dot wanted to arrange ours?' Grace stifled her laughter.

'Precisely.' Ted chuckled.

They drove along in silence for the next fifteen minutes or so, Ted's imagination running riot about how he and Grace might take advantage of his new freedom once Aaron had moved out. Things were different between them now from what they had been when Aaron was down in Brisbane, and he had expectations that… He glanced sideways at Grace again, but she showed no sign she, too, was anticipating the consummation of what was between them. *Had he been mistaken?*

'Is this it?' Grace asked, as the sign for the botanic gardens appeared on their right amid a profusion of grevillea and grass trees.

Drawn out of his musings, Ted turned off the road and into the car park which was almost empty.

Getting out of the car, they saw a sign pointing towards a bush path with the words, *Acacia Cottage* burnt into it. They followed the arrow to arrive at a glassed-in building with a few tables outside.

'This is lovely,' Grace said, 'but I think it's a bit cool to sit outside.'

Ted agreed and, pushing open the door, they found themselves in a large room with a marvellous view over a Japanese garden and koi pond.

'Oh, I read about this,' Grace said. 'Look, there's the roofed pavilion overlooking the pond, and the raked stone garden to the side. Bellbird

Bay has a sister agreement with a city in Japan and... Oh, sorry, you must know this.' She smiled. 'It's all new to me.'

Ted returned her smile, enjoying her enthusiasm. 'It's a long time since I've been here. It must have been on a school excursion. The place has grown a lot since then, and this café's new. Shall we sit down and order?'

'Oh, of course.'

They took a seat next to the full-length window from where they could feast their eyes on the view. There was a blackboard menu on the wall listing a variety of healthy lunch options.

After they'd ordered bowls of chunky potato and leek soup with crusty bread, and glasses of white wine, Ted took Grace's hand, rubbing his thumb over the back of it. 'You know how I feel about you, don't you?' It was the closest he'd come to revealing what was in his mind. This wasn't the venue he'd have chosen, but they were almost alone – only one other couple sitting in the far corner who were engrossed in each other and probably wouldn't have noticed if the roof blew off.

Grace blushed prettily and looked down at the hand he was holding. 'I've guessed, and... I enjoy your company... a lot.' She looked up to meet his eyes. 'After Russ died, I never thought I'd feel like this again. It's been a shock.'

'A pleasant one, I hope. I'd never expected it either. I've been happy, living a solitary life, seeing Aaron and Zack from time to time, surfing, painting...'

'Volunteering with your turtles.'

'That, too.'

A waiter appeared with their wine.

'To us, and to us seeing more of each other.' Ted raised his glass.

Grace raised hers, too. 'To us,' she said with a smile.

Their meals arrived and the conversation ceased as they enjoyed the thick soup and crusty bread.

'Coffee?' Ted asked when they had finished.

'Please.'

'What exactly did you mean before?' Grace asked, when they were sipping delicious cups of coffee.

Ted raised one eyebrow.

'When you mentioned seeing more of each other. Did you mean...?' Grace blushed again.

He loved it when she did that. It made her look about eighteen. 'How would you feel about it if I did?'

Grace didn't immediately reply.

Ted's heart plummeted. *Had he spoken too soon?* He waited.

'I think… I think perhaps it might be time. But I have to warn you, I… It's been a long time since… Before Russ died… he was sick for a long time.'

A wave of relieve flowed over Ted. *If that was all…* 'For me, too,' he said, putting his hand over hers on the table.

Thirty-three

Grace was still reeling from her conversation with Ted over lunch when her phone rang, and she saw Lou's number. She was so busy wondering if she'd been too quick to agree, if she was really ready for a full-blown relationship, if she was too old, if she could bear to reveal her sixty-one-year-old body to Ted, she missed Lou's initial words.

'Sorry, honey. Could you say that again?'

'I'm pregnant, Mum.'

Hearing Lou's excited voice on the phone was balm to her soul. Her news created such a different feeling from the one provoked by Mel's similar announcement. This time, it was easy to be glad for her daughter.

'Oh, my darling, I'm so pleased for you. You must be over the moon. Have you been to see your doctor?'

'Not yet. I will, but I did one of those tests from the pharmacy, and it came back positive. I almost wept when I saw the thin blue line. I screamed so much Greg thought I was dying.'

Grace laughed. It was such a relief to hear the happiness in Lou's voice. She did a quick mental calculation. The baby would be due around April – an Easter baby. She'd go down to Sydney for the birth and… She was getting ahead of herself. 'Greg must be pleased, too.'

'He's delighted, more so than I am, if that's possible. It was him who wanted a child in the first place, then I came around to the idea.'

Grace was surprised, though on reflection didn't know why. Lou had never been interested in babies growing up, never been one to play with dolls as a child. She'd always been keener on her career and had made a success of it, too. Would she change once the baby was born, choose to be a stay-at-home mother or take the minimum amount of maternity leave before returning to work and put the child into day care?

They chatted a bit more before Grace rang off, but not before reminding Lou to make an appointment with her doctor, despite knowing she sounded like a nagging mother.

'Fancy that, Tige,' she said to the cat who was sunning himself by the window. 'Another grandchild. Now it only needs Ben and Gemma to…' She bit her lip. There had been no news from Ben for some time. It wasn't like him to be out of contact. But perhaps he was busy at work. And now he was in a relationship, Grace realised his mother had to take second place in his affections. She sighed. All her chickens were grown. It was at times like this she missed Russ so much. How thrilled he'd be to know about Mel and Lou, and to see Ben with a serious girlfriend.

It was lovely to think of all three of her children settled, though she wasn't sure about Mel. She and Aaron spent a lot of time together, but Mel insisted they were only friends. 'How could we be anything else with me looking like this?' she'd asked only the previous week, gesturing to her growing stomach. But Aaron was a nice guy, not the irresponsible layabout Grace had first imagined. He was like his father, intelligent, quiet and gentle, and now he was working with his old schoolmate, he appeared to be happy with his life.

Grace hoped that perhaps, once the baby was born, the pair of them might make a match of it.

That only left her and Ted, and, despite their recent conversation, she didn't dare to imagine a future with him. He was so different from Russ, even though she was sure the two men would have got on well together and she knew Russ would approve of her finding a new relationship. He'd never want her to spend the rest of her life grieving for him. Dot would approve, too. Hadn't she been the one to introduce them in the first place?

The only fly in the ointment was Lou. But perhaps, with a new baby, even Lou might change her tune. Could Grace dare to hope?

*

'I'm bushed. What's up?' Mel came in, threw her bag down on the floor and collapsed into a chair to have Tiger immediately jump up on her lap. 'Not now, Tige.' She pushed the cat off. 'What are you looking so pleased about, Mum?'

'It's Lou. She just called. She's pregnant.'

'Wow! She finally did it. She might get off my back now. Bet she's pleased.'

'Delighted.'

'When's she due?'

'April, I should think. We'll know more when she's seen her doctor. She just did the pharmacy test and wanted me to know right away.'

'Wanted *me* to know more like.' Mel grimaced. 'But I'm glad for her.'

'How was your day?' Grace asked belatedly, realising Mel looked exhausted.

'Tiring, but…' her eyes brightened, '…John has suggested I do a degree in art history. He thinks I have potential. How about that? I'm going to check if I can do one online, so it won't interfere with the bub.' She looked down at her baby bump and stroked it lovingly. 'How was yours?' she asked. 'You were having lunch with Ted at that new café.'

'It was good. The botanic gardens are interesting. There's a Japanese influence in part of them.' They had walked around a bit after lunch, but the conversation they'd had dominated her thoughts, making it difficult to think of anything else. 'Ted said Aaron's looking at a townhouse closer to his work.'

'Yeah, he told me. He asked me to go to see it, but I don't see the point. He's the one who'll be living there.' Mel slipped off her shoes. 'Oh, that's better.'

'You're not seeing him tonight?'

'No way.' She rubbed one foot. 'Dinner, a bath and bed for me. Did you get exhausted when you were pregnant with us?'

Grace tried to remember. It had been so long ago, and unlike Mel, she hadn't been working outside the home. Russ had insisted she stay home, and she'd been happy to agree. It's what a lot of women did those days, especially in the country town. 'It was different for me,' she said after a pause. 'I didn't work and could have a nap in the afternoon.' She thought for a moment. 'Ted said his grandson – Aaron's son – will be coming to visit. Has Aaron said anything about him?'

'Not a lot, only that his ex is difficult about letting Aaron spend time with him. He didn't mention a visit. I wonder if he looks like his dad?' Mel feigned disinterest, but Grace could see she was curious. 'What's for dinner? Maybe I'll have a bath first.' Without waiting for a reply, she pushed herself out of the chair and wandered off.

Left on her own, Grace picked up Mel's shoes and shook her head. Mel might appear to be growing up, but she still had a long way to go. She'd get a rude shock when she had a child of her own to look after. Lou would, too. Grace stopped in her tracks as it suddenly hit her. This time next year she'd be a grandmother twice over, maybe three times if Ben and Gemma decided to follow suit.

Meantime there was her own life to consider. If Ted's grandson was coming to visit, they wouldn't be able to get together until after the school holidays. Her heart beat faster at the thought of being with a man again. She was concerned and excited in equal proportion. She'd met Russ when they were both young and innocent. There had never been anyone else. What would it be like to make love with another man?

Thirty-four

It was like Easter all over again, but this time Zack's visit had been arranged with Tanya's full agreement. Ted had stocked up on his grandson's favourite food and drinks, and Aaron had driven down to Brisbane to collect him.

Ted couldn't settle while he waited for them to arrive, and he couldn't dismiss the thoughts of Grace which were always in the back of his mind. Now she'd agreed to taking their relationship to the next level, he couldn't wait for it to happen, but wait he must. Aaron had signed a lease on the townhouse but wouldn't be moving in until after Zack's visit. And while Ted was eagerly anticipating spending time with his grandson, he was also counting the days till he was on his own again.

He looked at the new surfboard leaning against the wall in the hallway, designed to be the first thing Zack saw when he walked in. Will Rankin's son, Owen, had done well in the surfing championships the previous year and had used his winnings to set up a workshop to manufacture boards, complementing his father's surf school. He was an enterprising young man who was already making a mark for himself with his designer boards which were now sought after by surfers from as far away as Western Australia. This one for Zack was one of his premier designs.

Ted had completed all his chores and was wondering if there was time to work on his current painting – one he was doing from memory of Zack on a surfboard – when he heard a car stop outside, followed by footsteps and voices.

'Hello there.' Ted opened the door to see Zack heading towards him. The boy had grown since Easter and would soon be as tall as he was, but he still hugged his grandad.

'It's good to be back,' he said, pulling away and running inside only to stop at the sight of the surfboard. 'Wow! That's a beauty.' He went over to stroke the smooth surface. 'Bet you go good on this one, Grandpa.'

'It's for you, Zack. Thought you might like one of your own this holiday. Save you hiring one from Will.'

'For me? Really? Wow!'

Aaron came in behind him carrying his bag. 'Forgot this, Zack?'

'Sorry, Dad. Did you see what Grandpa Teddy got for me? Can we go surfing this afternoon?'

'Maybe not today, Zack,' Ted said, smiling at his enthusiasm, 'but if you get up early tomorrow morning, I'll take you out.'

'Wow!' Zack couldn't seem to say anything else.

'Have trouble getting away?' Ted asked Aaron while Zack was settling into his room.

'The usual,' Aaron said, frowning. 'Though I got the feeling Mark was glad to see him go. Zack was pretty quiet on the drive up. There's something bugging him, but I couldn't get him to open up. He became a different person when he saw that surfboard. Good idea, Dad.'

'I got my first surfboard when I was his age. I'll never forget the thrill of it. It's something you missed out on. I regret that.'

'I had other things.'

'True, but there's nothing like the excitement of your first board.'

Zack joined them in the kitchen, but he couldn't resist stroking the board again first as he walked past.

'Coke, Zack?' Ted asked. 'And I got some of those chocolate biscuits you liked so much last time.'

'Tim Tams. Now I know I'm on holiday. Thanks, Grandpa.'

Instead of the surf Zack wanted, after a snack they took a walk up the boardwalk to the headland where Ted pointed out the wilder beach on the other side. 'Once we get you more confident, we'll have a go out there.'

'Really?' Zack gazed out at the small group of experienced surfers sitting on their boards waiting for the next big wave.

Ted chuckled at his enthusiasm. He was looking forward to having Zack's company for the next couple of weeks.

They were on their way back down when they met Grace and Mel on their way up. Ted's heart rose at the sight of the woman he was fast falling in love with. 'Fancy meeting you here,' he said.

'This must be your grandson.' Grace nodded to Zack.

'Zack,' Ted confirmed.

'Hi, Zack. I'm a friend of your grandad. I live along here, too.'

'Hi,' Zack muttered, head down.

'And this is my daughter, Mel.'

'Mel's a friend of mine,' Aaron said, before Zack could respond.

Zack looked at Mel, his eyes dropping to her stomach. 'Oh!' he said. 'Hello.'

Ted could see something was worrying him. He waited till they were back home then asked, 'Something the matter, son?'

Zack shook his head then threw himself down on the sofa. 'Your friend,' he said to Aaron. 'She's having a baby, isn't she? You won't want me anymore either.' He knuckled away the tears which were forming.

'What do you mean? It's not my baby. And, even if it was, why wouldn't I want *you*?'

There was no reply. The boy's chest heaved.

'It's your mum, isn't it?' Ted asked. 'She's having a baby.' His eyes met Aaron's over Zack's head.

Aaron shook his head and mouthed, 'She didn't say.'

'Listen to us, Zack.' Ted crouched down beside his grandson and gently pried his hands away from his eyes. 'Your dad and I love you. Nothing can change that. We'll always want you. Now, why don't you tell us why you think we won't?'

'You're right. Mum's having a baby. They don't think I know, but I heard her and Mark talking. He wants me to board at school, says Mum won't have time to take care of me and a baby. I don't need taken care of. I'm twelve. I can't face becoming a boarder. It would all get worse.'

Ted met Aaron's eyes, seeing his own anger reflected there.

It was Aaron who spoke. 'I won't let that happen, Zack. You can come and live with me.'

'But... Mum...' Zack blinked.

'I don't give a damn what your mum will say, or what she might think. You're not going to board at a school in Brisbane when you can live here with me, if I can help it. I'll speak with her, take it to court if necessary.'

Zack's eyes brightened. 'Really, Dad? You'd do that?'

Ted felt tears come to *his* eyes. Aaron was finally taking a stand. He was proud of him. It was high time he stood up to Tanya, but he hoped it wouldn't come to a court battle. He'd seen too many of those in his days as a solicitor. They never ended well and often it was the child who suffered.

Thirty-five

The next week passed uneventfully for Grace. She rarely saw Ted and, when she did, he had his grandson with him. Zack seemed a nice boy, eager to please and clearly very fond of his grandfather, but she often saw a cloud in his eyes. A quiet word with Ted revealed a challenge with his mother and stepfather which Ted was sure could be resolved, but Grace could tell it worried Ted, too.

Children! The problems never seemed to cease. At least her three were settled now.

She was feeling jubilant. A class of primary children had come to the library today and with the teacher's permission and her heart in her mouth, Grace had taken the opportunity to read them the first few chapters of her book. They'd loved it, clamouring for more before the teacher insisted it was time to return to school, but not before they'd extracted a promise from her to read more on their next visit.

'Just think, Tige,' she said to her cat when she walked in, 'they really liked what I've written.' She picked up her pet and danced around the kitchen before he leapt out of her arms and ran off to hide in a corner. Grace laughed. She was filling the electric jug to make herself a cup of tea and wondering how soon she could call Ted to share her good news, when the front door opened.

'You're back early, Mel,' she yelled. 'I'm making tea. Want a cup?'

But it wasn't Mel who answered her.

'It's me, Mum.' Ben walked into the kitchen. He hadn't shaved and looked as if he hadn't showered for days either.

Grace knew he often went like this for days on a dig, but he was always fastidious about his appearance when he came home.

'Ben, darling. What's wrong?' She tried to hug him, but he moved away. 'Tea? Coffee?'

'Coffee.' His voice was flat and lifeless.

Silently, Grace prepared tea for herself and coffee for Ben. Then she popped a few brownies on a plate. She'd picked them up on her way home in a mood of celebration.

Ben took his mug of coffee through to the living room and slumped onto the sofa, his head back, his eyes closed.

Grace took a seat opposite and sat watching him for a few moments. She'd never seen Ben like this. He was normally full of life, the happiest and most content of her three children. She waited.

Gradually, he opened his eyes and took a gulp of coffee. 'Thanks, Mum.' He fell silent again.

'I won't ask, but I'll listen if you want to talk.' It took all of Grace's patience to say this. She was desperate to know what ailed him, what had turned her happy-go-lucky son into this zombie-like figure.

Finally, Ben looked across at her. 'It's Gemma. She's gone.' He took another gulp of coffee.

She should have guessed. Grace's heart went out to him. He wasn't the first to suffer heartache and he wouldn't be the last, but it didn't make it any easier to bear. From somewhere in the back of her mind, Ruby Sullivan's words came back to her – something about her son and heartache. A bolt of anger shot through Grace – anger with Gemma for hurting Ben and anger with Ruby for predicting it. How did the woman know?

'Gone? Gone where?' she asked.

'She and another teacher. They've gone to teach in East Timor.' He banged his mug down on the arm of the chair, some of the liquid overflowing. 'I don't understand her, Mum. I thought… I wanted… I was going to ask her to marry me. But not content with working with groups of aboriginal children here in Queensland, she's decided she can do more good by going off to work in a developing country. She must have been planning this for some time. She had to apply, arrange a visa, etcetera. I bet she knew, even when she was here.'

'Oh, Ben.' Grace shared Ben's frustration. She'd known he was smitten with the girl, but hadn't realised how far it had gone, though she had hoped. Now those hopes were dashed. There was no use telling him he was better off without her and he'd meet someone else. He was still too wounded for that conversation.

They were still sitting in silence when Mel burst in. 'I saw Ben's car. Oh!' She stopped in the doorway, sensing something was wrong.

Grace rose and, taking Mel by the arm, led her away, closing the door behind them. Ben didn't appear to notice them leave.

'What's up?' Mel asked, when they reached the kitchen. 'Ben looks awful. Is he sick?'

'Gemma's left him.'

'Huh! Know what that feels like. At least he's not pregnant.'

'Mel!'

'Sorry, but it's different for a guy. I suppose he's devastated and thinks he'll never get over it?'

'I suppose so.' Grace sighed. 'He hasn't said much, only that she's gone to teach in East Timor.'

'I thought she was a bit odd when she was here.'

'You did?' Grace recalled her own misgivings. 'In what way?'

'Dunno, but there was something. Anyway, how was the library? Weren't you going to read your book to some kids this morning? How did it go?'

Grace was immediately reminded of her earlier feelings of accomplishment, and how she'd risked Mel's ridicule to share her ambitions with her over breakfast. To her surprise, Mel had been encouraging. She smiled. 'They loved it.' Her forehead creased. 'But I'm worried about your brother. I've never seen him so down.'

'He'll get over it. Now, I'm going to have a shower. Don't make dinner for me. I'm going to the surf club with Aaron and Zack. He's a good kid. Isn't having an easy time of it with his mum and stepdad.' Mel became serious for a moment. 'I hope Aaron manages to get custody. He's planning on going to Brisbane to talk with his ex on the weekend.' She picked up one of the brownies Grace had left lying on the table and wandered off.

Grace sighed again. She was conflicted. She dearly wanted to talk with Ted, but needed to spend time with Ben, to try to bring him out of his depression. As her mind filled with possible ways to help him, she set to preparing dinner.

Ben was quiet during their meal, but he did manage to eat some of the salmon bake Grace had cooked. It was one of his favourite dishes, but he made no comment whereas he would normally have praised her. He even refused the glass of wine Grace offered. Surprised, she poured one for herself, needing something to sustain her.

They had finished eating, and Grace was contemplating another awkward silence until bedtime, when there was a gentle knock on the glass door leading out to the deck, and she saw Ted's face peering in.

Grace's heart leapt. How did he know she wanted – no, needed – his presence to break the painful situation?

'Who is it?' Ben asked, the first words he'd spoken since they sat down.

'It's Ted,' she said, her relief evident in her voice. 'I'll let him in.'

Ted hesitated in the doorway. 'Oh, I didn't know your son was here. Aaron said he and Zack were going to the club with Mel and I thought you'd be alone. I can leave.'

'No, please come in. A glass of wine?'

'Thanks. Hello, Ben. Good to see you again,'

Ben merely grunted.

Ted met Grace's eyes. She shook her head.

Ben stood up. 'I'm off to bed. Same room as last time?'

'Yes, you'll find a towel in the linen closet and…'

'Don't fuss, Mum. I'm not an invalid.' Ben strode out.

Grace watched him go, wishing she could wrap him up in a blanket and keep him safe, like she did when he was a baby. But he was a twenty-eight-year-old man and had to find his own way of dealing with this.

'Woman trouble?' Ted asked, when they heard the bedroom door slam shut.

'How did you guess?'

'Been there with Aaron. At least your son isn't married with a child.'

'True.' Though the thought had passed through her mind.

It was so comforting to have Ted here, someone who understood her grief and the sense of helplessness in the face of her son's despair.

'Your glass is empty.'

Grace looked at it. She didn't remember drinking the wine. Her plate was empty, too, but Ben had only eaten a few mouthfuls, moving the rest around his plate like he did as a little boy when he didn't want her to know he wasn't eating.

'Refill?' Ted picked up the bottle of shiraz.

'Thanks. I'll get you a glass.'

'I know where they are.' Ted filled her glass then went to the cupboard for another and filled it, too, before joining her at the table.

'Want to talk about it?'

'Not really. I've never seen Ben so down. He's always been the level-headed one, the one nothing could bother, the one I could rely on.'

'He'll get over it,' Ted said, echoing Mel.

'I know, but it'll be tough for him for a while. I wish there was something I could do to help.' She sighed.

'You're here for him. That's enough. Drink your wine and be grateful.'

'Grateful?'

'Didn't you tell me your older daughter was pregnant? You'll have two grandchildren to love and indulge. Isn't that something to be grateful for?'

'You're right. What about you? What do you have to be grateful for?'

'I have a healthy son and grandson who, with a bit of luck, will soon be living close to me.' He took a gulp of wine. 'Aaron's going down to Brisbane on the weekend to talk with his ex, Zack's mother. With a bit of luck, he'll manage to persuade her to let the boy live with him – avoid a nasty custody battle.'

'You think she'll agree?'

'This time, I think she might, if only to placate her new husband. Mark's never been keen on Zack and now he'll have a child of his own, I believe he'll be delighted to be shot of him.'

'I hope so, for your sake and Zack's. Mel says he's a good kid.'

'Mmm.'

They sat in companionable silence for several minutes, sipping wine, each thinking about their children and how strange life was.

Grace looked across at Ted. She wanted to feel his arms around her, comforting her. But she was conscious of Ben lying upstairs, of Mel about to arrive home.

Seeming to read her mind, Ted drained his glass. 'I should leave.

You have enough going on without me here to complicate things. Just remember what I told you. I'm here for you and, once Aaron moves out…'

A warm glow suffused Grace. He was such a good man. He'd made no attempt to rush her, waiting patiently till she was ready for a more intimate relationship. And now she was ready, their grown children seemed fated to put a spanner in the works. But their time would come, and it would be soon.

Thirty-six

'What do you think Mum will say, Grandpa?' Zack kicked the leg of the table, his eyes downcast.

Aaron had left early that morning, driving off just as the sun was rising, intent on catching Tanya and Mark before they had time to start their Saturday morning activities. From what Zack had told him, he knew they had a Saturday morning routine – a trip to the farmers' markets, then a visit to the gym.

'We can only hope and pray, Zack,' Ted said, taking a drink of coffee and grimacing to discover it had gone cold.

'Pray, Grandpa? I didn't think you went to church?'

'I don't, son. Never had much time for God, but it doesn't do any harm and it might help. But it won't do any good to sit here and worry. What say we see if we can catch one of the whale-watching cruises? I read they were starting this weekend.'

'Whale watching? Really? I've read about how the whales travel north to mate. Will we really be able to see them?'

'It's not guaranteed, but I understand you can often see acrobatic displays fairly close up.'

'Sick!'

'We'll just get cleared up here first, and you should make sure you're well wrapped up. It'll be cold out on the water.'

'Dad said if I can live with him, his friend might take us out on his boat sometimes. Maybe I can learn to sail, too.' He looked wistful.

'Maybe you can.' Ted wished he could reassure Zack, but it all depended on how flexible Tanya was prepared to be – or how willing Mark was to let go. Despite his apparent dislike of Zack, he seemed to enjoy maintaining his authority over him.

While Zack was donning a warm sweater and looking out his weatherproof jacket, it occurred to Ted to wonder how Grace was. He picked up his phone and pressed the speed dial for her number.

'Just checking in on my favourite lady,' he said when she answered. 'How's Ben today?'

'Still in bed.' Her voice was flat. He guessed she hadn't slept much.

'I have an idea. Zack and I are planning to go whale watching this morning. Why don't you join us – Ben too?'

'Whale watching? You can do that here?'

'A local guy – Mick Roberts – set it up a few years ago. Seems to do well in the season which is starting this weekend. You up for it?' Now he had made the suggestion, Ted was hoping Grace would agree.

'I don't know… Ben…'

'It would do him good, take his mind off things.'

'You think so? Wait a minute…' There was a pause, then, 'I think I hear him stirring. Can I call you back?'

'If you make it quick. We need to leave soon.'

'I will – and thanks.'

Ted could hear the smile in Grace's voice. He was glad he'd made the call.

*

'When are we going?' Zack shuffled his feet impatiently.

Ted checked the time. They'd need to leave, and Grace hadn't called back. Perhaps it hadn't been such a good idea after all. He stared at his phone willing it to ring, but it remained persistently silent.

'Who's that?'

Ted looked up to see two figures standing at the gate. Grace had a smile on her face, but Ben looked as if he'd prefer to be somewhere else, anywhere else. He was eating a slice of toast.

'I thought it'd be quicker if we just came,' Grace said. 'Glad we caught you.'

'Zack, you've met Grace Winter. This is her son Ben, Mel's brother.'

'I know who they are. Can we go now?'

'Sorry to hold you up,' Grace said. 'Hello, Zack. Good to see you again.'

Zack grunted.

'Sorry.' Ted rolled his eyes and grinned. He was delighted to see Grace.

They were an odd group, Ted thought, as they made their way down to where the cruise ship was berthed – a couple who many would call elderly, accompanied by an excited twelve-year-old and a bored young man who looked as if he hadn't slept – or washed – for a week. Perhaps he hadn't. Ted tried to make conversation with Ben on the way but, after a few fruitless attempts, he gave up and focussed on Grace and Zack.

At the terminal, they managed to buy tickets and were soon off on what Zack clearly considered to be an adventure.

There wasn't much to see as the boat made its way out to sea, but the skipper kept everyone entertained with an informative commentary on the habits of the humpback whales who, each year after a summer of feeding on krill in Antarctic waters, migrate north to sub-tropical waters where they mate and give birth, often travelling distances of up to 10,000 kilometres.

Zack was standing at the rail, gazing out to sea while Ted, Grace and Ben were seated in one of the rows of seats along with several other passengers.

Suddenly, Zack yelled, 'Look, there's one! Grandpa, I can see a whale!'

His yell brought others to join him at the rail including to Ted and Grace's surprise, Ben, who emerged sufficiently from his despair to show some interest in the marine creature.

Ted and Grace followed more slowly, Grace clasping Ted's arm in delight at the sight of the antics of several whales who were frolicking and breeching close to the ship.

'Thanks for inviting us,' Grace said, the wind almost whipping her words away. She looked so youthful and excited, her eyes glowing with pleasure, that Ted wanted to pull her into his arms and kiss her over and over again. But he had to be content with putting his hand over hers and squeezing it.

She gazed up at him and smiled, a smile filled with so much affection he felt breathless.

'Thanks, Ted,' Ben said, when they reached the wharf again. 'I needed this. Seeing these magnificent creatures… it helps put things in perspective. Thanks, Mum. I didn't want to come along, but I enjoyed it.'

'Lunch?' Ted asked, unwilling to lose the companionship they'd established.

'Can we go to Maccas?' Zack asked, still filled with the exhilaration of the trip.

Ted looked at Grace and Ben, a question in his eyes. It wouldn't have been his first choice of venue.

'Why not?' Grace said. 'Ben?'

'Sure.' Ben seemed to have withdrawn into melancholy again. But at least the whales had drawn him out of it for a time, Ted thought. It was a start. He remembered how Aaron had been when Tanya told him about Mark. He hadn't got out of bed for days, hadn't spoken even, then suddenly, he'd realised life had to go on. He had a job and a son who loved him. It would be the same for Ben, he was sure.

They were sitting in McDonald's – Ted, Ben and Zack were eating Big Macs while Grace had chosen a chicken burger; the three adults had ordered coffee, Zack a Coke – when Ted's phone rang.

'Is it Dad?' Zack asked, his mouth full of burger.

For once, Ted didn't tell him not to speak with his mouth full. He checked his phone and nodded before accepting the call.

'Aaron?' There was a rendering of Happy Birthday from a group at the next table preventing Ted from hearing his son's voice. 'Just a moment.' He gestured to the others and went outside.

'Sorry, we're having lunch at McDonald's. I couldn't hear. What's happened?'

'She's agreed, Dad. Zack can stay.' Aaron's voice broke.

'Oh, son, I'm so glad.' It was as if a huge weight had been lifted.

'Tanya wasn't keen at first. She put up all sorts of excuses – school, his friends, how she'd miss him. I thought she was going to refuse totally. But it was Mark who changed her mind.'

Ted nodded, not surprised.

'He reminded her how difficult it would be for her – them – to have a twelve-year-old and a young baby in the house, said a lot of rubbish about how demanding Zack was. But he persuaded her in the end. I have most of Zack's stuff in the car. Mark couldn't wait to be rid of it. He helped me pack.'

Ted frowned. He was glad Zack wouldn't have to stay where he wasn't wanted, but how could his stepfather be so eager to have him leave? 'So, you'll be on your way back?'

'Setting out now. I'll see you for dinner.'

'Do you want to speak to Zack?'

'If he's there.'

'Hold on.' Ted went back inside and handed the phone to Zack. 'Your dad wants to speak to you. Best take it outside.' He joined Grace and Ben at the table and pushed the remains of his burger away.

'Good news?' Grace asked.

'The best. Aaron's on his way back with Zack's belongings in his car.'

'Oh, I'm so glad. You've met Aaron, Zack's dad,' Grace said to Ben. 'Zack's been living with his mum and stepdad and hasn't been happy.' She turned back to Ted. 'He must be thrilled. You, too,'

Ted grinned.

Thirty-seven

It had been a whirlwind two weeks. First there had been the news about Ted's grandson, resulting in a mad rush to have him enrolled in Bellbird State College, the same school Ted had attended almost fifty years earlier. Then Ben seemed to reenergise himself and went back up north, vowing he was finished with women.

Lou still hadn't been to see her doctor, arguing her own doctor was on holiday and she was waiting till she got back. But she claimed she was sure she was pregnant as she was exhibiting all the symptoms. Grace wasn't happy, but Lou had always been a law unto herself.

The other thing was that only a few days earlier, Aaron and Zack had moved into the townhouse Aaron had leased, and Ted was on his own again.

This was probably the most momentous of the things that had happened, and Grace wasn't sure how she felt about it – and about what it meant for her relationship with Ted.

It was all very well to agree to take their relationship to the next stage when the next stage was off somewhere in the future. But now it was here, it was a daunting prospect. When she was with Ted, Grace ached to be closer to him, but making love to him was a different matter. Russ was the only man she'd been with, both innocents, learning about love together, and it had been years since she'd shared a bed. Ted said it had been a long time for him, too, but it was different for a man, wasn't it?

And there was her sixty-one-year-old body. While Ted had seen her in a swimsuit, the lycra outfit with the reinforced stomach panel hid a multitude of sins. She'd seen his almost naked body – the male swim gear left nothing to the imagination – and he had the physique of a twenty-year-old. How would he react to her flabby skin, stretch marks and age spots? What would he think? Would he be repelled?

Tonight was the night, and they'd agreed to go out to dinner before returning to Ted's for *afterwards*. Grace was a bag of nerves as she showered, then tried to decide on what to wear. She had an empty feeling in the pit of her stomach, her mouth was dry, and she couldn't imagine how she was going to manage to eat dinner.

After selecting and discarding several outfits, she finally settled on a soft blue wool dress Russ used to tell her was the colour of her eyes. Then she brushed her hair into its usual style and applied light make up, finishing with her favourite pink lipstick. When she examined herself in the mirror, she saw an outwardly elegant, confident woman. Her anxiety was well-hidden.

She was just ready when she heard a knock at the door. Taking a deep breath, she picked up her bag and popped her head into the living room where Mel was engrossed in watching some reality television show, a bowl of potato chips on her lap. 'I'm off now. I may be late.' She felt like a teenager going on her first date.

'Okay.' Mel didn't look round. 'I'll most likely be in bed. I can't stay awake late these days.'

Grace smiled. Mel was in for a rude awakening once the baby was born. She slipped out of the house.

*

The meal at *The Beach House* should have been delicious, but it could have been made of cardboard as far as Grace was concerned, though the Elephant in the Room Pinot Noir which accompanied it – an appropriately named wine for the occasion, Grace thought – did help calm the fluttering in her stomach.

Ted was kindness itself, telling her about Aaron's new home and Zack's first week in his new school which he was enjoying immensely, having found some kindred spirits who enjoyed surfing, and he'd joined the chess club. He enquired about Ben's return to the dig, whether or not Lou had consulted her doctor, and if Mel had settled on a name for the baby. It was all very civilised, designed to put Grace at ease, but she couldn't help wondering if she was making a mistake.

When they got back to Ted's house and he put the key into the door, Grace was tempted to turn and run, run back down the road to the safety of her own house. But she didn't. She followed Ted in, then stood awkwardly in the middle of the kitchen. It was all too cold-blooded. Where was the passion, the spontaneity? Were they going to go straight to the bedroom, or make more small talk? She just wanted to get it over with.

Sensing her uneasiness, Ted went to the fridge. 'I thought you might enjoy a glass of bubbly on the deck. It's a lovely evening and not too cool. Why don't I fetch a throw and we can sit outside and watch the stars?'

Relieved, Grace went outside. Ted dragged two chairs together, pulled the grey throw around their knees, then handed her a glass of sparkling wine.

It was peaceful, sitting there in the moonlight, drinking wine and gazing up at the stars. Grace's nerves began to disappear to be replaced by a sense of anticipation and excitement.

When Ted reached over to remove her glass and take her hand, Grace felt a flash of the desire she'd felt several times before in his company. With one hand in hers, his other snaked around her shoulders, their lips met. It seemed so natural, her fears disappearing as her limbs turned to jelly and a fierce passion surged between them.

*

Grace opened her eyes and turned to look at the man who had changed her life, made her feel desirable again. Making love with Ted had been more than she could have imagined, much more. She'd never expected anyone to find her aging body beautiful, but Ted's words and actions forced her to accept that, to him, she was. Their lovemaking had been a revelation. She gazed into his eyes wondering why she had been afraid, why they had waited so long.

'Happy?' he asked.

'Mmm. Very.' She kissed him, the touch of his lips reminding her of the passion they'd shared.

The sky outside the window was turning light, reminding her she hadn't intended to fall asleep, to stay all night. 'I need to go.' She pushed herself into a sitting position only to find Ted's legs wound around hers.

'Must you?' Ted stroked her arm, the touch of his fingers sending tingles of delight through her body.

Who would have thought she could have felt like this again?

But she had to get home before Mel woke and realised Grace had been out all night. She made a determined effort to rise, and this time managed to extricate herself sufficiently to put her feet on the floor and get out of bed.

Dressing in the half-light, Grace felt like the woman in a movie she'd once seen, in which the woman left her lover in bed to return home to her husband. But Grace was returning home to her daughter, and Ted was getting up and pulling on a pair of jeans and a sweater.

'I'll walk down with you.'

'There's no need.'

'But I'd like to.'

They walked down the boardwalk together hand-in-hand, Grace scarcely able to believe what had happened between them. It was quiet in this time between night and morning, before the day began, the only sound the waves pounding on the shore.

'Thanks,' Ted said, pulling her to him for a farewell kiss, a kiss which seemed even sweeter than those they'd shared before their night together. 'See you again soon.'

Grace nodded and crept into the house, closing the door quietly behind her and slipping off her shoes to avoid disturbing Mel who was a light sleeper. Reaching her bedroom, she threw herself on the bed, her face splitting into a wide grin at the memory of how Ted had made her feel, how all her fears had been baseless and how she couldn't wait to see him again.

Thirty-eight

Ted had a smile on his face as he packed away his painting gear for another day. He hadn't stopped smiling since he and Grace had consummated their relationship almost two weeks earlier. He had to admit – if only to himself – he'd worried about how it would go. He was no spring chicken – nor was Grace – but he'd worried needlessly. All went well and since then, they'd repeated the performance several times. Each time, it got better and better. Ted could scarcely believe it.

He was still thinking about Grace and working out when he could see her again – she sometimes found it difficult to get away – when he heard a voice at the door leading in from the deck.

'Grandpa Teddy?'

'Zack!'

Was it that time already? Since settling into his new school, Zack had taken to calling in on Ted some days when he had no after-school activities. The young boy would cycle over to his grandfather's, eager for a game of chess or to share some of the day's events with him. It brought a lump to Ted's throat to think Zack wanted to spend time with him when he could be with his mates.

'What's up, son?' he asked, seeing Zack's eyes clouded.

'Can we talk?'

'Sure.' Ted fetched a can of Coke for Zack and a beer for himself and carried them into the living room where the chess set was already set up waiting for them.

But today, Zack ignored the board, focussing instead on fiddling with his phone. He didn't speak.

Ted waited, knowing Zack would tell him what was bothering him when he was ready.

'It's Mum,' he said at last, looking up to meet Ted's eyes. 'The baby… there's two of them… twins.' His mouth twisted into a wry grin. 'I'm going to have two little brothers or sisters… or one of each, I suppose. She won't love me anymore.'

Ted thought for a few moments before replying. In his opinion, Tanya had never given Zack the attention he needed. He wasn't sure how she would cope with two young children, but perhaps Mark would take charge. 'Does it upset you?' he asked.

'I don't know.' Zack rubbed his eyes. 'She rang just as I was leaving school. She sounded excited. And she said Mark was ecstatic. He would be. He never had any time for me.' He grimaced. 'What I can't understand is why it has to take over her life, why she and Mark wanted me to board at school. Dad's friend Mel is pregnant and she's still able to spend time with Dad… and me. She's cool.'

Ted chuckled inwardly. 'Game of chess?' he asked, gesturing to the board.

'Okay.' Having got the news about his mum off his chest, Zack appeared happier.

After a hard-won game, Ted gave a rueful grin. 'You're getting better. You'll be beating me soon.'

'You taught me well, Grandpa.'

Ted smiled, thinking back to the days when he'd used chess to draw out his shy grandson – that and surfing. Now they were Zack's favourite hobbies.

'Are you staying for dinner? I can ring your dad.'

'No, better get back. I've a lot of homework to do, and Mel's coming to dinner.' He hesitated for several moments. 'Grandpa, Dad sees Mel a lot. Do you think he'll get married again? I mean, if it was to Mel, I don't think I'd mind, even if there is going to be a baby. It wouldn't be like Mum and Mark.'

Ted had wondered when this would come up. Aaron was seeing a lot of Mel. Both of them insisted they were only friends, but it didn't look that way. 'I don't know, son. They're good mates. Who can say what might happen in the future? I imagine Mel will find everything changes when her baby is born.'

'Why does everyone have to have babies?' Zack made a face. 'Noisy, messy creatures.'

'You were one once,' Ted reminded him with a grin.

'I guess.' Zack gave such a heartfelt sigh it was all Ted could do to stop himself laughing out loud. Instead, he cleared his throat.

Tanya and Mark had a lot to answer for. But Zack was going to be okay.

Thirty-nine

Grace stretched her arms above her head as the sun streamed in through her bedroom window. It was going to be another glorious day and she was feeling full of energy. Her thoughts went back to the previous evening when she and Ted had managed a few hours together. Mel had been out with Aaron again – something which was becoming a common occurrence, though she still insisted they were only friends – and she and Ted decided to make the most of the opportunity to be together without awkward questions being asked.

This wasn't one of her days at the library, and she planned to spend it editing her book again, then she and Ted were meeting for lunch – a perfect day.

Mel was already eating breakfast when Grace wandered into the kitchen. 'Morning, sweetheart. Sleep well?' she asked.

'Not really. I don't seem to be able to get comfortable. I'll be glad when it's over and Isla is finally here.'

'You've settled on Isla, have you?'

'I think so.' After choosing and discarding several possible names, Mel had recently watched a rerun of *The Great Gatsby* on television and had decided to call her baby Isla after Isla Fisher. 'Isla Winter sounds good, don't you think?'

'I do,' Grace said, repeating what she'd already said about Chloe Winter, Jacinta Winter and various other combinations.

'Good.' Mel seemed satisfied. 'Aaron thinks so, too.' She gave a secret smile which raised Grace's antenna. Was there more to this friendship with Aaron?

*

Grace was engrossed in her editing, lost in the world she'd created, when she was pulled out of it by her phone ringing. She was tempted to ignore it until she remembered this was the day of Lou's doctor's appointment. She picked it up, smiling when she saw her daughter's number. 'Hi, Lou,' she said, expecting to hear her daughter bubbling over with good news. Instead, there was an initial silence. 'Lou?' she repeated.

'Mum!' Lou's voice sounded strange, strangled.

Grace's heart plummeted; her throat tightened. *Wasn't she pregnant after all?* 'What is it, Lou? What did the doctor say?'

Lou's voice sounded as if it was coming from the end of a tunnel. 'I'm not pregnant, Mum. She wants me to have more tests. I… I might have ovarian cancer.'

Grace's hand gripped the phone tighter. Cancer? It couldn't be true. This was Lou, the daughter who was always telling Grace about how healthy her diet was, the daughter who went to the gym on a regular basis, the daughter who… It must be a mistake. 'Oh, my darling. Tell me exactly what she said.'

Half an hour later, Grace put down her phone, her face wet with tears. Lou had been crying too before the call ended, seemingly more devastated by the fact she wasn't pregnant than by the possible cancer diagnosis. It seemed the doctor wanted Lou to have a biopsy to confirm her diagnosis, then there would most probably be surgery to remove the tumour.

Grace rose unsteadily and made her way to the kitchen where she stared out the window, but was unable to see the view, her eyes still blurred with tears. She couldn't think straight. Her Lou had cancer. Although it had still to be confirmed, Grace knew the doctor would never have mentioned the C word if she'd been in any doubt. Thank goodness Greg had been with Lou. They were both in shock. Sensing her distress, Tiger was winding himself around Grace's ankles and purring loudly.

A tap on the glass door brought Grace back to the present. She focussed her eyes to see Ted's cheerful face. It must be lunchtime. To think, only a few hours ago, she'd been looking forward to enjoying lunch with him, without a care in the world. She opened the door.

Ted greeted her with his customary kiss on the cheek, then held her at arm's length. 'What's wrong? You look as if you've seen a ghost.'

'I'm sorry, Ted. I've had bad news. I don't feel like lunch.' In fact, Grace felt sick. She thought she might throw up if she had to sit in a café, make conversation, pretend to be cheerful, and eat something.

'Come and have a seat and tell me what's happened.'

Grace allowed herself to be led into the living room.

When they were both seated, Ted asked again, 'What's happened? Is it Mel?'

Grace shook her head. 'Lou.' She began to cry again, her body wracked with sobs.

Ted took her in his arms and rocked her like a baby, patting her back and murmuring, 'There, there,' till she calmed down. Then he found a tissue and patted her eyes and cheeks. 'Now, are you able to tell me what's wrong?'

'It's Lou,' Grace hiccupped. 'She's not pregnant.' Then she repeated the conversation and what Lou had told her. 'I can't believe it,' she said finally. 'Not Lou; she's always been so health-conscious.'

'Oh, Grace, I'm so sorry.' Ted hugged her and buried his face in her hair. His nearness was comforting but did nothing to alleviate Grace's fears.

'I'm sorry about lunch,' she said, sniffing.

'Forget lunch. But you should eat. You'll feel better with something in your stomach. Let me fix something.'

Grace watched as Ted went to the kitchen. As if in a dream, she heard cupboard doors open and close, then there was silence till he returned with a tray containing two mugs and a plate of crusty bread thickly buttered. 'I don't think…' she began, but the enticing aroma of chicken soup was rising from the mugs. It reminded Grace of her mother's remedy when she felt sick as a child. Taking the mug Ted handed her, she clasped it in both hands and took a sip.

Ted was right. The soup did make her feel a little better, but it didn't change anything. Lou was still sick, and she was miles away in Sydney. For the first time, Grace wished she hadn't been so determined, so pig-headed as to follow her own dreams and move to Bellbird Bay. Perhaps if she'd been there, in Sydney, she could have…

Sensing her thoughts, Ted said, 'There was nothing you could have done, even if you'd been living closer.'

But it didn't stop Grace feeling guilty.

'What are you going to do?'

Do? Grace couldn't think straight, never mind make any plans. She needed to tell Mel and Ben… and Dot, who'd be devastated, too. She and Kev had only recently returned from their trip earlier than anticipated, citing difficulties with their motor home but giving no details. Grace didn't know how she was going to deal with all their reactions.

'One thing at a time,' Ted said, the voice of reason.

Grace wanted to cling on to him and never let go. But she couldn't expect him to tell people for her. Lou wasn't part of *his* family. 'I need to tell…' She began to rise then fell back into her seat again.

'Shall I call Dot?' Ted asked.

'Please.' Her sister might have a lot of faults, but she was good in a crisis, and she loved Lou. Both Mel and Ben were at work. Grace didn't want to disturb them, and Mel needed to stay calm for the baby. Grace felt tears come to her eyes again and blinked them away.

Dot arrived in a flurry of concern, and Grace was happy to see her. 'Poor Lou,' Dot wailed as soon as she arrived, but she soon pulled herself together.

'It's Lou who needs your concern, not me,' Grace objected, as Dot rushed around making a hot toddy and suggesting Grace lie down. But she was grateful for her sister's fussing, knowing if she was left alone, she'd fall apart, imagining the worst.

'I'll go now,' Ted said, unwilling to show Grace affection in Dot's presence but his eyes were filled with what Grace recognised as love, even if the word had never been mentioned between them.

Forty

Two days later there was another call from Sydney. It was Greg this time, to let Grace know Lou's surgery had been scheduled for the following Monday. They talked a bit about how Lou was coping – not very well – and how Greg had arranged to take time off work. By the time Grace ended the call she was in a quandary. She was sitting in the living room, gazing into space, absentmindedly stroking Tiger, when Mel came home from work.

'Is there news?' Mel asked, sitting down beside her mother, and scratching Tiger's ears. The cat purred with pleasure.

'Oh, Mel! Lou's surgery is on Monday.' Grace's eyes filled with tears, which she brushed away with her hand. 'Lou needs me in Sydney, but you need me here. I don't know what to do.'

'Don't worry about me. I'll be fine. There's Aunt Dot. She'll be in her element and on call if I need anything.'

Grace frowned, but it was true.

When Dot and Kev returned from their trip, it was clear to both Grace and Mel that they couldn't hide Mel's pregnancy from them any longer. They'd both been apprehensive when they called round to *Bay Village* to welcome the travellers back home. But, far from the critical reaction Grace had anticipated, in an unexpected show of affection, Dot had thrown her arms around an astonished Mel.

'Oh, my dear, I'm going to be a great-aunt,' she'd announced with delight, and almost immediately brought her sewing machine out of storage and begun to make tiny garments, determined Mel's baby would be the best-dressed in Bellbird Bay. Mel now had a growing pile of small outfits which wouldn't have disgraced a member of the royal family.

'And there's Aaron,' Mel said with a wicked grin.

Grace's head shot up. 'Aaron? But you said you were only friends.'

'We are… were, but lately it's become more than that. Seeing him with Zack. He's a good dad. He wants me to go to live with him after the baby's born. He's good with it.' She gave Grace a sideways glance. 'I did what you said. I emailed Jason and told him about the baby. I shouldn't have bothered. He was horrified, suggested it wasn't his, was terrified his wife might find out. He's a real shit. Isla and I'll be better without him.'

'Oh!' Grace collapsed into a chair. This was almost too much to cope with right now. She was in the process of working out how she could leave the life she'd made for herself here for an unknown length of time to be there for her older daughter in her time of need. Meanwhile her younger daughter was planning to shack up with the son of the man for whom she had developed feelings. Life played some strange jokes.

'Well, if you're sure.'

'I am. Lou needs you more than I do right now. Isla and I'll be fine.' Mel rubbed her stomach. 'It sounds as if she and Greg aren't coping very well.'

How did one cope well with a cancer diagnosis? Grace was on the verge of falling apart herself. But if Mel felt confident she could manage on her own here, it would leave Grace free to go to Sydney. 'Thanks, sweetheart. Though I don't know how long I'll be gone. It'll depend on…' She couldn't contemplate what the result of the surgery might be, how long Lou might need her. This was the first time Lou had ever really needed her, Grace reflected. She'd always been such a self-sufficient little girl, bossing her younger siblings around and refusing help, even when she found herself in difficulties.

'You'll keep me informed, let me know what's happening. I know we have our moments, but she's my big sister.'

Grace squeezed Mel's hand. 'I'll ring every day.' She put a protesting Tiger down on the floor and took out her phone. She should call Ted, let him know she was going to Sydney. She fingered the phone, then put it away again. This wasn't something to tell him on the phone. She needed to see him.

*

Ted was having a beer before deciding what to cook for dinner. Zack had dropped in for a game of chess but hadn't wanted to stay. Why should he? The young boy had more to do with his time than spend it with his grandfather. Ted was only grateful to welcome him for a game of chess from time to time, and a surf on the occasional weekend.

He was anticipating a quiet evening by himself and had checked out his evening's viewing. SBS were playing a rerun of the second series of *The Bridge* which he'd missed first time around, and he was looking forward to this week's episode. He'd have preferred to spend the evening with Grace but, since she'd learned of her daughter's diagnosis, she'd been unsettled, preferring to stay home with Mel. When he heard her familiar tap-tap on the door out to the deck, he rose quickly to let her in.

'Grace, this is a surprise – a pleasant one.' He took her in his arms, feeling her body melt into his, smelling the faint floral aroma which always surrounded her, and thought for what must have been the hundredth time how lucky he was to have found her – for them to have found each other. Because it seemed she felt the same way.

For several moments, Grace allowed herself to be enfolded in his embrace, her lips soft on his with the promise of further intimacy, then she pulled away.

Ted knew something was wrong. 'You've heard from Lou again?'

'Greg. Lou was too upset to speak to me. Her surgery is on Monday, Ted, and…'

'You're going to Sydney.' Ted said the words with an air of finality. He'd known all along she'd want to be with her daughter. It was only natural. He'd do the same if Aaron was sick. But it didn't make it any easier. 'When will you leave?'

'As soon as I can. I'll let the library know tomorrow. Mel can take care of Tige, and Dot will be there for Mel. The thing is…' she wrinkled her brow, '…I don't know when I'll be back. This has hit Lou – all of us – hard and she needs me.' She looked up at Ted, her eyes wide, pleading with him to understand.

'I understand. She's your daughter. You need to go to her.'

Released from his embrace, Grace seemed unable to remain still. She moved around the kitchen as if in a daze. 'I'm worried about Mel, too. I wish…'

Sensing she felt torn in two, Ted went over to Grace and took her in his arms again, holding her tightly against him. 'I'm sure you're doing the right thing. Now, why don't I pour us both a glass of wine? Have you eaten?'

'Yes. No. Oh, Ted, I don't know.'

Ted gently led Grace through to the living area and put her into a chair, before pouring them both a glass of wine. He waited till she'd taken a few sips then, 'Better now?'

'A little. Thanks.' She managed a watery smile.

'I was about to make myself a bite to eat.' He thought quickly about the narrow range of options in his cupboard; it was some time since he'd done a grocery shop. 'Could you eat an omelette?'

'I think so. Mel…' She tried to rise.

'I'll call Mel.'

Grace subsided into the chair again. 'Thanks.'

By the time the omelette was ready, and Ted had added buttered toast, Grace was looking slightly brighter. He topped up her glass and his own.

'You're too good to me.' Grace met Ted's eyes. Hers were filled with emotion.

Ted cleared his throat. Now wasn't the time to profess his love for Grace, much as he wanted to. But at least he could comfort her.

When they had finished eating, and Grace rose to go, Ted took her in his arms again. Suddenly, it was as if everything else faded into insignificance and they were two people alone in the world as their passion for each other took over and they were engulfed in a frenzy of desire.

Forty-one

Next day, everything moved like clockwork. Grace's manager at the library was very understanding, Dot agreed to keep an eye on Mel and be there if she needed her, and Grace was able to secure a seat on a plane to Sydney that afternoon.

Grace wasn't able to relax till she was on the plane, seeing the coastline disappearing below them. Shaking her head to the offer of drinks from the hostess, she leant her head back and closed her eyes, remembering her night spent with Ted. They'd made love before, but last night had been different. It was as if it might be the last time and they had to make it one to remember.

Grace shook her head and opened her eyes. How foolish. Of course, it wasn't the last time. But when Ted stroked her forehead and said sadly, 'I love you, Grace Winter. You're the best thing that's happened to me for a long, long time,' there had been a tear in his eye, and she had been filled with a strange sense of regret.

All too soon, they were descending into Sydney where Greg, who seemed to have aged ten years since she last saw him – grey streaks in his hair and lines around his mouth that weren't there before – was waiting for her with a hug.

'Lou decided to stay home,' he said, as they drove to the townhouse in Forest Lodge. 'She couldn't face the crowds at the airport.'

Grace's forehead creased. It didn't sound like Lou, who was a social animal and had always loved being in the centre of things. 'How is she?' she asked.

'Not good. She's worried about the surgery, worried they might do a hysterectomy and put paid to any chance of having a baby. I've told her it doesn't matter. Her health is the most important thing, more important than any baby, but you know what she's like.'

'Oh, dear!' Grace blinked back the tears. How she wished there was something she could do for her daughter, wished it was her who was sick. She'd had a good life. Lou was only in her thirties; she had lots of years ahead of her – or should have. Grace swallowed and prayed Lou would come through this safely.

'Hi, Mum.' More subdued than usual, Lou greeted Grace with a warm hug.

'Lou, my darling girl.' Grace returned the hug, then held her daughter at arm's length and examined the face which, only a few weeks ago would have been alight with happiness. Today it was white and drawn.

'Thanks for coming, Mum,' Lou sobbed, gripping Grace tightly.

Grace patted her daughter's shoulders as she used to when Lou was a child. It reminded her of Ted doing the same to her. She dismissed the memory. She needed to focus on Lou now.

The townhouse was as cramped as Grace had imagined. A combined living and dining area backed onto a tiny kitchen which looked out onto a paved courtyard in which sat a round, white wrought iron table and matching chairs. A series of plant pots had been placed around the edges in an attempt to provide some colour, but today none were in bloom. To one side of the living area, a steep narrow stairway led up to what Grace could only suppose were the bedrooms.

'I'll show you your room,' Lou said, suddenly appearing to regain some of her former confidence and desire to be in control. She led Grace up the steep stairway to where there were three doors. One was open, revealing a desk containing a computer and printer and a futon made up as a bed. A small window looked out onto the neighbouring yard where some sort of renovation was taking place. 'It's really the study,' Lou said, apologetically, 'but there are only the two rooms. The bathroom is across there.' She gestured to the door opposite.

'I'm sure it'll be fine.' Grace tried to dismiss the image of the open, airy house and the ocean view she'd left behind.

*

Next day, Lou and Greg took Grace out to lunch, insisting she should see some of the city, but as they drank coffee, ate the requisite smashed avocado on sour dough bread, and wandered around the edge of the harbour, the following day was in each of their minds.

'Let's go back,' Grace said eventually, when she thought if she saw one more dog being wheeled around in a pram by its owner, she'd throw up, and her feet were beginning to ache. 'I'm sure you'd like a rest before tomorrow, Lou.'

Greg gave Lou a worried look, then said, 'Good idea. Why don't we grab an ice cream on the way? We usually have one when we come along here.'

Grace understood what he was trying to do – to pretend this was a normal Sunday and she'd just come to visit. But it was no good. The looming spectre of the surgery to take place next day couldn't be ignored.

However, she duly agreed, and they stopped to enjoy cones of mint chocolate chip for Grace, boysenberry swirl for Greg and double choc brownie for Lou, before heading home.

Once there, Lou retired for a rest, and Grace joined Greg in the small courtyard.

'It's tough for Lou,' he said. 'She was so thrilled to think she was pregnant at last – we both were – now this.' He plucked at the knees of his pants. 'Do you think… do you think she'll be okay? I couldn't… I love her, Grace. She's my whole world.'

'I'm sure she'll be fine,' Grace said, with a confidence she was far from feeling. What did she know of the risks of surgery?

'The doc said they'd caught it early. It's stage one. Does that mean…?'

Grace had no idea, though she had googled it before leaving Bellbird Bay and had been heartened to learn it had a good survival rate. 'We can only hope and pray,' she said, shocked to hear herself mention prayer. She hadn't prayed since Russ got sick and she'd wished she had a stronger faith. It was what people turned to in a crisis.

'That's what my mum says,' Greg said. 'She was here last weekend but had to get back to Dad. He hasn't been well.'

'I'm sorry.' Grace recalled Greg's parents were around ten years older than she was and lived somewhere on the north coast. She and Russ had met them at Lou and Greg's wedding, but the two couples had little in common and only kept in touch at Christmas. She felt for Greg with his dad sick, too.

'It's not… he's not…' His voice choked.

Grace put her hand on his as he wiped away the tears.

*

Next morning there was little time for conversation, and none of them felt much like talking. Lou had to be at the hospital by eight-thirty and wasn't allowed any breakfast. Grace and Greg choked down a slice of toast and vegemite and drank a cup of coffee before heading off.

At the hospital, Grace felt helpless as the hospital routine took over. Lou was admitted and taken to a room where she was visited by a series of medical staff. Then Grace and Greg were ushered out and told the surgery would take some time.

They walked into the corridor where Greg paced up and down then said, 'I can't stand it. I'm going to go into the office for a bit. Try to take my mind off it. It's only five minutes away. They'll call me when there's any news.' And, to Grace's surprise, he was off, striding down the corridor as if the hounds of hell were after him.

She supposed grief affected people in different ways. There was no sense in sitting here by herself. She checked someone would contact her when Lou was out of surgery and set out to find somewhere for coffee and something more to eat. She wasn't feeling hungry, but it would help fill the time.

Grace walked out of the Royal Prince Alfred Hospital onto the busy Missenden Road. As the traffic whizzed past, she reflected how different it was from the peace of Bellbird Bay and Granite Springs. This was where Lou spent her life, the inner city she loved. Seeing a café on the other side of the road, Grace waited for a gap in the traffic and dashed across, relieved when she made it to the other side safely.

The café was little more than a hole in the wall with only a few tables and it was empty apart from a couple of hospital staff – recognisable in their blue uniforms – buying takeaway coffee. Grace took a seat and picked up a menu, then ordered a cappuccino and a ham and cheese croissant and picked up a copy of *The Sydney Morning Herald* someone had left lying around.

But she couldn't concentrate on the news. Her thoughts kept veering back to Lou, wondering what was happening in the operating theatre and hoping it would go well. She couldn't bear it if the unthinkable happened. For a moment she wished that, like Greg, she could try to lose herself in her work, but she suspected he'd be no more successful than she was in dismissing the image of Lou being operated on.

'Your coffee and croissant.' The waiter – a young man with a distinct Italian accent – produced her order with a flourish. 'Enjoy.' Then he was gone, and Grace was left looking at the food she had no intention of eating. She pushed the plate aside and took a sip of coffee, her second in as many hours. If she continued like this, she'd become hyper. She normally preferred her herbal teas but today her body called out for caffeine. Even in her distressed state, she recognised this one was particularly good.

Grace's phone rang. Taking it from her pocket, she recognised Ted's number and, with a sense of relief, pressed to accept the call.

'Ted!'

'How are you, Grace? I've been thinking of you this morning. What time is Lou's surgery?'

'It's happening right now.' Grace clutched her phone like a lifeline. Just hearing Ted's voice was such a comfort. It brought him and Bellbird Bay closer. 'I'm having a coffee and trying to distract myself. It's so good to hear your voice.'

'How is Lou?'

'I think she'll be glad to get today over. Fingers crossed the surgery will be successful. She's been more subdued than normal, not her usual self. Greg has been wonderful.'

'And how are you?'

'Oh, I'm coping.' But Grace felt tears come into her eyes again, hearing the concern in Ted's voice. 'What's happening with you?' She tried to inject a positive note into her voice.

'Not a lot. Surfing, painting. I had coffee with Kev this morning at *The Greedy Gecko* and bumped into Mel.'

'How is Mel?'

'She's worried about her sister – and you. But she's looking well, blooming.'

Grace felt a pang of regret that life was going on in Bellbird Bay without her. She would much rather have been there, having coffee with Ted, perhaps chatting about Mel's baby, Ted's latest painting, or some inconsequential happening in Bellbird Bay. Instead, she was waiting to hear if the surgeon had managed to remove all of the cancer which was threatening her daughter's life.

'We're all thinking of you and praying for Lou's recovery.'

'Thanks.' Ted was such a caring man.

'Let me know when you have news. I miss you. Hurry home.'

'I will. I miss you, too. I hope I can come home soon,' she whispered, before hanging up. Home. It was strange, but after only a few months there, she had begun to think of Bellbird Bay as home.

Grace drank the rest of her coffee and ordered another. She nibbled on the croissant, but still didn't feel like eating. The time passed slowly.

It was late afternoon, and Grace was wondering what had gone wrong and was preparing herself for the worst, her mouth dry, her stomach a fluttering mess, when her phone rang.

'Mrs Winter?'

'Yes.' Grace's heart was in her mouth.

'Your daughter's out of surgery and should be back in the ward in around half an hour. You can see her then.'

'Thank you. Was…' But the call had ended. Her phone rang again. It was Greg.

'Did the hospital contact you? Lou's out of surgery. They didn't give me any more information, but surely…?' His voice was filled with hope, and Grace's spirits lightened.

'I'll see you there.'

They met at the entrance to the ward, and with her hand on Greg's arm, Grace walked in to see Lou's white face on the pillow.

Greg immediately rushed forward to the bedside. While Grace wanted to follow, she forced herself to wait a few moments to give Greg time with his wife. She saw Lou smile and take Greg's hand, then moved to join them.

'Mum.'

'Lou, my darling.'

A doctor wearing a blue gown joined them.

Grace turned towards him expectantly. 'Was the operation a success?' she asked in a trembling voice.

'We managed to remove the tumour and don't believe there is any need to perform a hysterectomy. It was fortunate we caught it so soon.'

Grace heard Lou give a sigh of relief.

'However,' the doctor continued, 'we do recommend a course of chemotherapy to ensure we have caught all of the cancer.'

Grace's stomach twisted at the realisation this was only the beginning of what could prove to be a lengthy process, but seeing Greg squeeze Lou's hand and smile, she managed to smile, too.

Forty-two

Ted wandered around the house which felt very empty. Aaron was living in his own place with Zack, and now Grace had gone to Sydney with no hint of when she might return – if ever. He felt as if his second chance of happiness had been torn from his grasp even before it had really begun.

Grace had been gone for three months now, and although she kept in touch with texts, emails and the occasional Facetime call, it wasn't the same as having her with him. He missed her gentle smile, her conversation, the fragrance which always surrounded her. He missed holding her close and whispering into her ear. He missed their lovemaking.

He knew Lou needed her, that Grace wanted to be there to support her as she underwent her chemotherapy, but her other daughter needed her, too. Mel was close to giving birth. Only last night, when she and Aaron had dropped in with Zack, she'd complained, 'I look like a whale. It won't be long, now.' And, although Mel declared she was happy with the support of Dot and Aaron, Ted knew she missed her mother.

But, he brightened, it was Saturday and Zack was planning to cycle over for a surf with his old grandad. The boy's surfing had improved in leaps and bounds. This was partly due to the fact that, to Zack's delight, his new school included surfing as part of the PE curriculum and, even at this time of the year, they were out on the ocean on a regular basis. Today, after much nagging on Zack's part, they were to take their boards to the beach on the far side of the headland.

Ted fixed himself another cup of coffee and took it out to the deck. Normally, sitting here, contemplating the view, the sound of the surf in his ears, was a calming experience, but this morning it failed to have the usual effect. Instead, it reminded him of sitting here with Grace, enjoying a glass of wine together in the twilight, anticipating the pleasure of taking her to bed. Would that ever happen again?

He was drawn out of his musings by Zack's arrival, and the excitement on his grandson's face sent everything else out of his mind.

'Ready, Grandpa?' Zack asked. 'I came as early as I could. Dad's still asleep.'

'Just waiting for you, son. Park your bike and we can get moving.'

Ted loaded their boards onto the roof rack – Zack kept his here – and they were off. There was no need for Ted to make conversation on the way, Zack never stopped talking. Ted couldn't help but reflect on the difference from the buttoned-up young boy who had visited from Brisbane. Now he was living with his dad and attending Bellbird State College, Zack was a different person from the reticent one who was bullied at school, ignored by his stepfather and found it difficult to make friends.

When they reached the parking lot for the beach, several vehicles were already there – mostly rusted out vans or utes – and the ocean was dotted with other surfers intent on making the most of the waves.

'Wow, it's sick out there.'

Ted grinned and unloaded the boards, before leading the way down to the beach.

By the time they'd spent an hour in the surf, even Zack was ready to call it a day. 'Thanks, Grandpa,' he said, tossing his hair out of his eyes as they made their way back up the beach. 'That was gnarly. When can we do it again?'

Ted chuckled. Zack had managed the wild surf better than he'd expected. The boy had the makings of a really good surfer. 'Soon,' he said.

Zack didn't stop talking again, all the way back. By the time they reached Ted's home, Ted had heard all about the proposed drama production at school, Zack's hope he'd be given a part, and the annual chess competition which was to take place in the coming weeks.

They were unloading the boards, when Zack became more serious.

'Grandpa,' he said, 'do you think Dad's going to marry Mel?'

Caught off-guard, Ted didn't reply immediately. Instead, he continued what he was doing and asked Zack to take his board inside, before doing the same with his and locking the car.

But once inside, Zack asked him again. This time Ted said, 'I don't know, Zack. How would you feel if he did?'

Zack thought for a moment. 'It'd be okay,' he said at last. 'At least I think it would. With the baby, we'd be like a real family. And I like Mel. She's cool, not like Mark.' He scowled.

Ted chuckled. He remembered a previous conversation which had been somewhat similar. It was clearly on Zack's mind. And anyone less like the uptight Mark than Mel would be difficult to imagine. But was Aaron really thinking of marrying Mel, or even living with her? What might that mean for him – and Grace?

Forty-three

Grace gazed out of the café window, before taking another sip of cappuccino and nibbling the Italian biscotti of which she had become fond. It had been over three months since she'd first sat there, waiting for the result of Lou's surgery and now it seemed as if she belonged there. Since Greg had been unable – or unwilling – to take more time off work, it had fallen to Grace to accompany Lou to her chemo appointments, and the café provided a respite from the clinical atmosphere of the hospital while she waited for the sessions to be over.

The three months seemed like for ever. The hustle and bustle of the inner city which at first had been so alien was now part and parcel of Grace's day, and to her surprise she was becoming accustomed to it. She even enjoyed the noise of the city which greeted her on her early morning walks along the harbour, the buzz of the traffic, the hooting of the ferries, the drone of the planes flying overhead. It was only at times like this, when she sat contemplating the future, that she wondered if she'd ever again experience the peace and tranquillity of Bellbird Bay.

Her phone pinged with a text, and her lips curled into a smile as she read Ted's message. These messages which appeared every morning without fail, provided her with comfort. Reading them, it was as if she was back in Bellbird Bay with the sound of the ocean in her ears and the salty smell of the sea in her nostrils. She could almost feel the sand between her toes. But she was aware how the distance between them had lengthened as the days and weeks passed, and there was no sign of her returning. It was lovely to see him on their infrequent Facetime calls, but each time their call finished, Grace felt further and further away from the future she'd imagined they might have together. Maybe it had all been an impossible dream. This was real – to be here with Lou in her time of need – even if she couldn't dismiss the fact that Mel needed her, too.

This morning, Ted reported he had been surfing with Zack, and the boy had asked about Aaron and Mel, reminding Grace how Mel had mentioned Aaron's wanting her to move in with him. Was that what would happen? And would she remain here in Sydney with Lou? Six months ago, she'd never have envisaged such a move, but things had changed. Mel had become more independent, while Lou's confidence had been shattered and she had come to rely more and more on her mother.

Grace checked her watch. It was time to collect Lou. She rose and paid for her coffee and biscotti, farewelled the Italian café owner who'd become used to seeing her there on a regular basis, and made her way across to the hospital.

*

Two days later, Grace decided to check out rental properties in Sydney. While it had been good to stay with Lou and Greg, it was cramped in their tiny townhouse, and she knew her presence in what was their office would eventually begin to wear thin. It had sufficed while Lou was sick and receiving treatment, but now the treatment was almost over, it was time for Grace to look for alternative accommodation.

As she marked the few rentals which met the criteria of being within her budget and within easy distance of Lou and Greg's townhouse, Grace sought to suppress the memory of Ted and how it had felt to be in his arms. Family must come first, and for the moment, that meant Lou. Grace knew Ted would understand. He had his own family to care about. But it wasn't easy to dismiss the thoughts of what might have been.

She put down her pen and remembered the conversation with Lou and Greg when Lou came home from hospital after her surgery.

'At least they didn't do a hysterectomy, that means…' Lou sobbed.

'Oh, sweetheart. I'm just so grateful they seem to have caught it in time. I can stay for as long as you need me,' Grace said, hoping any plans to have a baby might be put on the back burner for a while at least.

'Thanks, Mum, but… maybe…' She looked across at Greg, then seemed to weaken, '…maybe for a bit, just until I get on my feet again.'

Then there had been the course of chemotherapy and no more talk of a baby, but Grace had caught Lou looking longingly at women with prams as they drove to and from hospital or went to the local shops.

Although Lou's course of treatment was now over, Grace was aware how fragile her daughter still was, and all her mothering instincts were at play in her decision to look for a way to stay close by. She'd been a fool to imagine she could make another life for herself, have a fresh start. The episode with Ted had been just that, a brief reminder she was still desirable, but there was no sense in trying to recapture her youth. This – being with Lou in Sydney – was what she was meant to do.

She did still worry about Mel, but in her latest call, Mel had sounded cheerful and optimistic. Dot was keeping in touch every day, John had allowed her to drop back her hours in the gallery, Aaron was a great comfort, she was getting to know Zack better, and she'd applied for a place in a degree in Art History online through Open Universities Australia. It sounded as if she had really got her life together.

The baby wasn't due for another couple of weeks. Grace could take a trip up for the birth. She wanted to be there for Mel then, but it seemed her younger daughter no longer needed her support.

Grace had given up browsing through the list of possible rentals when, picking up her phone, she realised she had a missed call from Dot. Worried it might be about Mel, she quickly pressed to return the call.

'Dot, is it Mel? Is she all right?' Grace's throat tightened.

'Mel's good, but what about you?'

'Me? What do you mean?' Grace felt the familiar irritation her sister often provoked.

'How long do you intend to stay in Sydney?'

'As long as Lou needs me.' Grace could hear herself sound defensive. What was it about Dot that made her always feel the need to justify herself? Ever since they were small, Dot had tried to tell her what to do. But she and Kev didn't have children; she didn't understand.

Dot read her mind. 'You think I don't understand, but I do. You feel guilty for having sold Brigadoon against the girls' wishes, guilty Mel became pregnant, guilty Lou developed cancer. But, Grace, none of it is your fault. You said yourself, Russ and you intended to sell your property. It would have become too much for you both as you got older. You only did what you had to do. And coming here to Bellbird Bay was a good move. You became a different person, a person in your own right. You blossomed.'

Dot took a breath, and Grace gazed at the phone in surprise. Was this really her sister saying all these things?

'I know you don't want to hear this,' Dot continued. 'But it's time you let your children live their own lives. I love them dearly, as dearly as if they were my own, but they're grown now, Grace, and have to live with what fate has dealt them.'

'But Lou…'

'I know a bit of what Lou's been through. Remember I had breast cancer twenty years ago?'

Grace swallowed. How could she have forgotten? But it had been just when Russ began to be ill, and she'd been so wrapped up in her own little world.

'You need to come home, home to Bellbird Bay,' Dot continued. 'You're not helping Lou by staying there, when she and Greg should be working out the rest of their lives. You have a life, too. I love Lou but you can't put your life on hold while she gets hers back together. There's Mel to consider, too – and Ted.' Dot paused, making Grace want to wring her sister's neck. How dare she treat her as if she didn't know what was best for herself and her children? Grace wasn't a child anymore – hadn't been for over forty years. She'd been married, managed an acreage, reared three children, two of whom Dot seemed to think she knew more about than did Grace. 'At least she's left Ben out of her meddling,' she muttered to herself.

She spoke too soon.

'And there's Ben,' Dot went on. 'The poor lad has been let down by that girl. He needs you to be here for him. Remember how delighted you were when he took the job in Queensland?'

Damn Dot! She knew how to turn the screw. Ben was Grace's weak point, her youngest, her favourite.

Grace was furious when the call ended. Unable to settle to anything, she pulled on a jacket and, checking all was well with Lou, she slipped her phone and house key into her pocket and set off for a walk. She needed fresh air to get rid of the bitter taste left in the wake of Dot's call.

The air was brisk as Grace made her way down to the edge of the harbour, the overcast sky matching her mood. She took a seat on the low wall surrounding the water, Dot's words ringing in her ears, the famous Sydney Harbour Bridge, often called The Coathanger, reaching high behind her, a beacon to ships.

At first, all she could think of was how angry Dot had made her, then the anger began to subside, and Grace began to feel calmer. She watched as a pair of seagulls fought over a few crumbs, then a mother appeared holding her small child by the hand. The girl pulled away in an attempt to catch the birds who flew up out of her reach before landing again further along. A pair of young men passed, their phones held to their ears, then an elderly couple walking slowly and holding hands. It was a normal Sydney morning.

Grace closed her eyes, remembering the sounds and smells of Bellbird Bay. Was Dot right when she said Grace needed to consider her own life? What would Russ say if he was here? She could almost hear his voice telling her to listen to her sister. 'You've done your best, Gracie. It's up to them now. They need to stand on their own two feet. That's what we wanted for them.'

'But…' she wanted to protest, but it would be no use. Russ wasn't there to hear. He never would be again.

'Are you all right?'

Grace looked up to see a young woman peering down at her. The girl's hair was tucked up under a pink helmet, her bare arms were covered in tattoos, and she was wearing a pair of inline skates. To her, Grace must appear like a mad old woman, sitting here talking to herself.

'I'm fine, thanks.'

The girl looked doubtful but skated off, no doubt muttering to herself about weird old women.

The incident startled Grace and thinking of Russ helped her come to a decision. Rising, she checked her phone. The message from Ted today was a short one.

When are you coming home?

Forty-four

Once she'd made her decision, it was easy for Grace to make arrangements to leave Sydney. Did she imagine the look of relief Lou and Greg exchanged or was it a trick of the light coming through the kitchen window?

If Grace needed any confirmation she had made the right decision, the joy and relief in Mel's voice was it. 'Oh, Mum, I'm so glad. You'll be here for me and Isla. I have a feeling it won't be long now.'

But the best part was when she rang Ted to tell him she was returning to Bellbird Bay. Grace almost wept to hear the delight in his voice. 'I'm so glad,' he said, his voice almost breaking. 'I thought… I was afraid… You don't know how happy I am to know you're coming back.'

Even so, it was a wrench to leave Lou. During the past few months, they'd grown closer. The gulf which had widened between them when Grace revealed her plan to leave Granite Springs had healed, and they were able to talk openly again. Lou hadn't even flinched when Grace mentioned Ted's name, but she had quickly changed the subject.

Now the day had come. Grace looked around the small room which had been her home away from home. While sorry to leave Lou and Greg, she wouldn't be sad to leave the confines of the townhouse and get back to the renovated beach shack she now called home. Now she was about to leave, she had difficulty in imagining she'd ever considered staying in the city.

'Bye, Mum, and take care. Give my love to Mel.' Lou hugged Grace as the call for boarding came across the loudspeaker.

'*You* take care,' Grace replied. 'Don't try to do too much, and don't…'

'Mum!'

'I'll make sure she doesn't.' Greg put a loving arm around Lou's shoulders. 'And I'll make sure she takes care of herself, too.'

Grace was reassured to see the love in Greg's eyes mirrored in Lou's.

'Sorry.' Grace kissed Lou on the cheek. 'I can't help but worry about you. And remember, I can be back in a tick if you need me – for anything at all.'

All three became serious at the reminder of a possible return of the cancer, then Lou grinned. 'You can come back when we finally are pregnant.'

In no time, Grace was settled into her seat and the red roofs of Sydney were disappearing below her. This trip, she accepted a glass of wine from the hostess and leant back in her seat with a smile on her face, a bubble of excitement building up at the prospect ahead of her.

*

As the sight of the coastline of Southeast Queensland appeared below her, Grace felt as if a load had fallen from her shoulders and she was coming home. To her surprise and delight, Ted was waiting for her at the airport. As she fell into his arms, felt his lips on her forehead and heard his heartfelt, 'Welcome home,' Grace felt she truly had come home.

'Mel can't wait to see you,' he said, as they drove along the coast. 'She says the baby is only waiting for you to arrive.'

Grace chuckled. It was good to be back. She was looking forward to seeing Mel again and to breathing in the sea air. She'd missed it so much. She turned to gaze at the man by her side. He hadn't changed. He was still the lovely, gentle man he'd been when she left. Grace shivered at how close she'd come to losing him, to losing this chance of happiness.

'There's a surprise waiting for you, too,' Ted said, as he steered round one particularly sharp corner, and Bellbird Bay came into view.

'A surprise? Can't you tell me what it is?'

'Wait and see.'

With that, Grace had to be content. She didn't need a surprise. It was enough to be back here with the people she loved. For the first time, she admitted to herself that she loved Ted Crawford. She only hoped her absence hadn't made him change his mind.

'Here we are.' Ted pulled up outside the familiar house. The door opened, and Mel ran out – a larger Mel than the one she had left – and behind her…

'Ben! What are you doing here?' Grace got out of the car to be enfolded in a warm hug from her two children, while Ted watched on with an affectionate smile.

When they laughingly pulled apart, Grace's eyes were filled with tears – tears of happiness.

'I heard you were flying back, and I was due some time off, so here I am.' Ben laughed at Grace's surprise. 'I wanted to see the little mother again, too.'

'Not so little,' Mel said ruefully. 'I'm so glad you're here, Mum.'

Grace was glad, too. This was where she belonged.

They all piled into the house where Mel had prepared a welcome home lunch. 'All from *The Pandanus Café*,' she said with a grin. 'I've been practically living on their food, plus takeaways from *The Greedy Gecko*. I've been too exhausted to think of cooking for myself.'

After lunch, Ted disappeared to allow Grace time to catch up with Mel and Ben, but he promised to return and suggested they all go out to dinner together to celebrate Grace's return.

However, when Ted arrived ready for dinner, Mel confessed she was too tired to go out, and Ben offered to stay home with her. So it was only Grace and Ted who walked down to the surf club together.

'I'm glad it's just us,' Ted said, taking Grace's hand as they sat on the deck of the surf club with glasses of prosecco to celebrate her return.

Grace smiled, a warm glow enveloping her. She gazed at the man sitting opposite, then her eyes travelled to the sand and breakers, just visible in the fading light, wondering again how she could have imagined leaving all this.

'I am, too,' she said, smiling. 'I missed you. Missed all this.' She waved her hand in the air.

'I missed you too, more than you can imagine. I never thought I'd feel like this again. I hope we can…' Ted cleared his throat. 'I love you, Grace. Can I hope you…'

'I love you, too, Ted. For a time there, I thought I had to put my family first, that Lou needed me, but...' she grinned, '...it was Dot who made me see sense.'

'Dot?' Ted raised one eyebrow.

'My sister has her faults, but her heart is in the right place. She made me see I have the right to a life of my own, that sometimes we need to let go, to allow others to live their own lives, make their own mistakes.'

'If it was Dot who helped you decide to come back, then I have to give her more credit than I have before now.' He took both of Grace's hands in his and squeezed them.

They sat there enveloped in a bubble of love and contentment, only releasing their clasped hands when their meals arrived.

They were drinking coffee and contemplating going back to Ted's to renew the intimacy which had been interrupted by Grace's trip to Sydney, when her phone rang. Tempted to ignore it, Grace glanced at the screen to see Mel's face.

'Mel?' she asked, signalling to Ted who seemed about to ask a question.

'Mum, it's time. It's the baby.'

'Oh, my darling.'

'Ben's going to drive me to hospital. Can you...?'

'I'll meet you there.'

'It's Mel's baby,' she said to Ted as soon as she finished the call. 'I need to get to the hospital.'

'I can drive you.'

'But the car...'

They left the surf club and hurried back up the boardwalk where Ted reversed his car out of the garage and an excited and trembling Grace hopped in.

At the hospital, leaving Ted to park the car, Grace raced in and along to the maternity ward where she found Ben pacing up and down in the corridor as if he was the prospective father.

'Mel?' she asked.

Ben pointed to an open door.

Grace went in, to see Mel being tended to by a midwife.

It was a long night and, even though Grace suggested to Ben and

Ted several times that they go home and get some sleep, they stayed at the hospital till, just as dawn was breaking, they heard the sound they'd been waiting for.

'Isla's here!' Grace announced from the doorway. 'And she's beautiful, just like her mum.'

Exhausted, but having been fortified by numerous cups of coffee throughout the night, Ted and Ben hugged a tired and happy Grace.

'You can go home now,' she said. 'Mel won't be ready to see you till later. She needs to rest, too.'

'What about you?' Ted asked.

'I'll come home, too.' Grace smiled wearily.

'How does it feel to be a grandma?'

'It feels wonderful. It still hasn't sunk in. We need to tell Lou.'

'And Aaron,' Ted said. 'He's been waiting for news. Zack's excited, too. I rang them last night to tell him we were here. Aaron really cares for Mel, Grace. I think we may all be about to become one big happy family.'

To Grace's relief, Lou expressed delight at the news of Isla's birth, promising to visit as soon as she felt able. She sounded happy on the phone, leading Grace to believe her decision to leave Sydney had been the right one.

Later that day, Grace returned to the hospital to see Mel and her baby – her first grandchild. Shedding a tear that Russ hadn't lived to see his granddaughter, she looked around the bed to where Ben, Ted, Aaron and Zack were vying to take turns to hold the baby. She gave thanks for the way things had turned out, for the new life that stretched ahead – for her, Mel, and little Isla – and was filled with gratitude at the realisation that, at last, she was home again with the people she loved.

The End

If you've enjoyed Grace's story, I'd really appreciate it if you could leave a review on Amazon and/or Goodreads. A few words will suffice, no need for a lengthy review. It will mean a lot to me and help other readers find my books.

If you enjoyed this book, you'll also enjoy the next book in the series, *Starting Over in Bellbird Bay*. It features Will and Cleo who you have already met, and also other characters from this book and from *Summer in Bellbird Bay*.

Following the death of her husband, *Cleo Johansen* and her daughter moved to Bellbird Bay determined to make a new start. Having carved out a new life, Cleo is shattered when a shadow from her husband's past throws their lives into disarray.

Will Rankin has lived in Bellbird Bay all his life. Now widowed, the former surf champion runs the local surf school and enjoys a close relationship with his son. Content to lead a single life, the appearance of an undesirable stranger is quick to upset his peaceful existence.

While neither Will nor Cleo is interested in forming a new relationship, an unexpected attraction surfaces when a mutual friend suggests they spend more time together.

Set against a background of sun, sea and sand, can Cleo and Will find a way to move forward together?

A heart-warming tale of family, friends, and how a second chance at love can happen when you least expect it.

You can order it here getbook.at/StartingOverinBellbird

From the Author

Dear Reader,

First, I'd like to thank you for choosing to read *Coming Home to Bellbird Bay*. I hope you've enjoyed this trip to Bellbird Bay as much as I've enjoyed writing it. It was fun to locate my fictional town in the part of Queensland where I live and to populate it with characters who I hope you will come to love. It's the second book in this new series.

If you'd like to stay up to date with my new releases and special offers you can sign up to my reader's group.

You can sign up here

https://mailchi.mp/f5cbde96a5e6/maggiechristensensreadersgroup

I'll never share your email address, and you can unsubscribe at any time. You can also contact me via Facebook, Twitter or by email. I love hearing from my readers and will always reply.

Thanks again.

MaggieC

Acknowledgements

As always, this book could not have been written without the help and advice of a number of people.

Firstly, my husband Jim for listening to my plotlines without complaint, for his patience and insights as I discuss my characters and storyline with him, for his patience and help with difficult passages and advice on my male dialogue, and for being there when I need him.

John Hudspith, editor extraordinaire for his ideas, suggestions, encouragement and attention to detail.

Jane Dixon-Smith for her patience and for working her magic on my beautiful cover and interior.

My thanks also to early readers of this book – Helen, Maggie and Louise for their helpful comments and advice. Also, to Annie of *Annie's books at Peregian* and Graeme of *The Bookshop at Caloundra* for their ongoing support.

And to all of my readers. Your support and comments make it all worthwhile.

About the Author

After a career in education, Maggie Christensen began writing contemporary women's fiction portraying mature women facing life-changing situations, and historical fiction set in her native Scotland. Her travels inspire her writing, be it her trips to visit family in Scotland, in Oregon, USA or her home on Queensland's beautiful Sunshine Coast. Maggie writes of mature heroines coming to terms with changes in their lives and the heroes worthy of them. Maggie has been called *the queen of mature age fiction* and her writing has been described by one reviewer as *like a nice warm cup of tea. It is warm, nourishing, comforting and embracing.*

From the small town in Scotland where she grew up, Maggie was lured to Australia by the call to 'Come and teach in the sun'. Once there, she worked as a primary school teacher, university lecturer and in educational management. Now living with her husband of over thirty years on Queensland's Sunshine Coast, she loves walking on the deserted beach in the early mornings and having coffee by the river on weekends. Her days are spent surrounded by books, either reading or writing them – her idea of heaven!

Maggie can be found on Facebook, Twitter, Goodreads, Instagram, Bookbub or on her website.
https://www.facebook.com/maggiechristensenauthor
https://twitter.com/MaggieChriste33
https://www.goodreads.com/author/show/8120020.Maggie_Christensen
https://www.instagram.com/maggiechriste33/
https://www.bookbub.com/profile/maggie-christensen
https://maggiechristensenauthor.com/

Printed in Great Britain
by Amazon

80542204R00140